NAVY SEAL RESCUE

Susan Cliff

H HARLEQUIN®ROMANTIC SUSPENSE

Recycling programs
for this product may
not exist in your area.

ISBN-13: 978-1-335-45636-6

Navy SEAL Rescue

Copyright © 2018 by Susan Cliff

Printed in U.S.A.

Dear Reader,

While I was writing *Stranded with the Navy SEAL*, the first in the Team Twelve series, I became interested in a side character. The hero's friend and comrade, William Hudson, seemed like a perfect candidate for a thrilling romance. The only problem? He was dead.

Believed dead. He'd entered a building that exploded. No remains were recovered.

In *Navy SEAL Rescue*, Hud has survived the blast, against all odds, and been captured by the enemy. He's the first navy SEAL captive in the history of the organization, because SEALs never surrender. I learned that on Wikipedia. In addition to being a captive, and an elite soldier, Hud is an expert mountain climber. The heroine, Dr. Layah Anwar, desperately needs someone with his skill set. She helps him escape and their adventure begins.

Both Hud and Layah are resilient people who've endured personal hardships. He's divorced. She's a widow. Neither character wants to risk their heart again, especially when their lives are at stake. So of course they fall in love.

I hope you enjoy their story.

Susan Cliff

"Why did he want us to get married?" Hud asked.

"Yelda told him we were sleeping together," Layah said.

"Why would she do that?"

"I don't know. She thinks we are destined to marry."

His eyes narrowed with suspicion.

"I did not encourage her," she said, placing a palm on her chest.

"Right. You'd never force anyone to do anything against their will."

"I have no interest—"

"No interest? Really?"

"Not in marriage."

"You don't strike me as the casual-affair type."

She lifted her chin. "I feel desire, like any woman. I remember the pleasures of the bedroom. That does not mean I wish for a reluctant husband."

He didn't argue, so she continued walking. They seemed to have reached an understanding. She didn't want to say too much.

Admitting her desire for him wasn't a problem; he already knew.

* * *

Susan Cliff is the pen name of a longtime romance reader and professional writer from Southern California. She loves survival stories and sexy romance, so she decided to write both! Her Team Twelve series features men to die for—hot navy SEALs who live on the edge and fall hard for their heroines. Visit her at susancliff.com.

Books by Susan Cliff

Harlequin Romantic Suspense

Team Twelve
Stranded with the Navy SEAL

Chapter 1

Telskuf, Iraq

Hud was in hell.

He'd woken up here two months ago, buck naked and half-dead, caked in a mixture of blood and dust.

This particular corner of hell was an underground spider-hole with four walls, a solid dirt floor and no light. The only exit was an impenetrable metal door. It had a slot wide enough to push a tray through. He ate whatever they served with his bare hands. On good days, the gruel had bits of meat and gristle. On bad days, he went hungry.

Each week he was given a gallon of drinking water and an empty bucket. He'd learned to ration his water or suffer the consequences. He hadn't bathed since his arrival, unless he counted that extended waterboarding session with his new terrorist friends. One afternoon of this method had almost broken him, despite his extensive Navy SEAL training, but they hadn't continued. They must have decided it was a waste of water. Either that or they thought he'd die before he coughed up any useful information.

In addition to waterboarding, he'd been treated to periods of sleep deprivation, electroshock therapy and regular beatings.

He almost missed the beatings; they'd made him feel alive. He craved human contact, even in the form of fists. He preferred blood to dust. Blood was pain, hot and bright. Dust was oblivion. It was the dark nothingness that smothered him. It rained down on his head from the cracked ceiling like a slow burial.

Sometimes he closed his eyes and pretended he was back in Iowa, in the storm cellar on his grandparents' farm. He hadn't wanted to be cooped up underground, protected from the elements. He'd never been afraid of thunder and lightning. He'd wanted to chase tornadoes and climb mountains and touch the sky.

There weren't any mountains in his hometown, so he'd climbed every tree. He'd climbed the water tower and the soybean mill and the bridge across the river. He'd broken both arms one summer. His mother had been at her wit's end. She'd told him he was just like his father, a volatile race car driver with a taste for hard alcohol and low-class women.

Hud hadn't minded the comparison back then. He'd wanted to be fast and tough. Low-class women sounded pretty fun, too.

Until he met Michelle.

Thinking about her was a different kind of torture, twisting his gut into knots. She'd been a tempest, with her stormy moods and wild ways. Now she was another man's problem. Hud didn't envy the son of a bitch. He didn't envy the happy-family photos on Facebook, or the fact that Michelle looked better than ever.

Nope. Not at all.

What was there to envy? He was in a dusty tomb in Iraq, waiting to die, while those two cuddled up in a cozy apartment with the baby he'd thought was his. They were probably ordering takeout right now, and watching movies in bed.

Bo-ring.

He was so over her.

He was over this rat-hole bunker, too. The accommodations here left a lot to be desired. There was a gallon of water in one corner, a piss bucket in another. He had no blanket or sleeping mat. No clothes, other than a ragged pair of pants. No companions.

The isolation and monotony was a torture in itself.

It was the only torture, lately. He hadn't been dragged out of his cell in weeks. The first month they'd been more attentive. They'd kept him awake with loud voices and blaring alarms. They'd tried to wear him down with frequent beatings and hours of interrogations. He'd responded with the same rote answers, so they'd strapped him to a chair and started the electroshocks. That phase had been unpleasant, but it also rendered him unconscious, which wasn't the best way to make him talk.

He knew what would happen if he talked. He was a Navy SEAL from Team Twelve. His men were infamous for taking out enemy leaders in the dead of night. They'd killed three of the Islamic Front's top leaders in recent raids. Public beheading, after being dragged naked behind a vehicle, was how this story ended.

It might end that way even if he didn't talk, but he tried to stay positive. He had to wait for an opportunity to escape. He wouldn't give up. SEALs didn't quit.

They also didn't get captured—because they never surrendered. Hud was the first team member to be taken alive in the history of the elite military organization, and he wasn't proud of that distinction. He'd ruined a perfect record. Although he'd been unconscious when he'd fallen into enemy hands, it was still his fault. He'd been too eager to reach the target. His comm wasn't working, and his teammates had been delayed. He'd moved in anyway, assuming they were seconds behind him. They weren't.

Inside the compound was enough ordnance to blow up the entire block, and a fleeing terrorist with a remote trigger. Hud had chased the man into an escape tunnel. There was a huge explosion, and everything went black.

If any other SEAL had entered the building, they were dead now, and he was responsible.

The possibility haunted him. He'd started to torture *himself* with dark thoughts. He had too many deaths on his hands. Too much time spent in Iraq. Too much blood spilled into dust. The solitude was driving him crazy. He'd worn a path in his cell from pacing. He practiced martial arts for hours, which calmed his mind and boosted his morale. He did constant reps of low-impact strength exercises. He couldn't afford to sweat out his electrolytes with cardio, but he was still in good shape. He was lean and hard and ready to fight.

He just needed an opportunity.

Unfortunately, he had very little contact with the men outside. They came for him with Kalashnikovs and alert eyes. There was always an armed guard, even when they delivered water. He'd played sick once, lying facedown in the dirt for several meal cycles. No one bothered to check on him. It had been so long since his last interrogation, he suspected the terrorists had left him here to rot.

He had to get out now, before he was executed or became too weak to run. Because escaping this cell was just the first challenge. He also had to reach a base or safe zone. His team had been air-dropped into this place, a small town north of Mosul. It was a contested area between Iraqi Kurdistan and IF strongholds. The Islamic Front, known as "Da'esh" by the locals, was an extremist group that had been rapidly gaining territory. US forces had been working with local allies to push back against them, with mixed results. It was what the brass called a "liquid situation." Grunts like him called it something less polite.

Today was water day—he hoped. When the guards opened the door with a fresh gallon, he was going to fake a seizure and create some chaos. He believed in making his own opportunities.

He crouched in the shadows, conserving his energy. No one came with a gallon of water. He was about to give up and go to sleep when an explosion tore through the space above him. The impact knocked him off his feet. Dust rained down in a choking cloud and the ground shook beneath him.

Hud brushed off the dirt and scrambled upright, his pulse racing. Had his team arrived to rescue him? He waited for all hell to break loose, but it didn't. There was no gunfire, no secondary artillery. He didn't hear any voices.

He rushed to the door, which was still intact, and banged on the iron surface with his fist. "Hey! Down here!"

No one answered, but he kept shouting until someone arrived. Hud couldn't see who it was because the slot was closed. The only sound was the clink of metal as a couple different keys were tried. An ally would have announced his presence, so this wasn't a good sign. Hud swallowed hard, uncertain if the man on the other side was a friend or foe. After a tense moment, the door opened.

Hud gaped at his liberator in surprise. It wasn't a man at all. It was a boy. An Iraqi boy like any other, dressed in dusty Western clothes.

He stared back at Hud with a defiant expression. There was nothing friendly about him. He was about twelve, and brimming with antagonism. Maybe he'd come to loot the building, or to spill more blood in the name of jihad. Hud had seen younger boys with suicide bombs, so he couldn't dismiss this one as a threat.

He hardened his heart and braced himself for violence. He didn't want to hurt a kid, but he would.

He'd do anything to get out of here alive. He'd worry about the emotional toll when this ordeal was over.

The boy narrowed his eyes at Hud's fighting stance. Then he said something in Arabic and motioned for Hud to come with him. After a short hesitation, Hud went. Why not? He'd have gone through the door with the devil at this point.

They crept up a narrow stairwell before entering the main floor. Hud's eyes were sensitive to light, so the dusty haze almost blinded him. It was a mess of broken tiles and bricks, but most of the damage was limited to one wall. The explosive device appeared to have been deployed to gain entry, not to cause widespread destruction. There was a man in the corner that Hud recognized as a guard. He was dead or unconscious.

Hud squinted at the mayhem, eyes burning. The boy strode through the rubble with a reckless swagger. In the next instant, a second guard burst into the room holding a rifle. He took aim at the kid, who wasn't even armed. Hud didn't hesitate. He dived toward the guard and tackled him around the waist. Bullets peppered the ceiling as they rolled across the ground together. Plaster rained down on them and sharp bits of tile sliced into Hud's back. He ignored the pain, trying to gain control of the weapon. The guard didn't relent, so Hud climbed on top of him and held the rifle across his throat. He applied brutal pressure until the man's grip loosened. Then he yanked the weapon away and shoved the muzzle under his chin. He squeezed the trigger. The result wasn't pretty.

Hud leaped to his feet, brushing off shards of broken tile and bits of gore. He'd seen worse. The boy didn't seem fazed, either. He nodded his approval. Then he gestured toward the hole in the wall.

Hud followed him into the harsh sunlight. Two armed men came out of the shadows. They started arguing with the boy in a language Hud couldn't identify. They might have been Kurds. Or Turks. There were a lot of different ethnic groups in the area. It didn't matter to Hud. Whoever they were, he was going with them.

He stumbled forward on unsteady legs. He had cuts on his feet and blood dripping down his back. He was weak with hunger, shaking from dehydration. Maybe it was the stress of the situation, or the lack of proper nutrition, but he felt dizzy. When he careened sideways, the other men supported him. They dragged him across a cobblestone street and into a quiet alleyway, where a woman was waiting with a donkey cart.

She scolded the boy the same way the men did, adding a hard tug on his ear. The boy scowled and pulled away from her. Then she turned her attention to Hud, and a strange sensation hit him. It was like a red alert, or a premonition. This woman was important. She was central. He zeroed in on her as if they were the last two people on earth.

She was stunning, with intense dark eyes in an oval-shaped face. Her hair was covered with a simple blue hijab, her body draped in a shapeless robe. She had an elegant nose and finely arched brows. She looked like a desert princess in peasant garb.

Maybe any attractive female would have dazzled him into a stupor, after what he'd been through. This one was top-class, even swathed in fabric from head to toe. One glance at her brought him to his knees. She was that beautiful.

"This is him?" she said in accented English. She didn't sound impressed.

His vision went dark at the edges. He swayed forward, tumbling into oblivion.

Chapter 2

The locals must have exaggerated.

Layah Anwar had heard stories about Navy SEALs. Wild tales about death and daring. SEALs were the Da'esh's worst nightmare. They were mythical beasts that descended in the dark of night. They struck by sea, air or land, with an arsenal of weapons. They were rumored to have freakish strength. She'd pictured a genetic mutant in heavy chains. A thick-necked brute, hulking and indestructible.

This man wasn't indestructible. He was unconscious.

To be fair, he'd been held captive for months. He'd been tortured and beaten and deprived of basic necessities. He was covered in dust and blood. He appeared adequately muscled. But he was just a man, like any other. She'd seen larger specimens among her own people.

"Are you sure this is him?" she asked Ashur again.

"It's him. He has the tattoo." Ashur pointed. There was a geometric shape of a mountain on the inside of the man's forearm.

Layah helped her cousins lift the man off the ground. He was heavier than he looked. Even Ashur had to grab an arm. She'd made a place for him on the cart between straw bales. He groaned as his back hit the wooden platform. Beneath the dirt, his face was pale.

She hoped he wouldn't die before she got any use out of him. She'd paid a high price for the explosives. They'd been planning this breakout for weeks.

"Go," she said to her cousins. They raced into a nearby building to hide. She covered the man with a length of burlap and Ashur rearranged the straw bales to disguise his presence. Then she leaped into the driver's seat and took the reins. Ashur climbed in beside her. Her hands shook as she urged the donkey forward.

The streets were empty—for now. Telskuf had been evacuated months ago, before the town had fallen. The only residents who'd stayed had done so at great risk, for Da'esh militants patrolled the roads with automatic rifles. Although the Iraqi Army had attempted to regain control, they'd abandoned the effort after a few days. There were other, more important cities to protect. More important people. The Assyrian community wasn't a top priority in Iraq, or anywhere else.

Layah set aside her bitterness and focused on their escape. They had to reach the farm on the outskirts of town, where she could give the man medical attention. If he didn't recover from his injuries, she'd have to find another guide.

She glanced at Ashur, who sat like a stone beside her. She couldn't believe he'd defied her by rushing into the building. "You were supposed to stand watch."

"Yusef was afraid to go in."

"So he sent you?"

Ashur didn't answer. She knew he hadn't waited for permission. He'd just acted in his usual fashion, with recklessness and impatience.

"I heard gunfire."

"The American shot a guard in the head."

Layah's chest tightened with unease. Ashur had seen too much violence in his short life. He was becoming inured to it. Or worse, infatuated. He had a glint in his eye that suggested he'd enjoyed the excitement.

She wished she could shield her nephew from the most devastating effects of war. Instead, she'd recruited him as a spy. She hadn't expected any bloodshed on this mission, but the possibility always loomed. Maybe the narcotics they'd given the guards hadn't worked. Ashur had delivered the spiked tea this morning, after the usual errand boy had been delayed by her cousins.

"Did he recognize you?" she asked.

"I don't think so."

Ashur had met several Navy SEALs in Syria two years ago. His father, Layah's brother, had worked for them as an interpreter. Ashur remembered a SEAL with a tattoo on his forearm, blue and green lines in a distinctive mountain shape. Last month, Layah had learned that the Da'esh's new captive bore this tattoo.

He was exactly what she needed for the journey north. As long as he lived.

She led the donkey down cobblestone alleyways and dusty side streets. When the cart went over a bump, their passenger groaned in protest.

"Water," he said in a hoarse voice.

She was glad he was awake, but she couldn't give him water. "Tell him to be quiet."

Ashur leaned toward the injured man. "No water for you," he said in stilted English. "Now shut up or we die."

Layah frowned at his harsh words. "Speak with care, nephew. We need his help."

Ashur shrugged, unconcerned. He'd gotten his point across. The man fell silent. Perhaps he'd passed out again.

She focused on the road, holding the reins in a sweaty grip. It was a pleasant spring day, sunny and cool. No storm clouds loomed on the horizon. They were almost out of danger. She set her sights on the archway at the south end of town.

"Halt!" a voice shouted in Arabic.

The native language of Telskuf was Assyrian, so she knew the speaker wasn't local. He was a Da'esh invader.

Layah pulled up on the reins and reached underneath the wooden seat for the tar she'd hidden there. She stuck it over her front teeth. Then she grabbed a pair of dusty spectacles from her pocket. The thick lenses distorted her vision. When the Da'esh militants reached her, they found a homely creature.

"What are you doing?" one of the men demanded.

"Delivering a load of straw," she said. "My husband is too ill to accompany me, and my brother just died from the same sickness—" She broke off, hacking until she wheezed. "I hope it's not contagious."

The man retreated a step, his lip curled. "Who are you?" he barked at Ashur.

"I am someone who belongs here."

"What?"

"He's simple," she said, coughing again. "Don't mind him."

"How old is he?"

"Eleven," she lied. He was thirteen.

"Telskuf is under the control of the Islamic Front," the militant announced, as if she didn't know. "Those who enter without permission are considered enemy combatants. Even women and children."

She bowed her head. "Please forgive me."

He pardoned the trespass with a flick of his hand. She continued toward the archway, her heart pounding. Although the majority of townspeople had fled during the first strike, some residents had stayed. The sick, the stubborn, the desperate. They hid in their homes and prayed for the occupation to end.

Layah took off the glasses and put them in her pocket. Her eyes hurt from squinting through the dusty lenses, and her throat ached from fake coughing. A glance over her shoulder revealed an empty road. No one was following them.

When they arrived at the abandoned farmhouse,

Ibrahim opened the wooden gate and closed it behind them. Then he returned to his post, leaning heavily on his cane. She maneuvered the cart under the shaded awning on the terrace and turned to Ashur.

"Someone who belongs here?" she repeated.

"We are the native people of this land. Not them."

"You think pointing that out will make any difference?"

"You think making yourself ugly will stop them from raping you?"

She removed the tar from her teeth, rattled by the question. He knew more than a boy his age should. He was angry and difficult and he broke her heart daily.

"You'll never be too ugly for them. *Goats* aren't too ugly for them."

Laughter bubbled from her throat, despite the tension. Goat-fornicator was a common insult in their language. Ashur shouldn't repeat the crude talk of adults, but she didn't have the energy to scold him all the time. She was overwhelmed with other responsibilities. Her people were prisoners and outcasts in their own country. "If you worry about those men hurting me, you should not bait them."

"I will kill them," he asserted, thumping a fist against his chest.

She hoped he wouldn't get the chance. As the oldest male in her immediate family, he'd taken on the role of her protector. Which was ironic, because she was his legal guardian until she found a more suitable arrangement.

Their conversation was interrupted by the American, who shoved aside two bales of straw with a furious heave. His eyes were red-rimmed, his nostrils flared. He appeared larger and more dangerous up close, without her cousins holding him. She was pleased, and a little scared. Neither Ashur nor Ibrahim was capable of defending her against this man, who looked ready to tear her apart. He was bloody and disheveled, with a tangled beard that couldn't disguise his strong features.

"Water," he snarled.

"Bring it," she said to Ashur, afraid to break eye contact with the man.

Ashur filled a tin cup from the nearby barrel. The American drank in huge gulps, rivulets streaming down his dusty throat. Then he leaned against the straw bales, eyes closed. His face was pained, his breaths ragged.

Layah didn't think he felt well enough to attack her. He wouldn't try to run with bloody wounds on his feet. The gate was locked. He had nowhere to go. She motioned for Ashur to fetch the tray she'd prepared earlier. Ibrahim kept one eye on her and one eye on the road, squinting in disapproval. He didn't trust Americans. Neither did Layah, but desperate times called for desperate measures.

She unharnessed the donkey and pushed the remaining bales off the cart to make room. Then she climbed onto the platform and sat down. "Your wounds need to be cleaned."

He grunted, but didn't move.

Ashur returned with shawarma and the special tea. After delivering the tray, he led the donkey away to graze. Taking care of the American was Layah's job. She needed him to make a swift recovery.

He took an experimental sip from the teacup. "What is this?"

"Chai."

Nodding, he moved on to the shawarma. His appetite was promising. He ate in ravenous bites, barely chewing. She thought he might choke on the meat, but he didn't. She watched his throat work as he swallowed. He had another tattoo on his upper chest. It was a military symbol, a flying eagle with a trident and an anchor. She wasn't a fan of Western body art, but she recognized the quality in the work. She also saw beauty in the canvas. His hard-muscled torso was undeniably attractive.

Her gaze rose to his face and connected with his. Heat suffused her cheeks as she realized he'd caught her admiring his bare chest. She was no longer accustomed to being alone with strange men, or men in any state of undress.

"Who are you?"

"I am Layah Anwar Al-Farah," she said, bowing her head.

"Layah," he repeated. His voice was husky, with a pleasant rumble. She got the impression that he liked the way she looked, which was good. She wanted him to like her. She could use it to her advantage.

"What is your name, sir?"

"Hud."

"Hud?"

"Hudson. William."

"Hudson," she said, which felt more familiar on

her tongue than Hud. She had trouble with monosyllables in English. They sounded bitten-off and incomplete.

"Why did you rescue me?"

"I have a proposition for you."

His eyes darkened with interest. "What's that?"

"Please. Finish your tea."

He emptied the cup, eager to hear more. She wondered if he thought she'd rescued him to warm her bed. She found the idea amusing, considering his condition. He was unwashed, dehydrated, malnourished and wounded. And yet, still appealing.

"How do you feel?" she asked.

"Better. Thank you."

"You're welcome."

"You look familiar."

"We haven't met."

"I know. I'd remember. But there's something about your face…" He touched his own cheek with his knuckles, contemplative. Then he frowned into his empty teacup. "This is drugged."

"Yes."

He glanced around, as if searching for an exit. They were inside a small compound, surrounded by concrete walls. "Where are we?"

"In a safe place."

"In Iraq?"

"Telskuf."

He set the cup aside. "I have to make a phone call."

"You can't. The Da'esh cut all the phone lines and tore down the cell towers."

A muscle in his jaw flexed. He seemed agitated,

but unfocused. She'd given him a hefty dose of narcotic. "What do you want from me?"

"I want you to lie down and let me take care of you."

He blinked drowsily, studying her face. She patted the wool blanket she'd placed in the middle of the platform. He stretched out on his stomach with a wince. She waited a few moments, until his shoulders relaxed and his breathing deepened. She studied his sleep-softened features. His eyelashes were dusty, his forehead creased. The blood on his back had dried into a sticky red-black paste. He had a scar on his elbow from an old surgery. Faded bruises spanned his rib cage from his lean waist to the underside of his right arm. He'd been kicked by his captors. She felt the strange urge to soothe him, stroke his hair.

"What are you doing?" Ashur said, startling her.

She gave him a chiding look. "You should be at your post."

"I want a gun."

"What?"

"I can't stand guard without a gun."

She pointed at the far wall. "Go keep watch."

He went with a scowl, kicking a rock across the courtyard. Sometimes she didn't know what to do with him. She'd inherited a teenager who seemed hell-bent on destruction, and destruction was everywhere they went.

She gathered her medical supplies to tend to the American's wounds. First, she washed his feet, which were covered with shallow cuts. He stirred as she flushed out the debris, trying to push her hands away.

"I don't work for the government, you bastards."

She blinked at his harsh tone. He seemed to think he was still a prisoner, being tortured by the Da'esh.

"I already told you. I'm an independent contractor."

She applied some healing ointment and wrapped his feet in strips of muslin. As long as he didn't get an infection, the cuts would heal quickly. His back was a different story. He had a deep laceration that needed sutures. She knelt beside him and cleaned the area as best she could. The work was painful enough to make him lift his head.

"Be calm," she said. "It is Layah."

He stared at her blearily. "Layah?"

"I'm taking care of you."

"I should bathe, before we…"

"Hush."

She didn't have any local anesthetic, so she applied a numbing agent. Then she hiked her skirt up to her knees and straddled his waist, because she didn't trust him not to jerk away from her when she sank the needle in. The contact felt unbearably intimate. It reminded her of stolen nights with Khalil.

"This would be more fun if I rolled over."

She let out a breathy laugh, resting her hand on his back. She was surprised he had the energy for sexual suggestions. "I have to stitch your wound."

He groaned in protest.

"You are strong. Stay still."

His shoulder twitched as the needle penetrated his skin. "Are you a doctor?"

"Yes."

"Why are you here?"

"In Iraq? I was born here."

"In Telskuf."

She closed the cut with neat sutures. "I came for you."

"Why?"

"I want you to take me across the Zagros Mountains."

"I'm not a pilot."

"We go on foot."

"That's…impossible."

"I disagree," she said, placing a large bandage over the wound. "But we can debate later. First, we have to escape this town alive."

He slipped back into unconsciousness. She didn't expect him to go along with her plan. She had no money to pay him, and he wouldn't volunteer his services. He couldn't, even if he wanted to. SEALs were bound by professional regulations. They didn't do freelance missions. He would never be allowed to guide a group of refugees on a dangerous journey.

So she wasn't giving him a choice.

Chapter 3

Hud woke with a mild headache and a queasy stomach.

He jerked upright, almost falling out of bed. He was in a bed? It was a narrow bed with a pillow and a wool blanket, in the corner of a quiet room. He couldn't fault the accommodations. It was a hell of a lot better than an underground torture chamber. This place had air and light and even a window—an open window with muslin curtains that fluttered in the breeze. Goats bleated and bells clanged at a distance.

They weren't in Telskuf anymore. He wasn't in his cell, and he wasn't alone. There was a boy in a chair by the window, glowering at him. Hud searched his memory for a clue to his identity.

Shut up or we die.

This was the boy who'd rescued him, with the help of that woman.

"Layah," he said. He remembered *her*.

"She is not here."

"Who are you?"

The boy rose to his full height, which was about five and a half feet. He had hair that stood up on top and ears that stuck out to the sides. His thickly lashed brown eyes were set in a hard glare. He looked like Bambi, if Bambi were an angry adolescent.

"I am Ashur," the boy said.

"I'm Petty Officer William Hudson."

Ashur stepped forward. Instead of shaking hands with Hud, he brandished a dagger. "If you try to leave, I will kill you."

Hud studied the blade warily. He didn't know who these people were or what they intended to do with him. They could be allies. They could be opportunists. Ashur reeked of antagonism, but that didn't mean anything. Some Iraqis hated Americans as much as they hated the terrorist invaders. There was a lot of resentment about the involvement of foreign governments, most of which had done more harm than good. It was a goat-screw of a situation, as his comrades would say.

That didn't mean he was going to let this little punk threaten him. Hud reached out to grasp the boy's skinny wrist, lightning-quick. When Ashur tried to twist free, Hud applied pressure until the dagger fell from his hand. "You couldn't kill a turtle. You're slow and small, and your blade is dull."

The boy said something in Arabic, probably curse words.

"Also, your eyes reveal too much." Hud picked

up the dagger. "I know what you're going to do before you do it."

"Teach me."

"Teach you what?"

"How to kill like you."

Hud met the kid's fervent gaze. It was a chilling request, made more so by the fact that Hud had already supplied a brutal demonstration of blowing someone's head off. "You just point and shoot."

"Layah will not allow me to have a gun."

"Layah is a smart woman."

"Why do you say this?"

"Who do you want to kill?"

Ashur lifted his chin. "The men who killed my father."

Hud returned the boy's dagger, handle first. His old man had died when he was about this kid's age. After the funeral, Hud had taken an air rifle into the woods and shot at everything that moved. Every innocent little bird and squirrel. He didn't want to think about that day, or to relive those feelings. He certainly didn't want to teach this boy how to be like him. "I'll give you some tips if you do me a favor."

"What?"

"Bring me a cell phone."

"There are no phones in this village."

"Where are we?"

He rattled off an Arabic name with about twenty syllables. It might have begun with *S*.

Hud knew that they weren't in Telskuf anymore. Last night they'd loaded him into the bed of a pickup truck. He'd drifted in and out of consciousness while they traveled over miles of dark, dusty road with no headlights.

Ashur handed him a cup.

"What is this?"

"Water."

Hud drained the cup and passed it back.

"I bring food," Ashur said. "You want to eat?"

His stomach growled with interest. "Yes."

"Do you need a pot?" He mimicked the act of urinating.

"No," Hud said, putting his feet on the tile floor. They were sore, but they held his weight. "Is there a toilet?"

"Yes," the boy said. "Come."

The stitches on his shoulder tugged as he followed the boy through the door. There was a closet-sized space with a squat toilet at the end of the hall. No sink, just a bucket with cold water. He rinsed his hands and let them air dry. He wanted to pour the entire bucket over his head. He'd kill for a hot shower and clean clothes.

When he emerged, Ashur escorted him back to his room and disappeared again. Hud went to the window to look out. The ground was about six feet below. There was a walled courtyard with a simple wooden gate. He could escape easily if he wanted to. Which he didn't. He was safer here than out there, and he needed to regain his strength. He needed time to think about his next step.

Beyond the gate was a pastoral-type village with rolling green hills. He'd never seen this side of Iraq. It lacked the relentless dust and nothingness of Telskuf. He could feel moisture in the air, not just swirl-ing debris. Mountains rose up in the distance, with jagged edges and snow-capped peaks. In this little valley, it was a pleasant spring day. At higher eleva-tions, the weather would be harsh and unpredictable.

Had she really asked him to take her across the Za-gros? Maybe he'd dreamed up the request. Surely he'd exaggerated the beauty of the woman who'd made it, as well. Angels didn't appear out of nowhere in Iraq. They stayed hidden in voluminous black robes, faces veiled. He must have imagined the heat in her eyes as she studied him, as well.

His shoulders tensed when she entered the room. He knew it was her without looking. He could esti-mate height, weight and gender from the sound of footsteps. He also just felt her, like a whisper of breath at the nape of his neck.

He turned and saw that she was even prettier than he remembered. Her dark hair was uncovered, gath-ered in a sleek braid. She wore a long blue tunic and black leggings with Moroccan slippers. Her eyes were deep brown and thickly lashed, with a calm serenity that made him want to inhale her.

She was exquisite, but she wasn't really his type. He had lowbrow tastes, truth be told. He liked party girls who weren't afraid to show some skin. This one didn't even reveal her hair in public. When she crossed her arms over her chest, he got the impres-sion of nice curves hidden beneath layers of fabric.

"You should be resting," she said.

He sat on the bed dutifully. She took the chair across from him.

"Do you remember our conversation?"

His gaze traveled over her figure. He remembered her bare thighs straddling his waist, and her throaty laugh as he suggested a better position. He liked her bedside manner—a lot. "About the Zagros?"

"Yes."

"Why do you think I can help you?"

"You are a Navy SEAL, and a mountain climber."

"Who told you that?"

"My sources."

He didn't bother to deny it. The tattoo on his chest was a symbol of his military affiliation. The terrorists had known he was a SEAL. They'd enjoyed putting out cigarettes on his trident, searing his flesh with hot embers. He touched the spot absently and felt no remnant of the torture. No permanent scarring. He was lucky they hadn't used a poker or a cattle brand. The minor burns had healed, the pain fading into a distant memory.

"You are a SEAL, yes? Sea, Air, Land?"

"You need an experienced local," he said. "I've never climbed those mountains. I've never even seen a map of the route."

"There isn't one."

"No map?"

"No established route. I have topographic information and satellite imagery, but no climbing details."

"How do you know it can be done?"

"It has been done before. Just not chronicled."

"Because it's not legal."

"The Kurdish government does not allow travel in this region."

"I wonder why," he said drolly.

"They do not wish for tourists to come to harm, or for refugees to get stranded and need assistance."

"Are we in Kurdistan?"

Her lips pursed at the question. "That depends on who you ask. It is a Yazidi village, protected by Kurdish forces and threatened by the Da'esh."

He couldn't keep track of the different ethnic groups and shifting borders in Iraq. The map seemed to change daily, and he'd been out of the loop for months. *Da'esh* was an Arabic word that meant Islamic Front. He knew that much. "Is Mosul still under attack?"

"It was taken by the Da'esh, along with Telskuf and every other Assyrian town in the Nineveh Province."

"You're Assyrian?"

"I am."

If his memory served, the Assyrians were Christians. Being Muslim in Iraq was no picnic, with the different sects in constant conflict, but other religious groups were even more persecuted. They had fewer numbers and less power. "My condolences."

"Are you Christian?"

He shrugged. "I was raised that way."

"Then you will help us."

"Us?"

"My people."

He gave her a dubious look. Her idea to cross the Zagros was crazy enough without adding a passel of refugees, like that maniac kid and the hunchbacked old man. The fact that they were Christians didn't change his mind. He was loyal to his team and his country, period. "You can't hire a guide who knows the area?"

"I have tried. I paid two Turkish mountaineers in advance." She let out a huffed breath. "They came during the fall of Mosul and turned back."

He nodded his understanding. There weren't a lot of expert climbers in Iraq. It was a leisure sport that required time, travel and excess cash. They were in a war zone where people were struggling to survive.

"I need a man who will not quit." She placed her hand on his forearm. "I think you are that man."

Hud arched a brow at her touch. She was a beautiful woman, savvy enough to read the interest in his eyes. She knew he'd been denied every pleasure and comfort during his captivity. Although he liked having his ego stroked, among other things, he couldn't do anything for her. He was a Navy SEAL, not a mercenary. He didn't take money from refugees, and he doubted she had any to pay him.

"Why the Zagros?" he asked.

She removed her hand from his arm. "There is no other way. The Da'esh control the roads to the south and west. We cannot travel through Syria. We have to go over the mountains, into Turkey."

"Turkey is safe?"

"Turkey is the least hostile border country. But they are closed to refugees, so crossing illegally is necessary."

"What happens if I say no?"

"For your own sake, you must say yes."

"Is that a threat?"

"It is reality. We are both prisoners here. I need

you to get out of the country. You need me for the same reason."

He made a skeptical sound, even though he believed her. In a remote location, with no communication or support from the US military, striking out on his own would be unwise. He couldn't afford to get recaptured.

She offered a tight smile, aware of his dilemma.

He smiled back at her, determined to choose his own fate. She wasn't the most formidable opponent he'd ever faced. Compared to the psychopaths who'd tortured him, she was soft. Soft and lush, with her flawless skin and alluring mouth. If he wasn't so dirty and disheveled, he might try to seduce her.

"I need clean clothes and a shower."

She bowed her head. "As you wish."

He wondered what else he could get from her. She didn't look desperate, but her actions implied otherwise. She'd blown up the side of a building to rescue him. She'd risked her life for his. She was a daring woman, despite her modest dress and demure attitude. She'd drugged him and transported him against his will. That should have been a turnoff, but it wasn't. He'd always been drawn to danger.

After she left the room, Ashur came back with a tray of delicious food. It was a feast fit for a king, and Hud ate like a half-starved wolf. He devoured every morsel of kebabs and rice and hummus, his manners gone. He might have growled at one point. There was a green salad with tomatoes, pita bread, and other dishes he couldn't identify, but shoved into his mouth nonetheless. He ignored the tea in favor of water.

"I have *bira*, if you like," Ashur said.

"What's that?"

"It is beer. We brew. Very good."

"Beer, in Iraq?"

Ashur sneered at his ignorance. "My people invented beer, American."

Hud had been under the impression that alcohol was illegal here, or rarely imbibed. "Assyrians invented beer?"

"The ancient ones, in Mesopotamia."

"I didn't know that."

"Do you speak Arabic?"

"No."

"I speak three languages."

Hud grunted and kept eating. He'd learned a few words of Arabic from one of his teammates, but he didn't have an ear for it. Too many syllables and inflections. Too many different dialects, with sounds as unique and complex as the mix of cultures in the region. Interpreters were worth their weight in gold here. That was why the IF hunted them down and cut off their tongues.

Hud swallowed the last bite, with some difficulty. "You wish to shower now?" Ashur said. "Come."

Ashur led Hud down another hall and through a door that opened to a quiet courtyard. The shower was a rustic hut made of corrugated aluminum. Hud found a bar of soap and a nubby towel on a bench inside. He shut the door and stripped down. His trousers were bloodstained and stiff with dust. He stepped into the stall, cupping one hand over himself protectively. He wasn't disappointed by the lukewarm trickle that emerged from the pipes. It was clean and it was wet. Any kind of water was a luxury to him. He hadn't so much as splashed his face in weeks. He tilted his head back, eyes closed in rapture.

God.

His throat tightened with emotion as water flowed over him. During the darkest hours of his captivity, he hadn't believed he would ever see the light of day again. He thought he'd become a pile of bones in that dusty tomb. Now he was standing in an outdoor shower, his shoulders warmed by the sun.

He bent forward and let the water cascade down his neck, humbled by the experience. He washed his matted hair and battered body, which still felt strong enough to fight. He was alive. He wasn't sure he deserved to be, after what he'd done. But here he was.

He'd survived, against all odds. He'd endured weeks of near starvation. He'd been tortured and beaten and treated like an animal.

Now he was free, and determined to stay that way.

Chapter 4

Layah drummed her fingertips against her forearms as she waited for Hudson to return from his shower.

Her captive continued to surprise her. She'd expected more resistance. Navy SEALs were elite soldiers, but they were still soldiers. They followed orders from the higher ranks. She'd been prepared for him to cite United Nations regulations and demand transport to a US air base. Hudson hadn't done any of those things. He hadn't even turned her down.

She didn't trust him to cooperate, no matter what he said. He might be waiting for his wounds to heal before he attempted an escape. But if he left, he wouldn't get far. This village was sparsely populated, and the Yazidi guarded their land with rifles. They were more likely to shoot him than help him flee.

Hudson seemed to be playing along with her for now. Maybe he wanted money in exchange for his services. Maybe he wanted something else. He looked at her with desire in his eyes, the way men often did.

His interest wasn't unusual, but her reaction to it was. Her pulse raced in his presence. She felt nervous and short of breath, like a schoolgirl with a crush. She wasn't sure how to catalog her response. She hadn't been drawn to a man since Khalil. Her physical needs had been buried with her husband, along with her broken heart.

Layah didn't believe Hudson had resurrected her feminine longing. She was excited by the situation, not his searing gaze and hard-muscled body. He'd killed a guard yesterday. She'd rescued him from certain death. She wanted him to like her, and she had to keep him close. It was only natural to feel nervous around him. She'd been numb for so long that she'd mistaken an adrenaline rush for attraction.

Yes. That was it. Adrenaline.

She had to stay focused on her plan. Hudson was a means to an end, nothing more. She couldn't afford to get distracted.

He emerged from the outdoor shower in the clothes Ashur had given him. The items were borrowed from one of her male cousins, and they fit well enough. Hudson was tall and broad-shouldered, rangy like Khalil had been. About the same age. Her husband would have turned thirty this year, had he lived. Her chest tightened at the thought.

There was a large open sink next to the shower hut for washing hands, dishes and everything else. Ashur provided Hudson with a new toothbrush, still in the wrapper. Toiletries were prized items in this remote area, but she'd splurged on a few luxuries for her captive. He'd been beaten and tortured by the Da'esh. Under her care, he'd be treated well.

When he was finished, Ashur escorted him back to his room. She gathered her maps and notebook, along with her medical bag, before venturing that direction. Ashur was carrying an empty tray down the hall.

"He eats like a pig," Ashur said in Assyrian. "It will cost a fortune just to feed him."

"He's worth it."

"That's what you said about those thieving Turks."

She shooed him away in annoyance. Ashur thought he knew everything, and was quite happy to argue with her about any choice she made. From the start he'd insisted that they didn't need a guide, especially a foreigner.

She paused in the doorway. Hudson sat at the edge of the bed, hands folded in his lap. His trousers molded to his long legs and the polo shirt stretched tight across his shoulders. She found no fault with his appearance. He looked good. His hair was a honey-brown shade, like his eyes, and his skin had the same warm tone.

He was handsome. Striking, even.

She entered the room and placed her things on the table. "How do you feel?" she asked, aiming for a polite, professional tone.

"Almost human."

"Any pain from your suture site?"

"Not really."

"Can I take a look?"

He twisted at the waist to give her access. She sat

down beside him and lifted the hem of his shirt halfway up his back. The bandage was still clean and intact, so she left it alone. The bruises on his side had
darkened to an angry purple in some places. When
she touched him there, he sucked in a ragged breath.

"Does it hurt?"

"No."

She palpated his ribs gently. "Were you kicked?"

His expression was flat. "I can't remember."

She didn't believe him. Perhaps he'd learned to
give no information, even when pushed to the limit.
She was barely pressing him. She didn't feel any
broken ribs, just warm flesh over hard muscles. She
tugged his shirt down, trying not to imagine the horrors he'd endured. "I have painkillers."

"I don't need them."

Her gaze rose to his. He'd shifted toward her when
she finished her exam. Now they were side by side,
and too close for comfort. She could smell the soap
he'd used, which conjured an erotic image of water
flowing down his naked body.

She suppressed the urge to inhale deeper. "Do you
need…anything else?"

His eyes darkened at the question, dropping to her
lips. It wasn't difficult to guess what he was thinking. She'd been a wife for long enough to know what
men liked. What they craved, what comforted them.

"I wouldn't mind a haircut," he said.

"What?"

He let out a choked laugh and lifted a hand to his
head. He made scissors with his fingers. "A haircut,
you know. Snip snip?"

"Oh. Yes. I will get Ashur."

"No, not him."

"No?"

"I don't want him near me with sharp objects."

Her stomach fluttered with unease. "What has he done?"

"Nothing much. He's okay. I just prefer you."

"I apologize for Ashur. He is a difficult boy."

"Is he your son?"

She rose to her feet abruptly. Anguish speared through her. "He is my brother's son."

Hudson gave her an assessing look, but didn't ask more questions.

She busied herself by searching through her medical bag for a pair of utility scissors. "I will cut your hair." She gestured to the only chair in the room, a simple wooden stool by the table. "Come sit."

He sat down and stared out the window. A villager was leading his herd down the rocky hillside in the distance. She liked the deserts and the valleys of her homeland, but there was something tranquil about this mountain backdrop. She turned her attention to Hudson's hair. "How short?"

"I don't care."

She did her best to cut sparingly, in even amounts. There were matted tangles and singed ends, as if he'd been burned. She tried to remove the damage without leaving any bald spots. When she was finished, she set aside the scissors and touched his newly shorn head. His hair looked choppy, but felt nice. She murmured in approval, running her fingers through it.

He made a grunting sound of pleasure.

She glanced down and realized he was staring at her breasts, which were about an inch from his face. She'd been so intent on her task that she'd forgotten to keep a polite distance. She hadn't meant for this mundane act to become so intimate. The air between them turned electric, charged with sexual energy. He was leaning into her hands, like a cat that wanted more petting. She froze, her fingers still threaded in his hair.

He glanced up at her, his jaw tense.

"Sorry," she said, releasing him. Before she could step back, he slipped his arm around her waist.

"Are you?"

She was startled by his sudden movement. His expression revealed hunger, not anger, but she had to be careful with him. His injuries hadn't made him weak or slow. If he wanted to overpower her, he could.

"Are you sorry for touching me? For getting too close? Or for holding me against my will?"

Her eyes widened in surprise. "I'm not."

He arched a brow at this claim. When she tried to twist away, he pulled her closer. She braced her palms on his biceps, her pulse racing. Maybe he could sense her excitement, as well as her deception. Because she liked his arm around her, strong and immobile. She liked his taut face and hard body. She could lie to him, but she couldn't lie to herself.

He lifted one hand to her face. "Let's make a deal."

Her heart fluttered like a trapped bird in her chest. He didn't want to help her. He wanted to regain control of the situation by any means necessary. Although she might enjoy his methods, she couldn't let him manipulate her.

"I take you across the mountains, and you take me however I like."

"I rescued you," she choked. "You owe me."

"This isn't a rescue. It's forced labor."

"We help each other. It is fair."

"No. If you want my services, you have to buy them."

"I can't pay you."

He brushed his thumb over her trembling lips. "Sure you can."

Arousal coursed through her, unabated. Her body didn't care about his motives. It longed for a respite from grief and pain. One sensual interlude, to make her forget her troubles.

"You're not free until I am," he said in a low voice. "You can walk away from my deal as soon as I can walk away from yours."

She couldn't acquiesce to his demands, no matter how tempted she was. She couldn't allow him to gain the upper hand. He seemed excited about turning the tables on her and giving her orders. A flash of intuition told her he wanted freedom, not sex.

"Fine," she said, feigning defeat. "Take me."

His gaze darkened. "What?"

"Do your worst."

"My worst is the best you've ever had, guaranteed."

A thrill shivered down her spine at his boast, but she summoned a bored look. "Go ahead, if you must."

He stood abruptly, lifting her off her feet. In the

next instant, she was on the bed, flat on her back underneath him. He pushed her arms over her head and pinned them against the mattress. She didn't protest. He stared at her for a long moment, breathing heavily. She stared back at him, calling his bluff. He wasn't the dumb brute she'd expected. He had brains, as well as brawn. He thought he could pressure her into releasing him. What he didn't realize was that they were both prisoners here. The only way out was over those mountains, together.

His grip on her wrists loosened. He collapsed, burying his face in her neck.

She experienced a strange mix of emotions. Sorrow, relief, guilt, sympathy…disappointment. And kinship, maybe. He didn't want to help her, but they were connected. They shared a common enemy. They'd both suffered the traumas of war, even though he'd done so by choice, not because of a direct threat to his home and family.

She raised a hand to his hair, tentative. It still felt nice. So did his body, for that matter. The heavy weight of him reminded her of past pleasures, long forgotten. She stroked the nape of his neck lightly.

He lifted his head, his expression incredulous. She knew she was playing with fire, and she didn't care. She raked her nails through his hair, encouraging him. She thought he might shove her away in anger, but he didn't. His half-lidded gaze lowered to her lips.

Then his mouth descended.

The first contact was electric. She parted her lips under his, breathless. She'd wanted this from the first moment she set eyes on him. He was battered and bruised. He'd been in a dark place. So had she. Maybe that was what drew her to him. He needed comfort, and she ached to give it. He was her captive, her patient, her only hope.

His kiss wasn't gentle. He plundered her mouth with his tongue, taking what he wanted. He tasted like mint and soap and male heat, a tantalizing mixture. She clutched his hair and moaned. He feasted on her mouth the same way he devoured plates of food, without finesse. She reveled in the possession.

Had it been this way with Khalil? This urgent?

She couldn't remember, but it didn't matter. Hudson kissed away those thoughts and inserted himself back into them. His tongue delved deeper and his body pressed harder. She could feel the exciting length of his erection. Desire pulsed between her legs. She shifted her hips against him.

He groaned against her mouth, his big hand squeezing her waist. It roved to her hip and back up again, covering her breast. This simple pleasure seemed to undo him. He broke the kiss and fumbled for a way underneath her clothes.

She might have let him continue, but the sound of approaching footsteps snapped her to her senses.

Ashur.

He was coming down the hall.

Hudson heard it, too. He turned his head toward the open doorway, his hands still. They were about to get caught.

She pushed at his shoulders and he shifted to one side, allowing her enough space to move. She scrambled off the bed in a panic. He sat forward and folded his arms over his lap while she straightened her tunic. When Ashur appeared in the doorway, she made a face like a scolding auntie.

"Where have you been? I need a broom to sweep up this hair."

Ashur muttered something about cleaning up after swine and went to do her bidding. It was his typical attitude, so she didn't think he'd noticed her dishabille. She leaned against the chair, weak-kneed. When she glanced at Hudson again, his eyes were sharp.

"Are you married?" he asked in a hard voice.

"No."

He rubbed a hand over his mouth, as if the question had left a bad taste in it.

"I'm a widow," she said. "A recent widow, still in mourning."

His expression didn't change. "How recent?"

"Two years."

"Two years is a long time."

"In my culture, some widows stay in seclusion for the rest of their lives. Most do not remarry or keep company with men."

"Is that your plan? Never remarry?"

It wasn't what Khalil would have wanted, but she hadn't imagined moving on. She also hadn't imagined kidnapping an American and allowing him to take liberties. She didn't recognize the woman she'd become.

Ashur returned with the broom, saving her from responding. He swept up the clumps of hair, his eyes downcast. She wondered what he'd done to make Hudson wary. Ashur was so full of grief and fury.

He blamed all Americans for destabilizing the country. He blamed Hudson, in particular, for his father's death. She couldn't afford to get caught kissing the man. It might send Ashur over the edge.

"Do you require anything else, Queen Aunt?" Ashur asked.

She gestured for him to go. He did an exaggerated bow and left the room. She didn't think it was funny, but Hudson's lips quirked with amusement. She crossed her arms over her chest, studying him. "Are you married?"

"I'm divorced," he said. "It's what we do in my culture."

"It is not uncommon here, either."

"Really?"

She nodded and turned her attention to the map on the table. She was curious about his past, but she needed to focus on the journey ahead. "I can pay you after we reach our destination."

"I don't want your money."

She didn't ask what he wanted. She already knew. "Please, look at the map. Crossing the Zagros is not as dangerous as attempting to travel within Iraq."

"Why can't you stay here, in this village?"

"The Yazidi have offered a temporary meeting place, not a permanent refuge."

He stood and joined her at the table, his brow furrowed.

She pointed to a tiny dot on the map. "We are here." She traced the edge of the mountain range with her fingertip, until she reached the outskirts of Turkey. It wasn't her final stop, but he didn't need to know that. "I want to go there."

"What about the Kurds?"

"What about them?"

"They won't help you?"

"Kurdistan is not stable, due to border conflicts with Turkey and Iran. They have also taken Assyrian lands in the guise of protecting us. They are your allies, not ours."

"This country," he muttered.

"What about it?"

"It's a goddamned mess, that's what."

"Yes, it is. We live in rubble left by the US intervention."

He made a sound of skepticism. "Your wars go back centuries, before the US was even founded."

"Before your ancestors stole land from the natives, you mean?"

He tapped the surface of the map. "There's snow and ice on those mountains. We need special gear for that."

"I have gear."

"Do you have crampons for everyone?"

"Yes. Come see."

She escorted him to another room. She had tents, canvas packs, climbing rope, crampons for icy terrain, and a pile of boots in the corner. He picked up a boot, arching a brow. They were desert-style cast-offs from a US military base. Or perhaps stolen. She'd bought the gear in bulk and not asked questions.

"These aren't for snow."

"They are all we have."

He pulled out one of the tents and studied it. "What about sleeping bags? We'll freeze to death at night."

"We will use wool and sheepskin, like the nomads." She showed him her stack of sheepskins. There were two rectangular pieces for each hiker. One covered the front of the torso and one covered the back. There were ties at the shoulders and on the sides. "This can be worn and used as a sleeping mat."

"How?"

She laid the two panels flat on the ground. The sheepskin offered warmth and padding. "The wool cloaks are versatile also. They become blankets."

"What if they get wet?"

"I have ponchos." She found the plastic hooded ponchos. "See?"

He rifled through one of the packs, studying the gear. It was a mix of modern, traditional and low-budget items, all painstakingly collected. She had stainless steel water containers that could be used for cooking. Food rations in sealed tins. He tossed out whatever he deemed unnecessary. When he was finished, he lifted the pack with one hand to test its weight. His bulging biceps mesmerized her.

He dropped the pack with a thunk.

"Is it too heavy?" she asked.

"How do you expect that old man to strap on a fifty-pound pack without falling and breaking a hip?"

"Ibrahim is not coming. He returned to his home in Telskuf."

"No old people? No kids?"

"Only Ashur. He will have a lighter pack."

Hud grunted in response, his gaze moving down

her body. "You don't know what you're in for. Grueling fourteen-hour hikes. No rest stops. Elevation sickness. Dangerous terrain. Bad weather."

"I walked across the Syrian Desert for sixteen days. I think I know."

"This won't be like that."

"It is a journey my people have taken before."

"Yeah, who?"

"My mother and father. They guided Assyrian refugees from other countries *into* Iraq when they were young."

He cursed under his breath at this revelation.

"We will make it. I am confident."

"Do you have guns?"

"Of course." Those were easy to get here, unlike climbing gear. "As many Kalashnikovs as you like."

"Great," he muttered. "When do we go?"

"As soon as the others arrive. Four or five days."

"I can't wait."

She followed him back to his room, feeling giddy. His sarcasm didn't bother her. It meant he was going to cooperate. She was eager to discuss the itinerary, but he stopped at the threshold, barring her entry.

"Unless you want to finish what we started, get away from me."

She flushed with embarrassment. "Good night, then."

He slammed the door in her face.

Chapter 5

Hud spent the next three days recuperating.

Recuperating, seething in silence and fantasizing about Layah.

He couldn't believe she'd played him like that. He'd intended to play her, not the other way around. He thought he could convince her to abandon her half-cocked plan by demanding sex, but she hadn't blinked an eye at his crude proposition. She wasn't afraid of him, and she wasn't innocent. She was a young widow, ripe for pleasure. She'd stroked his hair and rubbed her generous breasts against him.

Damn it.

All he'd gotten for his efforts was an erection that wouldn't quit. He kept reevaluating the kiss they'd shared, searching for signs of deception. She couldn't fake chemistry. They had that in spades. The feel of her hands in his hair had turned him into mush. When their mouths met, it was like fireworks.

She'd wanted him, in that moment. They'd been on the same page, hungry for each other. He hadn't imagined her heated response.

Then they'd almost been caught by Ashur, and she'd jumped up from the bed in a panic, as if she might get stoned in a public square for kissing him. A cold weight had settled in his stomach at the sight, and a little voice in his head whispered: *She's married. She looks guilty because she's married.*

She'd said she was a widow, and that made sense, but he didn't trust her to tell the truth. She was holding him hostage. She'd kidnapped him and drugged him. Lying was a minor offense compared to her other infractions. Intuition told him she was hiding something, and he'd been burned by beautiful women before.

His cheating ex, for example.

He'd searched Layah's room at the first opportunity. He hadn't found a cell phone or any useful items among her personal effects, which he'd inspected thoroughly. The damp lingerie in her washroom had smelled like jasmine water, clean and intoxicating. It wasn't his finest moment of reconnaissance, but no regrets.

This morning, he'd woken up antsy. He'd paced the room, considering his options. He didn't want to cross the Zagros with a bunch of refugees, but he didn't want to stay in this village. It was an insecure location, nestled against the mountains. He had no local contacts. The closest military base was hundreds of miles away.

After breakfast, he tested his stitches by doing a basic captivity workout. Fifty push-ups, two hundred curl-ups, five minutes of cardio. Halfway through, he heard a knock at the door. He paused, wiping the sweat from his face.

Ashur looked in on him. "Are you sick, American?"

"No, I'm training."

"Kill-training?"

Hud smiled at the boy's hopeful expression. He'd given Ashur a basic self-defense lesson yesterday. The boy was an apt pupil, eager to learn more close-quarters combat techniques. "What do you want?"

Ashur entered the room and dropped a pair of boots on the floor at Hud's feet. "Layah says we go today."

"Go where?"

"On our journey."

His gut clenched with unease. He hadn't expected to leave so soon. "Have the others arrived?"

"The others?"

"The other people in our party."

"They came weeks ago."

Hud dragged a hand down his face. She'd lied to him. The other refugees had been here all along, waiting for *him*.

"You are strong," Ashur said. "The weather is good. We must go now."

He tried on the boots. They were the right size, and almost new. Layah had waterproofed every pair with beeswax and oil, on his orders. He could argue that he was still too weak to climb, or simply refuse to leave, but neither option appealed to him. He didn't feel secure here. His best option was to travel with Layah. He'd act as her guide, for now. He'd do whatever she wanted. A part of him was excited by the prospect.

A very stupid part of him that sometimes made his brain shut off.

He knew he shouldn't touch her again. He was a Navy SEAL, and she was a refugee. He might be able to get away with seducing her as an escape strategy. Doing it for his own pleasure was a clear violation. It was unprofessional, unethical and unwise. Not to mention dangerous. He couldn't afford to let down his guard with this woman. Bedding her would be hot, but he had to stay cool and keep his distance.

She'd been giving him a wide berth, so it shouldn't be difficult. They'd hardly spoken since the kiss. She never came into his room. Maybe she didn't trust herself to be alone with him. He smiled at the thought.

At some point, he'd get a chance to sneak off on his own. He'd have the advantage in the higher elevations. He didn't know where they were, exactly, but they had to be close to Iraqi Kurdistan. The Kurds were reliable US allies, with an army of well-trained soldiers. They would take him to an air base.

He stood, rolling his shoulders in anticipation. His injury wasn't bothering him. He'd done little but sleep and eat for two days straight. He could feel his body recharging, gaining back the weight he'd lost. A glance in the mirror in Layah's washroom had revealed a stranger with sharp cheekbones and a delineated rib cage, but plenty of lean muscle. He touched his flat stomach, which was still full from breakfast.

"Hungry again?" Ashur asked as they left the room.

"I don't think you've fattened me up enough," Hud said.

Ashur made a snorting sound. "You eat more than ten men, American. You will be fat as a *qurād* soon."

"What is that? A king?"

He laughed, shaking his head. "Yes, a king. Do you wish to learn Arabic? I teach you."

Hud didn't plan on being in the country long enough to bother. "You can be my interpreter."

Ashur flinched at this suggestion, his smile fading. Hud was reminded of his last interpreter, who'd died a grisly death. Ashur couldn't know that, but he seemed offended. "I will never work for you," the boy said.

"I work for you, is that it?"

"Yes. That is it."

Hud stared back at him in silence. Ashur had a quick temper and a chip on his shoulder the size of Iraq. Hud recognized a bit of himself in the boy. He'd been angry at the world as a kid, unable to control his emotions. Climbing had been his only outlet until he'd joined the military, where he'd learned to channel his aggressions.

Now Hud was adept at staying calm and focused, after years of practice. He'd worked hard to master his mind and body. The strategies he used to maintain equilibrium had kept him sane in captivity. It was ironic, he supposed. His mother had worried constantly about his combative nature, and his affinity for danger. She'd thought climbing would be his downfall. Instead it was his salvation. His troubled adolescence had been a training ground, honing him into an elite solider who could withstand extreme duress.

Hud moved around the boy and continued outside. Ashur wasn't a serious threat, and he wasn't responsible for Hud's predicament. Layah was. She stood by the gate with three backpacks at her feet. Bulky layers of clothing disguised her figure and a pale brown hijab covered her hair. She might look unremarkable from behind. Straight on, her beautiful face shone like the desert sun.

He felt a stirring of desire and resented it.

"Good morning," she said.

He nodded curtly. They were getting a late start, by his standards. Most climbing expeditions began before dawn. He picked up his pack, which was loaded with ropes and equipment. He'd examined every item yesterday. The sutures on his shoulder tugged as he balanced the weight.

"How are you feeling?"

"Do you care?"

She lifted her own pack with a frown. "I wish I could give you more time to rest, but it is important to begin our journey now, before the Da'esh come, or the ground thaws and the terrain becomes unstable."

He glanced at the white-capped peaks in the distance. It was the middle of spring, so he understood her urgency. Snowmelt turned the ground into slippery slush and caused rock slides. They needed the weather to stay cool and clear, but there were no guarantees. At the summit, the temperature could dip to below freezing, with swirling snowstorms and zero visibility. "Where are the others?"

"We will meet them on the mountain."

Ashur opened the gate for them. Two men stood outside, guarding the exit with Kalashnikovs. Hud recognized them as the men who'd carried him away from the rubble of the torture cell.

"This is Yusef and Aram," she said.

"My executioners?"

"My cousins," she corrected. "They will not harm you."

Hud gave both men a quick examination. Layah's cousins appeared comfortable with their weapons, but they were no match for him physically. He could disarm one and kill the other in the blink of an eye.

"You must stay with us," she said, as if she could read his mind. "The Yazidi have taken a great risk by giving us refuge. They know you were a Da'esh prisoner, and they will not allow you to endanger them by getting recaptured."

"So your men won't shoot me, but the Yazidi will?"

"If you leave our group, yes. They will shoot you to protect their families."

He adjusted the straps on his pack. She'd chosen to begin their journey at midmorning for a reason. She wanted him to be seen by the villagers, who would help her keep him in line. "How convenient."

"You fault me for warning you?"

"No. I fault you for threatening me with violence while pretending you're above it."

Her cheeks flushed a dusky rose. "I pretend nothing."

He studied her face, remembering her heated response to their bedroom tussle. She might not be a faker, but she wasn't honest, either. And his body didn't seem to care. If anything, his anger and resentment had stoked his desire. He felt outmaneuvered by her, and the caveman in him wanted to flip things around. He wanted to get back on top and pin her underneath him.

But that wasn't going to happen, so he dropped the subject and started walking. Challenging her wouldn't improve his situation. It would only make him want to crush his mouth over hers in retaliation. He told himself it was a normal reaction. Any man who'd been taken prisoner by a beautiful woman would think about doing her, and she'd encouraged him to kiss her. She'd given him signals. Of course he was going to fantasize about getting even. Or at least, getting off.

Layah trailed behind him, followed by Ashur and the two cousins. Hud continued down the dirt road, which couldn't have been more than a mile long. He could see a well-worn path from the village into the mountains, used by goats and sheepherders. It would take a day or more to hike beyond the grazing hills.

After a few minutes, his muscles warmed up and his tension eased. It felt good to be outdoors again. It felt good to be alive. The air was cool and the land was green. He loved climbing. He'd rather die on the side of a mountain than in a dusty tomb. Forced labor wasn't so bad, and the scenery was excellent.

He could almost hear his comrades' mocking voices in his head: *You're mad about getting res-*

cued and bossed around by a sexy woman? Dude, what is wrong with you? Did you lose your balls in that explosion?

Thinking about his team members gave Hud pause. Some of them might have died in that explosion—because of him. Because of his choices, his mistakes. He'd been so intent on catching the terrorist who'd killed their interpreter that he'd risked his own life, and the lives of his best friends. That didn't sit well with him. He needed to stop lusting after Layah and concentrate on his main objective. He could still ditch her in the mountains. He felt strong, like he could hike forever.

As they started up the goat path, Layah fell into step beside him. "You are unhappy about our partnership."

He arched a brow. "This isn't a partnership."

"I would like it to be."

"I think what you'd like is for me to follow your orders with a smile."

She gestured toward the summit. "Up there, you will be giving the orders."

He glanced that direction, trying not to feel excited by the prospect. The lure of a dangerous challenge beckoned.

"The journey will be difficult, but it is the best way. Soon we will all be smiling in celebration of our success." Her lips formed a tentative curve that was half peace offering, half propaganda.

"You don't have to sell it to me, Doc. The threat of being shot by Yazidis already did the trick."

"I wish for harmony between us, not strife."

He squinted at her wording. "Did you learn English from a brochure?"

"No. I learned it in Baghdad."

"Why do you cover your hair?"

She blinked in surprise. "What?"

"You aren't Muslim."

"Many non-Muslim women wear a hijab."

"Out of fear?"

"There are other reasons. Assyrian women have been wearing them since Biblical times. I do it to be respectful, to keep the dust out of my hair and so I can travel without attracting attention."

He doubted she could travel anywhere unnoticed, with that face. He wanted to ask more questions, to interrogate her about every detail of her life. Instead he pulled ahead, ending the conversation. She was a fascinating woman, but he couldn't afford to get sucked in.

The steady climb kept him busy for the next few hours. He set a punishing pace to see if they could match it. They couldn't, but there were no complaints. No one requested a break. Soon he was sweating, his leg muscles burning.

He spotted a plateau where they could rest. A glance over his shoulder revealed Layah in front of the others, flushed with exertion and struggling to catch up with him. He accelerated, leaving them behind.

When he reached the plateau, he found a motley group of refugees awaiting him. Two sturdy-looking, dark-haired men stood in front of a half-dozen women. Packs were scattered around in a circle. The men looked wary, uncertain if he was friend or foe. They hadn't expected him to arrive alone.

Hud said hello in Arabic, which was about the extent of his vocabulary. Then he took off his pack and sat down to drink water. He was light-headed from the last push. All the refugees approached to introduce themselves, saying names he couldn't make sense of. It was an incomprehensible mix of sounds.

"Hudson," he said, touching his chest.

"American," someone said. "American, yes?"

He gulped more water. "American. Yes. Hoorah."

There were several cheers, as if he was here to save them. A weight settled into the pit of his stomach, making him queasy. He shouldn't have pulled ahead of the others. Taking a deep breath, he did a quick head count. There were two extra bodies here.

An old woman and a girl.

God*damn* it.

Layah appeared with Ashur and her two goons. They were sweaty and winded, like Hud, but they'd done well. Better than the current party would do. He gave Layah a dark look, because she'd promised him a team of healthy adults. They were going to have a very *unharmonious* discussion about this as soon as she caught her breath.

The extra woman was pushing sixty, with a sturdy shape and a careworn face. The girl was Ashur's age or younger. She was too big to carry, too small to carry her own weight.

The grandma brought him a flatbread sandwich loaded with meat and goat cheese. It was delicious. He devoured every bite. Then he stood and gestured for Layah to come with him. They walked about ten yards away for a private chat. He didn't think anyone else spoke English, but he wasn't sure. Ashur accompanied them, eating his sandwich. Layah's cousins watched from a distance, their rifles close at hand.

"I can explain," Layah said.

Hud crossed his arms over his chest, waiting for it.

"The girl and her grandmother asked to join our party."

"So you just said yes?"

"They are Yazidi. I could not refuse."

He understood her dilemma. The Yazidi had sheltered Layah and her people. She owed them a favor. "I can't guide a team of children and old people."

"We have no choice. We cannot send them back."

"Why not?"

"I gave my word."

"You gave *me* your word," he said in a low voice.

Ashur stepped in front of Layah protectively. "She does not answer to you, American."

Layah nudged Ashur aside. "The girls in the village are being taken as brides by the Da'esh."

Hud was no stranger to the horrors of war, but this news shocked him. "That young?"

"As young as thirteen. She is twelve."

Hud swore under his breath. He'd heard about IF militants targeting women and girls. The highest-ranking members collected as many wives as they wanted, and murdered any male relatives who protested.

"One of their leaders has already claimed her,"

Layah added. "He said he would come back for her in the spring."

Ashur studied the girl as he finished his sandwich. "She is pretty, for a Yazidi."

"I can't carry her," Hud said.

"You won't have to," Layah replied. "She is strong enough to make the journey."

He rubbed a hand over his mouth, uneasy. Layah had no idea how many things could go wrong on a climbing expedition. This entire country was a jinx, as far as he was concerned. His last mission had been a disaster. He'd left two good men behind. He'd let down his team by getting captured.

He wasn't ready to play the hero again, physically or mentally. Four days ago he'd been struggling to survive in an underground dungeon. Now he was carrying a heavy load of equipment and a staggering amount of responsibility. Innocent lives were at stake. He closed his eyes, swallowing hard.

"Is your shoulder sore?" she asked.

"It's fine."

"Any dizziness?"

He shook his head and moved past her. If he pushed them hard, someone might get injured or quit before they reached the point of no return. He could push Ashur off the side of a cliff while he was at it. "Let's go."

She agreed with an easy nod. "I would like to reach the edge of the snow by nightfall. How does that sound?"

He squinted into the distance. "Optimistic."

They set out again five minutes later. Hud led the

pack, followed by Ashur and Layah. Everyone else marched behind them in a neat row, with the armed guards at the rear. Hud didn't expect any gun battles out here in the middle of nowhere, but it was possible. If they did get shot at, he planned to grab a Kalashnikov and return fire. The rocky terrain offered very little cover. The best defense was excellent marksmanship.

As they reached higher elevations, the conditions worsened. Loose pebbles shifted beneath his feet and he struggled to catch his breath in the thin air. Tomorrow they would add snow to the mix. Then ice. At some point, he'd need to use his climbing gear on the rock face. Without his technical skills, they wouldn't make it.

Hud might have enjoyed tackling this mountain range with Team Twelve. SEALs were all experienced climbers and expert outdoorsmen. He could lead his team across the Zagros with confidence. Refugees and children were another story. He kept glancing over his shoulder, expecting injuries.

They settled into a steady rhythm. He pushed as hard as he dared, and they pushed themselves harder. No one fell down the hill or collapsed in exhaustion. Layah, in particular, impressed him with her stamina. She had a body like a centerfold, not an athlete, so he hadn't expected her to keep up.

About an hour before sunset, he spotted a possible campsite. It was a little early, and they hadn't yet reached the edge of the snowcap, but they were close. He knew they were tired, because he was tired. The excited chatter he'd heard all afternoon had died down.

He paused on a flat stretch of land and studied the

area. There was a trickle of water running down the side of the cliff nearby. It was a good place to stay, sheltered from the wind on three sides.

"We can stop here for the night," he said to Layah.

She smiled her relief. "Bless you."

He took off his pack and sat with his back against the rock, muscles aching. He was beat. She pressed a handful of dates into his palm. Although he was ravenous, he chewed slowly, savoring each bite. The others rested with them, drinking and eating their own snacks. The setting sun glowed on the horizon.

"Beautiful, isn't it?" Layah murmured.

Before today, he'd have said Iraq was the ugliest place on earth. But this stretch of land was a rich tapestry of colors, dancing with light. He turned his gaze to her face and found more beauty there. "We have to set up the tents."

"My cousins will do it." She gave the order with a wave of her hand.

Aram and Yusef fumbled with three tents, two medium-sized and one small. They were clearly out of their element, but Hud left them to it. Layah had a tiny stove to boil water for a meal of dried meat and couscous. It was a time-consuming process. They ate in batches, refilling their water bottles from the stream. When they were finished, it was almost dark, and the temperature had dropped considerably.

Hud knew at a glance that there wasn't enough space for everyone. There was a tent for women and a tent for men, both full. Hud, Ashur and Layah were left with the smaller tent. "This was supposed to be for the Turks," Layah said.

"I'll take it," Hud said.

"You can't. The women's tent has no space because of Hanna and Yelda. Ashur and I have nowhere else to sleep."

"Ashur can sleep with your cousins."

"The men are taking turns keeping watch."

"So? He can take a turn."

Ashur was pleased with this arrangement, which gave him man status and access to the Kalashnikovs.

"I don't want him handling weapons," Layah said.

"I'll give him a safety lesson tomorrow," Hud said. He didn't trust Ashur not to shoot him accidentally. Or even on purpose.

"Very well," she said, ruffling the boy's hair. "Good night."

Ashur joined the other men in the tent while Yusef came outside for first watch. He narrowed his eyes at Hud in warning, but said nothing.

"My cousins don't approve of us sleeping together," Layah said.

"Your cousins aren't in charge."

She didn't disagree. Hud suspected she had her own reasons for agreeing to share his space. Maybe she wanted to keep tabs on him.

Hud crawled into the two-man tent after Layah. He didn't care about her overprotective family members or her martyred-widow reputation. He just wanted peace and quiet. She settled in next to him, stiff as a board.

Two minutes later, he was asleep.

Chapter 6

Layah dreamed of Khalil.

They'd met in Damascus, at the university where she attended medical school. He was studying law. She used to sit and read beneath an olive tree near her favorite café. She'd noticed him watching her one day, and she liked what she saw, so she'd left her book behind. He'd picked it up and followed her.

That was before he joined the Free Syrian Army. Before everything fell apart.

In her dream, she was following him. He was weaving through the crowded market, staying one step ahead of her. He skirted around traffic and ducked into an alleyway. He was tall and broad-shouldered, easy to spot but hard to catch. She ran after him and found a dark-haired stranger in his place.

She fell to her knees and wept.

Then his strong arms wrapped around her and she was safe again. She hugged him closer, clinging to his lean form. She pressed her lips to his warm neck. He inhaled a sharp breath.

She woke with a start, her limbs tangled with his. Her mouth on his skin. Only it wasn't Khalil. It was Hudson. The two men were about the same size, with rangy builds, but they didn't feel the same. Hudson's body hummed with energy, as if he had a live wire inside him. A spark of passion, ready to ignite.

They didn't smell the same, either. She didn't remember what Khalil smelled like, but this wasn't it. This was a heady combination of rough wool and male heat and earthy minerals. She moistened her lips, tasting salt. His grip tightened on her upper arms. A vein pulsed at the base of his throat, where her mouth had touched.

Sleeping with Hudson was a bad idea, but it wouldn't ruin her reputation. Her marriage to Khalil had already done that.

She eased away from him, moving as far as she could in the cramped quarters of the tent. Although she'd attempted to keep as much distance between them as possible, they'd drifted together in the night.

"I'm sorry," she said. "I was dreaming."

"About your husband?"

"Yes."

He scrubbed a hand down his face. It was chilly inside the tent, especially now that they'd separated. "How did he die?"

"He was shot on the outskirts of Palmyra with a group of opposition fighters."

"He was in the rebel army?"

She nodded, swallowing past the lump in her throat. "He left the university to join them a few months before graduation. I begged him not to go. I said he would get shot the first week." She sat forward and reached for her boots. "He lived more than a year."

Hudson braced his weight on his elbows, watching as she tied her laces. She couldn't meet his eyes. Her emotions were on edge, she was sore from the hike and she hadn't slept well on the hard ground. He seemed impervious to discomfort, but he'd been trained for extremes. She couldn't imagine the conditions he'd endured in the torture cell.

He didn't ask any more questions. She unzipped the front flap and looked out. Aram was awake, keeping watch as dawn broke over the horizon. She could see her breath in the cold air. Before she left the tent, she grabbed her wool poncho.

It was still difficult to speak of Khalil, to dream of him and remember him. She'd loved him so much. After his death, she'd buried herself in work at the hospital in Damascus. They'd needed all the help they could get. The day of the air strikes, she'd stayed on duty for forty-eight hours. She'd seen things she could not bear. And, like many medical professionals before her, she'd fled the carnage and never returned.

She'd walked to Jordan. She'd worked in a tea house to pay for room and board. The weeks had passed in a blur of nothingness. Then she'd received the devastating news about her brother and his wife. She'd picked up the broken pieces of herself and returned to Syria, for Ashur's sake. She'd planned to bring him back to Jordan, but the roads had become impassible. They could travel only one direction, toward their ravaged homeland.

She pushed aside the memories and collected water for breakfast. Hudson thought the refugees were ill-equipped for this journey, and they were. But they wouldn't give up. Everyone here had a story of hardship and loss. A lifetime of diaspora. They were all seasoned warriors, the same as him.

She visited the women's tent, which was crammed with six females sleeping head to toe. Two were her cousins' wives. Although Layah felt uneasy about sharing a tent with Hudson, she couldn't fit here. She also suspected he would try to leave the group if given the opportunity. She needed to keep him close, but not too close. He was a virile, attractive man. If she wasn't careful, she might find herself in a compromising position. Again.

They shared a breakfast of hot tea and dehydrated eggs. Hudson finished his rations quickly. She knew it wasn't enough to satisfy him. She hoped they could hunt at some point, because the food wouldn't last. They had milk powder, bouillon cubes, dates and several handfuls of dried meat. In three or four days, they'd have nothing.

She approached him for a consultation while her cousins broke down the tents. "How far will we go today?"

He glanced toward the snowy mountaintop. "How far do you want to go?"

"I want to reach the summit."

"The summit is the high point. We want to cross at the lowest elevation."

"I want to reach the crossing place, then."

"We can't get there in one day."

"Why not?"

"You're a bunch of amateurs, and I'm still recovering. We'll be lucky to cover half that distance."

"Will we get there tomorrow?"

"I doubt it."

"When?"

"Let me see the map."

She retrieved the map from her pack and presented it to him. It showed natural topography and nothing else. No roads, borders or towns. She'd marked a dotted red line along the route she wanted to take.

"What the hell is this?"

"It is a suggested path."

"You don't have the other maps?"

"No." She'd left them behind on purpose, because she thought he might try to take them from her and use them to aide an escape.

He stared at her in disbelief.

"I think we are here," she said, pointing to a spot.

"You *think*?"

His reaction didn't surprise her. She'd anticipated this argument yesterday. She folded the map and put it away.

"How am I supposed to be your guide without GPS or a real map?"

She gestured toward the peak. "What more information do you need? We are climbing this mountain in front of us."

"We're traveling through a conflict zone," he said in a low voice. "I need to know which side of the god-damned border we're on."

"We will cross in an area too remote for fighting."

"Then what?"

"Then we will all be free."

He narrowed his eyes at this claim. When she touched his arm imploringly, he shook off her hand and walked away. She told herself it didn't matter what he thought of her as long as he cooperated, but that was a lie. She wanted him to like her for personal reasons. She wanted him to like her because she liked *him*. The spark he carried within him had caught inside her. She found him thrilling, from every angle.

She had to smother this feeling, of course. It was an insult to her husband's memory, and it made their journey all the more difficult.

They left camp just after sunrise. Her sore muscles warmed and became loose again. Ashur didn't complain about the hike, which concerned her. She remembered his silence during the long walk from Syria. They'd traveled over a hundred miles together, hardly speaking.

When they reached the snow line an hour later, Layah paused. Hudson didn't. He kept right on going.

"Do we need the crampons?" she asked.

"Not for this."

"Why not?"

"They're for ice or hard-packed snow."

She followed him across the thin white layer. The powder crunched beneath the soles of her boots and the hard ground. It was cooler here than in the village, but not cold. Sunshine sparkled on the snowdrifts in the distance. Soon she was perspiring beneath her wool poncho. Hudson started to pull ahead. His stride was longer than hers, his natural pace swift and steady. She couldn't catch him.

He glanced over his shoulder to watch her struggle. A muscle in his jaw flexed with impatience. He shrugged out of his pack and removed his fleece pullover. "Take off a layer," he said, when she joined him. "You don't want to sweat up here. Damp clothes will lower your body temperature."

She removed her pack and shed her poncho, instructing the others to do the same. They drank sips of water and started hiking again. Ashur took the second position instead of Layah. She lingered behind to make sure everyone was okay. Hanna smiled and nodded. This was a grand adventure for her. The Yazidi girl had probably never left her village before.

At midmorning, they reached the base of a snow-covered slope. Hudson paused to test it with a long stick.

"Now do we use crampons?" Layah asked.

"It's still too soft," Hudson said. "I'll have to kick steps."

"Kick steps?"

"It's like making a set of stairs in the snow. You follow my footprints."

She studied the slope warily. "What if someone falls? Do we need ropes?"

"No ropes," he said, sounding confident. "On snow, being tied together is more of a hindrance than a help. This slope isn't steep enough to bother with a fixed line. If someone falls, they'll slide down a few feet and get back up."

She nodded and put on her gloves. He was the expert.

He took out his ice ax and sank the point into the slope to anchor himself. Then he kicked two steps in the snow, repositioned his ax and moved up. It was a methodical process that he seemed comfortable with. When he'd formed about ten steps, he gestured for her to start climbing after him.

She began the ascent, her pulse racing. It wasn't as easy as it looked. Even though he was doing all the work, she struggled to keep up. Her pack felt top-heavy, her boots stiff and clumsy. Cold seeped through her gloves. She was afraid to look up or down. The climb stretched on, never-ending.

By the time he pulled her over the edge of a plateau, she was trembling from exertion. She collapsed on her back, sucking in cool air. She hadn't realized how difficult it was to climb over snow. She imagined several more days of slow, steady ascent.

Ashur joined her on the plateau. The others followed one by one. She dragged herself upright to study their surroundings. They were stranded in a sea of jagged peaks and slopes, flanked by a stretch of gritty, gray-streaked snow.

"That's a glacier," Ashur said in Arabic.

"Are you sure?"

"I've seen pictures."

The glacier appeared to follow the path of least resistance into steeper terrain. It was a mix of volcanic rock, blue ice and ashy-looking snow. It resembled a raging river, frozen in time. With crampons, they could travel over the surface.

They shared a lunch of dates and flatbread, taking a much-needed rest.

"Can we go that way?" she asked Hudson, pointing to the glacier.

"It would be faster, but more dangerous."

"I want to try it."

He stared across the icy expanse, contemplative. Although he claimed he was still weak from the months of captivity, he didn't look it. He glowed with health and manly vigor. Maybe it was the light reflecting off the surface of the snow that flattered him. Maybe it was the spectacular backdrop. He seemed very much in his element, framed by rugged mountain peaks. "I thought I was giving the orders up here."

"You are."

He fell silent, the corner of his mouth twitching. It dawned on her that he was enjoying himself. He didn't like the way she'd forced him into this journey, but he was clearly relishing the experience. He was the type of man who embraced challenges. His strength and resilience were undeniable.

She smiled back at him, her breath hitching with excitement. His gaze darkened and tension spiked between them. His words suddenly struck her as suggestive. She wondered if he wanted to order her around in the bedroom, not just on the mountain. The idea made her jaw drop.

He laughed at her scandalized expression. She knew then that danger was the spice of life for him. It was an aphrodisiac that allowed him to let go of his anger toward her and focus on the pleasure they might share together.

While she stood there, remembering the feel of his hard body against hers, a snowball came hurtling from Ashur's direction. It hit her right shoulder and exploded over her chest. She gasped in outrage.

No one spoke. The Yazidi girl's eyes widened. Seconds passed.

Layah did the only thing she could do. She dropped to her knees to scoop up some snow. Her cousins followed suit. So did Hudson. In the next instant, snowballs were flying everywhere. There was no escaping the onslaught. Layah launched hers at Ashur, who ducked to avoid it. The Yazidi grandmother was standing behind him, so she took a cold blast to the face. Ashur doubled over with laughter and got pelted by multiple assailants. Cousins targeted cousins. Hanna lobbed a snowball at Hudson.

At the end of the battle, they were all grinning and out of breath. Layah had snow in her ear and her hands were frozen, but she wouldn't have changed a thing. Because she hadn't seen Ashur this happy in years. She hadn't seen him play. The war had taken everything good they'd both ever known, and left them with only each other.

Hudson helped Ashur to his feet, brushing snow off his jacket. Ashur didn't protest. Maybe this was the beginning of a truce between them. Layah stuck her hands in her pockets, her throat tight.

"We need to gear up if we're walking over the glacier," Hudson said. "Do you have crampons and harnesses for everyone? And goggles?"

"Yes."

"How many ice axes?"

"Three."

"That's not enough."

She held his gaze. They didn't have enough food, either. He knew that, because he'd examined the contents of every pack. "I want to get over these mountains quickly. There is no safe path."

He studied the surface of the glacier, his brow furrowed. "We'll have to travel in roped teams, and watch out for crevasses. Most are exposed, and easy enough to avoid, but some are hidden under a layer of snow. The risk of falling is significant."

She nodded her agreement. They unpacked the gear and decided on three teams. The leader of each team would have an ice ax. The others would hold tent stakes and hope for the best. Hudson showed them how to self-arrest in the event of a fall. Layah translated his words for her cousins, but the physical demonstration was easy to follow. She admired his form as he modeled the proper technique.

Hudson chose Layah and the Yazidis for his team. The other two teams were led by her cousins. She helped the women with their harnesses before donning her own. Then she attached the crampon spikes to her boots and found her snow goggles.

Before they set off, Hudson checked their gear. He knelt to adjust Layah's harness, giving it a hard pull. She flushed as the straps tugged between her legs. Nodding, he clipped her to the rope with a carabiner. He repeated this process with every member of the group. Then he used his ax to hack some notches into the side of the glacier. It was a similar process to kicking steps in the snow.

After he made a safe access point, he climbed the ice stairs. The Yazidis followed, then Layah. They walked a short distance across the top. The surface of the glacier wasn't as slippery as she'd imagined. It was grainy and rippled, covered in a frozen layer of snow. Her crampon spikes crunched with every step. She felt like a true adventurer, and smiled at Hudson, pleased with their decision.

He waited for the other teams to join them. Then they moved forward once more. He started slowly, testing the conditions. The glacier seemed rock-solid beneath her feet. She didn't fall behind or let the rope go slack. There was about three meters of space between each team member, which limited conversation, but they were all within shouting distance.

So far, so good.

She glanced over her shoulder at Yusef, who flashed a grin. He was her favorite cousin, calm with a gentle spirit. Aram was more like Ashur, quick to anger. They both appeared comfortable in the lead positions. She turned back around and came to a halt. Hudson had paused with his left fist in the air. The stop signal.

She made the signal to the two other teams.

"Crevasse," Hudson shouted at her. "We can step across it."

She translated this message for Hanna and Yelda before they moved forward. There was a fissure in the snowpack, about the length of her arm. Hudson stepped over it easily. The grandmother went next, after a short hesitation. The girl leaped with grace.

Layah peered into the crevasse before she joined them on the other side. It was four or five meters deep, with smooth turquoise walls and strange, bulbous ice formations. She wanted to climb inside for a better look, but they didn't have time to explore. She took a big step over the gap and continued forward.

They encountered a second crevasse around the bend, also exposed and narrow enough to cross over. It had a slightly wider gap, which meant they all had to jump to the other side. The grandmother slipped and almost lost her footing as she landed. When she regained her balance, Layah moved forward.

The next crevasse was wide and shallow, with broken chunks of ice on one side. Hudson lowered himself into the space and climbed up the ice blocks against the far wall. At the top, he offered a helping hand.

"We have to look for a place to camp," he said, giving Layah a boost.

She glanced at the late afternoon sun with surprise. She was tired, but invigorated. They were near the summit. She prayed they would cross over the mountain range tomorrow. From there, it was all downhill.

They hiked on, searching for somewhere to stop for the night. Her stomach growled with hunger and her muscles ached from overuse, but her main focus was on their sleeping arrangements. She wondered if she'd drift into Hudson's arms again. Would he try to keep his distance, or pull her closer?

A strange sound caught her attention, snapping her back to the present. It was the crunch of shifting snow. Several meters in front of her, the path fell away.

Crevasse!

It had been hidden under a layer of fresh powder. Hudson grabbed Yelda by the arm, saving her from falling into the space. Layah froze in her tracks as Hanna dropped down into nowhere. She was there one second, gone the next.

Hudson sprawled on his belly and sank his ax deep into the ice to anchor the safety line. Layah got swept off her feet and dragged forward, as if a rug had been yanked from underneath her. She attempted to self-arrest with the metal stake. It skimmed over the surface and found no purchase. She went hurtling into the abyss.

She anticipated a hard slam into some wicked ice, but didn't hit anything. She sailed past Hanna in a blur of motion. Black space rushed up to greet her. The safety rope caught and held with a hard snap, cutting off her scream of terror. She dangled in space, disoriented. Blood rushed to her head.

She was upside down. She tried to flip over, but the weight of her pack held her captive. With shaking hands, she released the buckle across her chest. Her pack tumbled away and she careened upright.

Allahu Akbar.

She took a deep breath, trying to focus. Hanna was suspended above her, crying for her grandmother. Hudson had secured the line, but how long could he hold them? Layah removed her goggles and squinted into the dark interior of the cavern. The bottom of the crevasse was about two meters below her. The distance to the top appeared to be more than ten meters. It was too far to climb.

There was a promising ledge to her right. She stuck

out her foot and hooked her crampons on the edge, maneuvering toward it. When both boots found purchase on the ice shelf, she rested there, weak-kneed with relief.

Yelda appeared at the mouth of the crevasse, far above them. She spoke Kurdish too fast for Layah to understand. Layah was afraid the old woman would fall in with them.

"Listen to me," Layah said. "I will detach from the rope. You pull her up."

"What if I drop her?"

"She will not fall. Hudson has control."

The woman looked to him for confirmation. He might not approve of Layah removing the safety line, but she felt secure, and the grandmother couldn't pull them both up. They had to be rescued one at a time. Layah unclipped the carabiner, nodding at Yelda. The woman dragged her granddaughter to safety, probably with Hudson's help.

Layah clung to the wall of the cavern, gulping cool air. She was okay. The girl was okay. Hudson would throw her the rope in a minute. She wanted to be ready, so she looked around for her pack. It was at the bottom of the chasm, in plain sight. She couldn't leave her pack behind. Her entire life was inside it.

She crawled down from the ledge carefully. She took a tentative step forward. Then another. On the third step, ice cracked beneath her boots and water rushed over them. She went still, realizing her mistake.

A second later, she plunged into the glacier's bowels with a horrified shriek.

Chapter 7

Hud knew they were in trouble the instant he heard the ground move.

The hairs at the nape of his neck lifted and he glanced over his shoulder in time to see the Yazidi girl drop into the hidden crevasse. It wasn't an unusual occurrence, but he hadn't expected it. The other crevasses they'd encountered had been exposed, with little or no snow cover. This one was disguised under a snow bridge, a hard shelf formed over years of accumulation. He'd walked right over it, oblivious.

Cursing, he sprawled on his belly and sank his ax deep into the ice. The safety rope held. Two hard tugs on his harness told him that Layah had fallen with the girl.

Damn it.

The rope might have prevented them from plummeting to their deaths, but they could both be seriously injured, tangled together and bleeding. He looked back again. The other teams were a minute or two behind them. They appeared to be moving quickly, but they couldn't run on ice. He moved his gaze to the Yazidi grandmother, his jaw clenched. She was in danger of falling over the edge with them.

Jesus.

He didn't want to scare her by shouting orders, and she wouldn't understand him anyway. She exchanged words with someone in the crevasse, which was a good sign. Then he felt the unmistakable ease of tension in the line.

Not a good sign.

Yelda started tugging on the rope with all her might. Hud rolled over to assist her. Together, they brought the girl up easily. The grandmother hugged her, sobbing with relief.

Okay. Now what about Layah?

He yanked his ax out of the ice and scrambled to his feet. Yusef's team had almost reached the other side of the crevasse. Hud tore off his goggles as he approached the edge. Then he dropped to his stomach and shouted for Layah.

"Here!" she screamed.

She was in a glacier hole at the bottom of the crevasse.

His chest constricted at the sight. Falling into glacier water was no joke. It was like a river beneath a mountain of ice. The cold shock alone could be deadly. If she got swept under, he couldn't go after her.

Luckily, she seemed alert. She wasn't fully submerged. He could save her.

He shrugged out of his pack and bit off his gloves, trying not to panic. He needed a fixed line, immediately. He grabbed an anchor from his belt, then took several seconds to hammer it into the ice with his ax. He threaded his rope through the anchor with shaking hands and lowered himself into the chasm.

Heart racing, he rappelled to the bottom and braced his boots on either side of her. It was an awkward position, but the ice around her was thin and the walls felt solid. The glacier hole appeared shallow. When she reached up to him, he got a grip on her arm and yanked her out of the slushy water.

Her skin was cold, too cold. She managed to find a foothold, with his help. She climbed his body like a tree. He wrapped his arms around her, afraid to let go. She shivered violently, her face pale and her lips dark.

One of her cousins threw down another rope. Hud clipped it to her harness and shouted for them to pull. She clung to the line as it moved upward. As soon as she was safe, he retrieved her pack and climbed the fixed rope on the other side. The Yazidi girl and her grandmother watched him with tearful expressions.

Most of the snow bridge was still intact, so he used it to cross the gap and join the others. Everyone was huddled around Layah. She was on the ice with Ashur, her eyes closed and her head cradled in his lap.

"She is dying," Ashur said.

"She's not dying," Hud assured him. "She'll be fine as soon as she gets out of those wet clothes and warms up."

"I need the tent," she murmured.

Hud swore under his breath. She wouldn't undress

out in the open. He set up the small tent for her and she crawled inside. Her sluggish movements concerned him. He yanked off his jacket, preparing to climb in with her.

"Not you," Yusef said in broken English.

"She needs help," Hud said. "And body heat."

"Not you," Yusef repeated.

One of the women took over, nudging Hud aside. It was Yusef's wife. She joined Layah in the tent. Another woman gathered wool blankets and sheepskins for them. A third unpacked the camp stove and boiled water for tea.

The men stood around, faces tense. Hud couldn't tell if they were glad he'd rescued Layah or angry that she'd fallen on his watch. He felt responsible for the accident. Frozen terrain wasn't his forte. He never should have agreed to travel over the glacier. He'd done it only because she'd looked so goddamned beautiful, her eyes bright with excitement.

Hell.

She had a touch of the same ailment he suffered from—an overly adventurous spirit. Hud hoped she recovered, because they couldn't take her to a hospital. They couldn't stay here on the glacier, either. He'd have a hard time carrying her even a short distance. Now that the adrenaline had worn off, his strength was fading.

After about ten minutes, Ashur unzipped the flap to check on them. Yusef and Aram crowded closer. Hud waited for an update, his pulse pounding with trepidation.

Was she unconscious? Awake? Sipping tea, warm and naked?

Ashur gave a short order in Arabic. One of the women brought a bundle of clothes from Layah's pack and dropped it inside. Then he zipped up the flap again.

"Is she okay?" Hud asked.

"Yes, she is okay."

Aram glared at Hud.

"Is there a problem?"

Ashur paused, as if searching for the right words. "My cousins think you dishonor Layah with your familiar ways."

"What does that mean?"

"You should not touch her or share a tent with her. You should not look at her with desire."

Hud rubbed a hand over his mouth, stung by the criticism. No beating around the bush in their world. "How was I supposed to rescue her without touching her? Should I have left her to die in the crevasse, just to be polite?"

Ashur translated this sentiment to his cousins and listened to their response. "They thank you for the rescue."

He inclined his head.

"But you will stay away from her. She is not yours."

Hud crossed his arms over his chest, shrugging. He wasn't in the mood to concede anything. He'd gotten roped into this journey against his will. They were lucky he hadn't abandoned them. Somewhere between the first camp and here, he'd decided to go along with Layah's plan. Now it was too late to turn back. They couldn't move forward without him. If he walked away, they'd be stranded.

These men should be treating him with respect, not warning him off. He'd vowed to keep his distance from Layah for his own reasons, but she was a grown woman. If she wanted him to touch her, that was her business.

Layah emerged from the tent a few minutes later, fully dressed. She appeared steady on her feet and capable of walking a short distance. He didn't question her, because they needed to get going. It was almost sunset.

They packed up and headed to the edge of the glacier, where ice met land again. A sheer cliff rose up in the distance. Ascending it would be tomorrow's challenge.

Hud spotted a good place to camp nearby. He was exhausted. He'd done too much today. His shoulder felt like raw hamburger. As soon as they reached flat land, he shrugged out of his pack and sat down.

The women started cooking, while the men set up the tents. They had to melt snow for soup and drinking water. The meal wasn't as filling as last night's couscous, but it contained dehydrated meat, which Hud's body desperately needed. He ate three servings, earning a disapproving glance from Yusef. That guy was a real buzzkill.

Hud set up his own tent and crawled inside, disregarding their earlier conversation. He wasn't going to change his sleeping arrangements to suit Layah's cousins. He was too damned tired to dishonor anyone.

Layah crawled through the opening and settled in next to him. It was colder than the previous night. He could see her breath in the chill air. She didn't protest when he rolled onto his side and put his arm around her.

"Thank you," she said. "For everything you did."

He grunted an acknowledgment. "What happened to the safety line?"

"I removed it so the girl could be rescued."

"You should have waited."

"I did not realize the danger."

"Never do that again," he said. "When in doubt, stay put and wait for help. I could've set the anchor where I self-arrested, and rescued both of you."

She sighed, shifting into a more comfortable position.

"You make me feel like my mother," he muttered.

"Oh?"

"She was always telling me to be careful, to have patience, to stay safe."

"Did you listen?"

"No."

Layah laughed softly. "I say the same things to Ashur, for different reasons. I worry that he will join the fighting."

Hud had seen boys younger than Ashur in every local militia. "Has he threatened to?"

"Many times."

"Where are his parents?"

"Dead."

Hud remembered his promise to give Ashur a gun safety lesson. He hoped the instruction wouldn't encourage the boy to take up arms. "He's protective of you."

"Yes."

"He told me to stay away from you."

"He did?"

"He was translating for your cousins, but I think they all agree."

"They are overstepping. I am not a schoolgirl."

"How old are you?"

"Twenty-nine. How old are you?"

"Thirty-two."

"Do you have children?"

His gut clenched as if she'd punched him. "No."

"I wanted a child with Khalil. I wish we hadn't waited."

"You still have time."

"But no husband."

Hud didn't say anything. He certainly wasn't going to offer his stud services.

"Tell me about your wife."

He winced, rubbing his jaw.

"What passed between you?"

"It's a long story."

"Did you love her?" Layah asked, undeterred.

"Yes."

"You could not mend your differences?"

"No."

"Why not?"

"She slept with someone else. It was kind of a deal breaker."

Layah twisted to face him, her eyes wide with shock. "How did you know?"

He rolled onto his back and looked up at the ceiling of the tent. "She got pregnant while I was on deployment. I thought the baby was mine for the first couple of months. Then I went with her to an appointment, and the dates didn't add up. I finally figured it out."

"Did she confess?"

"Yeah, she did. She begged me to forgive her."

"Do you wish you had?"

"No," he said, after a pause. "I'm away a lot, and I couldn't trust her."

"That is very sad," Layah murmured, settling down again. "She must have so much sorrow and regret."

"I don't know. She looks pretty happy on Facebook."

"Really?"

"She's with the baby's father."

"Perhaps that is for the best."

"Yeah, it worked out great."

"You are angry."

He couldn't deny it, though the feeling had faded from a raging wildfire to a mild burn. In time, he might feel nothing. "It's not easy to talk about."

"Do you love her still?"

He didn't, so he shook his head. He might have fallen out of love with her before she cheated. They'd been drifting apart for years. Instead of confronting the problem, he'd ignored it and paid the price. "We were wrong for each other. She wanted someone to come home every night."

"And you are not that man."

"No."

Layah snuggled closer, resting her head on his chest. He put his arm around her again. The discussion wasn't as painful as he'd expected. He'd neglected Michelle, and she'd betrayed him. There were worse things to get over.

He'd lived through torture, after all.

He closed his eyes and breathed deep, clearing his mind. Layah's scent filled his nostrils. She smelled like warm woman and silky hair and snowflakes. Like a cozy wool blanket at the end of a perfect winter day.

Something melted inside him, and he slept.

Chapter 8

Layah didn't wake in Hudson's arms the next morning.

He wasn't cuddling her spoon-style with his male parts snuggled against her bottom. She wasn't all over him, fingers tangled in his hair. He wasn't breathing in her ear or nuzzling the nape of her neck.

He wasn't even there.

She sat up and rubbed her eyes, frowning at the empty space beside her. She hadn't heard him leave the tent. In her dreams, the night had passed in a sexy tangle of shifting positions. His hands on her curves. Her mouth under his.

She squeezed her legs together, swallowing hard. Her skin tingled with arousal. It was an unfamiliar feeling these days, but comforting. Life-affirming. The war hadn't taken everything from her. She was still a woman. She still had a heart pumping inside her chest and blood flowing to her limbs, making her flush with desire.

She was normal, healthy, human.

She emerged from the tent, stretching her arms over her head. Her entire body was sore from hiking. All the men were gathered at the base of the cliff, watching Hudson begin his ascent. He had a harness strapped with ropes and gear. Although he looked confident, and he was obviously an experienced climber, her stomach clenched with unease. The rock face loomed as high as the skyscrapers in Baghdad.

In the middle of camp, Yelda was making tea with her granddaughter. Layah accepted a cup and sipped it nervously. The Yazidis didn't speak Arabic, the universal language of the region.

"How are you?" she asked them in Kurdish.

Hanna said she was well. Yelda smiled and repeated the sentiment. After they exchanged pleasantries, Yelda held Layah's hand and said a prayer of gratitude. She asked the spirits to watch over Layah's husband.

Layah shook her head. "No husband."

"No?"

"He died."

She patted Layah's hand in sympathy.

"My grandfather died," Hanna said.

"I'm sorry."

"Wife?" Yelda asked, pointing at Hudson. "No wife?"

Layah pretended not to follow.

"You will marry him," Yelda said. "At the end of this journey."

Hanna nodded at this prediction. "She sees the future."

"What does she see for you?" Layah asked.

The girl glanced at Ashur, who was standing with his cousins. Then she looked down at her tea, cheeks flushed.

Layah wondered if Hanna had a crush on him. Ashur hadn't paid her much attention. He was more interested in guns than girls. Perhaps that would change when they were free again. She hoped he would give up on his quest for vengeance.

Yelda made a scolding remark, indicating that she did not see Ashur in the girl's future. Yazidis weren't allowed to marry outsiders, or even speak with them under most circumstances. Although Yelda had happily suggested a match between Layah and Hudson, a foreigner, the option wasn't open to her granddaughter.

Layah studied her nephew from the girl's perspective. He was handsome, even with that perpetual scowl. He had her brother's strong features, softened by youth and thick eyelashes. To Hanna, Ashur might seem forbidden and mysterious. Ashur, in turn, thought all Yazidis were backward and inferior.

The grandmother had nothing to worry about.

After a light breakfast of tea and powdered eggs, Layah brushed her teeth and washed her face in the snow. She'd given everyone a tiny tube of toothpaste and a bar of hotel soap at the start of the journey, but they'd had few opportunities to wash. If she wasn't sharing intimate space with Hudson, she might not have bothered.

By the time she joined the men, Hudson was half-way up the cliff. Although he made it look easy, she knew it wasn't. Every five meters or so he hammered a piece of gear into the rock, anchoring himself in place. Then he rested with his hands cupped over his mouth. The rock face was mostly smooth and free of snow, but it was a blustery morning. Without gloves, his fingertips must be frozen.

Near the top of the cliff, there was a difficult spot, with no convenient ledges or handholds. Hudson had to brace his fingers inside a crack in the wall and use that for leverage. Layah didn't take a full breath until he reached the summit.

When he pulled himself over the edge, cheers rang out in three or four different languages. She hugged Ashur, who frowned and pushed her away. She didn't take offense. She'd grown accustomed to his rebuffs.

"How are we going to follow him?" she asked, in awe of Hudson's feat.

"He will come back down to show us what to do," Ashur said.

Hudson hammered more anchors at the top of the cliff. Then he rappelled down the rock face the same way he'd rappelled into the crevasse, with swift efficiency. When he reached the ground, he gestured for her to join him. He took a device out of his pack to show the group. "This is a belay. It will catch the rope if someone falls."

He demonstrated the technique, while Layah translated. He picked Nadir, the heaviest man, to stand below and belay.

"We're using the fixed line to climb." He pointed to the rope he'd anchored to the cliff. "It's faster and safer. The safety line is just for backup. If someone can't make it on their own, the men on the ground can pull them up."

She repeated this information to the others.

"I'll climb first to show you what to do," Hudson told her. "As soon as I'm finished, you can start. I want the women to go before the men. I'll come back down to belay Nadir at the end."

"Who will belay you?" she asked.

"No one."

She nodded, accepting this risky decision. He started his second ascent and wasted no time getting to the summit. She committed every move he made to memory. When he was safe, he removed the belay rope and tossed it down the cliff. Then it was her turn.

She wanted to go first. If she climbed the rock wall without falling or needing help from the men, the other women were more likely to follow suit.

She attached the rope to her harness and started climbing. It was harder than she'd expected. Her body was sore from several days of travel, and the altitude didn't help. She had to rest on the second ledge to catch her breath. Then she continued to climb, using her leg muscles to walk up the wall. She focused on making steady progress. Step by step, hand over hand. Before she knew it, she was halfway there.

Then she made the grave mistake of looking

down. It was a sickening distance. One of her boots slipped and she almost lost her balance. Her stomach dropped about twenty meters. She clung to the fixed line, scrambling for a better foothold.

Hudson shouted down at her, "You're doing great. Just hang on."

She swallowed hard, trying not to panic. She kept her gaze locked on him. His eyes held hers and she felt the familiar jolt of chemistry between them. Her nerves settled and her chest swelled with exhilaration.

She could do this.

A few minutes later, she was at the top of the cliff. He dragged her away from the edge and unfastened the safety rope on her harness. She stared up at him in wonder. He had snow in his beard. He looked like an advertisement for an adventure magazine.

She'd never felt so alive.

He crushed his mouth over hers, making the best of an amazing moment. She laced her fingers through his hair, delighted with the bold choice. It was just the two of them, on top of the world together. No one else could see them.

He wasn't shy about parting her lips with his tongue. She wasn't shy about moaning her encouragement. They shared a snowflake-melting, life-affirming, toe-curling kiss.

His mouth left hers much too soon. "You're dangerous."

She sputtered with laughter. "Me?"

"I want you."

Her breath caught in her throat.

"I'm willing to risk getting shot by your cousins just to have you."

She raked her nails through his hair, biting her lower lip. "I think you like risk. I think it arouses you."

His nostrils flared and his eyes blazed with hunger. They were dangerous together. Combustible. She found herself saying and doing the most shameless things. Maybe taking risks aroused her, too. With a low groan, he rolled away from her. Then he picked up the end of the safety rope and started winding it around his elbow. When he had it gathered in a coil, he tossed it down the cliff for the next climber.

Layah rose to her feet and studied their surroundings. They were in Turkey, or close to it. This side of the Zagros wasn't as severe. Snowy, gradual slopes dissolved into rolling green hills. She was pleased with their progress. They were actually on schedule.

"You are an excellent guide," she said, smiling.

He arched a brow. "Do I get a bonus?"

She could imagine what he wanted, and she was tempted to give it to him. He was an ideal candidate for a short affair. Sexy, passionate, casual. He'd never expect more from her, and he'd leave well before she got attached.

In theory.

In reality, sleeping with him was a terrible idea. He was her hostage. He was connected to her brother's death. Hasan had worked as an interpreter for Hudson's team in Syria. She felt guilty about forcing Hudson on this journey, and for deceiving him. Using him for pleasure would only complicate things.

He stretched out on his belly to watch the next climber. She noted his broad shoulders and taut buttocks with a wistful sigh. Yelda said they'd get married at the end of the journey. Layah hoped they would not be enemies.

They spent the next two hours at the summit. Some of the women needed help, and Yusef fell once on his way up, but everyone reached the top safely—thanks to Hudson. She knew they couldn't have made the ascent without him. They wouldn't have survived the trek over the surface of the glacier, either. His expertise was priceless.

At midmorning, they started hiking again. Traveling downhill was a little easier, but she struggled with the terrain. It was a snowy slog over shifting slopes. The heavy pack dragged her off balance and the ground felt unstable. They skipped lunch because there was nothing to eat. Her stomach gnawed with hunger and her feet ached.

She was about to ask for a break when one of the men shouted a warning.

"Watch out!"

Layah turned to see loose rocks careening down the hillside. They all scrambled to get clear of the danger. Hanna lost her footing and almost fell in the direct path of the rocks. Ashur yanked her out of harm's way. They both tumbled to the ground.

Layah rushed forward as soon as the rocks settled. "Are you all right?" she asked the girl in Kurdish.

"I'm fine," Hanna said, nodding at Ashur. "Thank you."

He knew enough Kurdish to mumble a polite response. Then he rose to his feet and hurried away as if the girl had a disease he might catch.

Yelda helped Hanna upright and they continued to the bottom of the slope. When they were on stable ground, Hudson allowed them a short rest.

Layah joined him to discuss their afternoon plans. He was pushing hard, like always. "We need water," he said, studying the landscape. There was a valley with a cluster of trees in the distance.

She glanced around, surprised by the lack of snow in the area. They'd covered a lot of distance in a few hours. She took the map out of her pack and unfolded it. His eyes darkened at the reminder of their uneasy alliance.

"There's a lake in this region," she said.

"Yeah? What region is that?"

"Turkey," she said, ignoring his caustic tone. "There is a large body of water on the Turkish side of the border. If we see it, we know we are on the right path."

"Those trees look promising."

"I agree."

"Do you want me to scout ahead?"

"No. It is not far."

They set out again, moving forward with grim determination. Layah kept a close watch on Hanna, who trudged along behind her grandmother. They were all exhausted, but they needed water more than they needed rest. The distance to the valley seemed endless. The sun stayed suspended above the horizon.

Finally, they arrived at a cluster of trees which

overlooked a sprawling blue lake. It was a glorious sight.

Layah didn't feel her feet touch the ground until she reached the shore. She shrugged off her pack, laughing with glee. She gave Ashur a bone-crushing hug, and he hugged her back. With a triumphant cry, she ran to the water's edge and fell to her knees.

Tears coursed down her cheeks as she cupped her hands in the chilly liquid and drank deeply. Then she looked up at the sky and opened her arms wide.

This was freedom.

Chapter 9

Hud didn't join the celebration at the lakeside.

A strange feeling had settled in the pit of his stomach as he watched Layah exchange embraces with the others. It wasn't jealousy. It was aversion. He stood at a safe distance, his heart pounding with trepidation. Although no one tried to hug him, the very idea caused him to break out in a cold sweat.

He knew the symptoms of PTSD. He'd been trained to recognize the warning signs, and prisoners of war rarely escaped unscathed. But his recovery had been easier than expected so far. He hadn't suffered from nightmares, mood swings or delusions. His encounters with Layah hadn't triggered him. Her touch had a soothing effect, in fact. He'd convinced himself that he was strong enough to avoid the affliction.

His current reaction told him otherwise. He swallowed hard, struck by a wave of bad memories. During the first few weeks in his cell, he'd been forced to stay awake. He'd been kicked and punched and doused with water. Whenever he let his guard down and surrendered to exhaustion, he got punished.

Then the torture sessions stopped, and he missed them. He missed his captors. He couldn't stand the isolation. He'd craved human contact. One day, when a guard had been standing over him with a rifle, he'd bear-hugged the man around the ankles just to touch someone.

It was the same guard he'd killed, too. He felt more shame and guilt about hugging him than killing him.

Yeah. That was pretty twisted.

Now he felt like throwing up because people were embracing in his presence. His next psych eval was going to be fun. He could withstand waterboarding and dead bodies and sleep deprivation and extreme ops, but not hugging. Hugging was too much.

He staggered away from the joyful scene and disappeared in the trees. He walked until he couldn't hear happy voices anymore. He walked until he was alone, and he could breathe again. Then his shoulder muscles relaxed and his anxiety eased.

Wiping a hand down his sweaty face, he shook off the dregs of the episode. Then he approached the shoreline for a drink. He wouldn't normally take the risk, but a glacier-fed lake in a remote location was about as clean as you could get. He made a cup with his hands and drank straight from the source.

He spotted a set of deer tracks when he lifted his head. He crouched down to touch the soft mud, glancing into the trees. The tracks were fresh. His stomach growled with hunger. Now that his nausea had passed, he was starving again.

His detour into the woods didn't go unnoticed. Aram and Yusef burst through the trees, their rifles raised. Ashur followed close behind.

Hud stood slowly, raising his palms. He'd never believed Layah's claim that her cousins meant him no harm. He didn't trust her, but his desire for her hadn't waned. Whenever he looked at her, the ugliness of the world faded away, and nothing else mattered.

"Why are you alone?" Ashur asked.

Hud dropped his hands. "I was taking a piss. Maybe your cousins hold each other's dicks, but I don't need any help."

Ashur flushed at this response. He didn't translate.

"We should hunt," Hud said, changing the subject. "These are fresh tracks."

Aram lowered his weapon and studied the prints. He exchanged a few words with Yusef, who shook his head. After a short debate, Yusef gave his rifle to Ashur. The boy accepted it with reverence.

"I will hunt with you," Ashur said. "They want to stay here."

Hud shrugged. It wasn't what he'd expected, after being interrogated at gunpoint, but he didn't argue.

"Be careful," Yusef said in stilted English. Then he walked away with Aram.

"Why are they letting me go with you?" Hud asked Ashur.

"They think you are the best shot, and they are tired."

"Aren't you tired?"

"Yes, but I want to learn to kill."

"So you can avenge your father."

"And my mother."

Hud crossed his arms over his chest. "The first thing you need to know is that killing and emotions don't mix. Only a calm man has a steady trigger finger."

Ashur narrowed his eyes. "I am calm."

"You're angry."

"You are angry also. You insult my cousins and lust for my aunt. Do these feelings make you unable to kill?"

Hud rubbed a hand over his mouth. Ashur was too smart for his own good, and too determined to dissuade. Hud didn't know why he was trying to talk Ashur out of his revenge fantasy. What did he care if the kid went on a rampage? Hud wanted Layah. Ashur wasn't his problem. "Have you fired a gun before?"

"Yes. Aram let me shoot at cans once."

"Give me the rifle. You're holding it wrong."

Ashur passed it over. Hud checked the safety before he explained the parts of the rifle and showed Ashur how to handle it correctly. The boy was a quick study. He listened with interest and asked a few questions.

Hud insisted on carrying the rifle through the woods, but he didn't spot any deer. They lost the trail as soon as they moved away from the muddy shoreline. He continued uphill until they reached a clearing. There was a cluster of rocks to hide behind. It was as good a post as any. He got down on the ground and gave the rifle to Ashur.

"When can I shoot?"

"When you see an animal."

"You think the deer is here?"

"I have no idea."

"Where do I shoot it?"

"I'd go for the chest, and you have to wait for the right moment. If it stops to sniff the air, take the shot. Line it up and squeeze the trigger."

"Okay," Ashur said.

Ten minutes went by. It was almost sunset, and the temperature had dropped. They hadn't brought their jackets. Hud rolled over and tucked his hands behind his head, content to let Ashur keep watch. He doubted they'd have any luck.

"Can we make the deer come out?" Ashur asked.

"Not if we don't know where it is."

Ashur was quiet for another ten minutes. Then he shifted and flexed his trigger hand. "I do not like hunting."

"Do you like eating?"

"Not as much as you."

"What does Layah plan to do in Turkey?"

"We go first to the Yazidi village to deliver Hanna and Yelda."

"Then what?"

"Then we go to an Assyrian place."

Hud wondered where they would part ways. He could leave the group as soon as they moved away from the border. He didn't anticipate any trouble from the Turkish authorities in the country's interior. "You did a good thing for Hanna today."

Ashur grunted at the compliment.

"Maybe you can stay friends."

"Yazidi girls aren't allowed to be friends with boys from other faiths."

"Why not?"

"Because they are uneducated barbarians. Yazidis have little or no contact with outsiders. Marrying a non-Yazidi is punishable by death."

"Are Assyrians allowed to marry outsiders?"

Ashur glanced up from the rifle. "You think you can marry my aunt?"

"I didn't say that."

"Of course not. You only wish to use and discard her."

Hud bristled at the charge. He had no ill intentions toward Layah, despite the fact that she'd *kidnapped* him. If anyone was getting mistreated around here, it was Hud.

Ashur inhaled a sharp breath. "Look."

Hud straightened as a small deer trotted across the clearing. It paused to nibble on tender spring grass. He couldn't leave this golden opportunity to chance, so he put his arm around Ashur and made sure his sights were straight. Hud braced his weight against the boy's shoulders to absorb the kick.

"Now," he said.

Ashur squeezed the trigger. He kept his finger on it too long, peppering the ground with bullets, but that was fine. One reached its target. The deer's front legs crumpled. Then its hind legs went down, and that was it.

"I got it!"

"You sure did." Hud took charge of the gun and engaged the safety. "Good job."

"I was steady," Ashur said. "My hand didn't shake."

Hud grunted his agreement. "You're a natural. Let's go dress your kill."

"My kill," Ashur repeated with a smile.

They strode across the clearing together until they reached the deer. It was a male fawn, still twitching. Blood huffed from the animal's nostrils as it took a final breath. Then it went still, legs stiff.

Ashur didn't appear quite as pleased as he had two minutes ago. "It's a baby."

"It's a juvenile," Hud said. "A good size for our group. Nothing will go to waste."

The boy's dark eyes filled with tears. He blinked them away, seeming embarrassed by the display of emotion.

"There's no shame in feeling sad about taking a life."

"Are you sad when you kill a man?"

"No," Hud admitted. He hadn't cried over any of his kills, but he'd never shot a baby deer, or a defenseless man. "I killed a bunch of squirrels and birds one day, just because I was angry. I cried then."

Ashur nodded his understanding. He studied the speckled fawn, his face solemn. There was something familiar about his expression. Something that stirred Hud's memories.

Hasan.

It came to him in a flash of recognition. Hasan Anwar was the interpreter Hud had recruited in Syria.

Ashur looked like a younger version of him. Had Hasan been Assyrian? Hud couldn't remember. He probably hadn't asked. Layah and Ashur were well educated, like Hasan. They'd been in Syria. They'd known Hud was a SEAL.

The pieces fit.

But why had they kept this connection a secret?

The hairs at the nape of his neck prickled with unease. Hud had brushed off Ashur's anger toward him as anti-American sentiment and general teen angst. Now he realized it went far deeper. Hasan had been executed because he worked with Team Twelve. US forces hadn't done enough to protect him.

If Ashur was Hasan's son…he had every right to be angry.

"How do I clean it?" Ashur asked, kneeling beside the fawn.

Hud showed him what to do. The boy wasn't squeamish about the unpleasant task. When he was finished, Hud dragged the carcass away from the mess.

"I will carry it," Ashur said.

"Are you sure?"

"Yes. It is my kill."

Hud hefted the carcass onto the boy's shoulders. It weighed about twenty-five pounds, but Ashur didn't buckle. He held on to the hooves and started walking. The fawn's head flopped against his back with every step.

"How do I look?" Ashur asked, just before they reached camp.

"Like a badass," Hud said honestly.

Ashur flashed a grin. He had blood on his face, hands, neck and shirt. Layah screamed when she saw them. She rushed forward, speaking in their native language. She seemed concerned that he was hurt. Everyone else cheered with approval. Ashur put the deer down next to a pile of firewood someone had collected. Aram and Yusef patted Ashur on the back, ruffling his hair in celebration.

They were going to feast tonight.

Hud walked to the lake's edge to clean up. He had gore up to his elbows. Layah followed with Ashur. When she tried to scrub the boy's neck and ears, he jerked away from her to do it himself. After a sharp exchange of words, he left.

"You can wash me," Hud offered.

Layah's lips curved into a sad smile. She dipped the cloth in water and approached him. She swept the damp fabric over his forehead, the bridge of his nose, the nape of his neck. "You are not bloody. Just dirty."

"He doesn't like to be touched," Hud said.

"No."

"That's a common symptom of PTSD."

She dropped her hands. "I know."

He wanted to kiss her again, despite his earlier revelation. He wanted to kiss her and confront her at the same time. But he did neither. She could keep her secrets. They were in Turkey now. She didn't need his guide services anymore. As soon as they reached a developed area, he would leave her.

Damned if that didn't feel like a punch in the gut.

Yelda appeared to collect water from the lake, and they broke apart like guilty teenagers. Hud used the interruption as an excuse to walk away. The tents were already set up, so he ducked inside the smaller one. Her pack was sitting right there. After a short hesitation, he started rummaging through it.

Toiletries, makeup, panties, female products. Nothing suspicious.

He found the ridiculous map she'd been using, which had no borders or labels. She'd sketched a path across the mountains. There was a dot on the other side of the lake, perhaps to mark the Yazidi village where they were headed. The path continued along a U-shaped river and curved north again.

He wanted to tear the map into shreds. It embodied his feelings of anger and frustration. The journey had been stressful, dangerous and thrilling at turns. He liked Layah, and he admired her tenacity, but that didn't mean he forgave her deception. The only thing worse than being stranded in a war zone was being stranded in a war zone without clear borders.

He folded the map and put it back. As he pulled his hand free, he felt a distinctive rectangular shape against his fingertips.

Bingo.

He found the opening of a small pocket and searched it, his pulse racing. What he discovered inside wasn't the cell phone he'd expected. It was a pair of passports, secured with a rubber band.

He released the band and opened the first passport book. It was Layah's. She'd been to Syria, Jordan, Israel, Greece, even France. Her travel itinerary didn't scream "destitute refugee" to him. The second passbook belonged to Khalil Al-Farah. Hud studied his photograph. He was dark and handsome, with laughing eyes. Hud flipped through the pages, noting that Khalil had visited many of the same countries Layah had. He'd also been to places she hadn't, like Egypt and Saudi Arabia.

Hud pictured the stunning couple on sunny beaches together, or visiting ancient sites. He pictured them on a romantic honeymoon. This was the man Layah had married. The man who'd seen and touched all the places she kept hidden.

Hud was intensely jealous of Khalil Al-Farah, who seemed very much alive in her thoughts. Two years after his death, she'd stayed true. She spoke his name in her sleep. His passbook was intimately entwined with hers.

She was still in love with him.

Hud returned Khalil's passport to her pack and slipped Layah's into his pocket. He wanted to separate them for stupid, possessive reasons. He had strategic reasons, as well. He needed something of hers to use as leverage. A little insurance, in case she tried to screw him. She'd promised him freedom. He had to make sure she delivered.

He emerged from the tent with a darker outlook. He'd been dazzled by her beauty, and that was understandable, but he couldn't afford to get played. She was a very perceptive person. She sensed his desires, his preferences, his turn-ons.

She'd pegged him earlier. He *was* aroused by danger. He liked risky situations. And he'd always been attracted to the wrong women.

Take Michelle, for example. He'd met her at a bar, which wasn't unusual for him. SEALs were work-hard, play-hard types, and he'd indulged in his share of one-night stands. Michelle had been fun and hot and wild. He'd wanted to settle down, but not with someone boring. They went to Vegas one weekend for a quickie wedding. He'd known she was a handful—he just thought he could handle her. He'd imagined their marriage would have ups and downs, like a roller coaster. Instead it was a train wreck from start to finish.

He shook off the bad memories and sat down by the fire, near Layah. Yusef placed the skinned carcass on a rotisserie over the flames. For the next hour, Hud stared into the animal's dead eyes.

The mood in the camp was jovial, with lively conversations punctuated by laughter. Husbands cuddled wives. Layah stayed quiet, and she didn't translate for Hud. She seemed lost in her own thoughts. When Aram sent around a small bottle of liquor, she passed it to Hud. The bottle was almost empty, so Hud gave his share to Ashur.

The boy drained the bottle with relish. He sputtered and coughed uncontrollably. Everyone roared with laughter except Layah. Hud understood her concerns, but he also knew how it felt to be a sad, angry kid on the cusp of manhood.

They ate well that night. Hud went to bed early, his body sore and his mind in turmoil. When Layah joined him, he pretended to be asleep. She curled up on her side, facing his back. He sensed her reaching hand, suspended near his shoulder, but she didn't touch him. He waited until her breaths were deep and even.

Then he let himself drift.

Chapter 10

Layah woke up shivering.

It was dawn, or even earlier. She could see her breath in the chilly air. Hudson was crouched at the front of the tent, looking out. He'd taken her sheepskin and her blanket. All the bedding was folded and stacked in the corner.

He glanced over his shoulder and made a series of complicated hand signals. It appeared to be some kind of military communication that she had no hope of understanding. Then he returned his attention to the tent flap.

She rubbed her eyes in confusion. She didn't hear any sounds, other than someone snoring, and Hudson wasn't actually looking outside. The mesh panel at the top of the tent flap was covered by nylon, zipped up tight. He couldn't see through it.

He was dreaming.

She didn't want to startle him by speaking, but she was cold. She reached for the blankets he'd stacked in the corner. He caught the movement and leaped into action. Before she could draw a breath, she was facedown underneath him. He straddled her waist and wrenched her arms behind her back. Quick as lightning, he grasped both her wrists with one hand and grabbed a handful of her hair with the other.

She smothered a scream, trying not to panic. He could probably snap her neck like a twig. "Hudson, stop. It is Layah."

He loosened his grip on her hair. "Layah?"

"Yes."

With a muttered curse, he climbed off her. She rolled away from him and sat forward, straightening her mussed hair. He stared at her in horror. Then he looked down at his hands as if he didn't recognize them. "I hurt you."

"No."

"What did I do?"

"You were crouched like a tiger, and you jumped on me."

"I'm sorry," he said in a hoarse voice. "I thought you were someone else."

"The Da'esh?"

He nodded, swallowing hard. "There was a corner in my cell where they couldn't see me. I would practice attacking from that spot, over and over again. One day I surprised the guard and broke out, but I didn't get far."

"What happened?" she whispered.

"They caught me and beat me unconscious. I

couldn't move for a few days. After that they stopped coming in my cell. The beatings stopped. Everything stopped. No one came to kick me or spit on me or wake me up at all hours. They pushed a food tray through a slot in the door. That was it."

Her chest constricted with sorrow. She wanted to reach out to him, but she thought he might rebuff her, like Ashur often did. "I'm sorry."

He started putting on his boots, his jaw clenched.

"The bruises on your side were from the last beating?"

"Yes."

"How long ago?"

"I don't know. A month."

"I should check your sutures."

"They're fine," he said, tying his laces tight. "I'm fine."

She watched him leave the tent. He wasn't fine. No one could be fine after months of captivity. He was a strong man, mentally and physically, but he needed time to recover. She felt guilty about forcing him into this grueling journey. She grabbed a blanket to cuddle with, but she didn't sleep. She was worried about him. He'd hardly spoken to her since that kiss at the summit. Something had changed between them, and she wasn't sure what.

Did he regret telling her that he wanted her?

Getting involved was a bad idea for both of them. She assumed it was against the rules for a SEAL to have any kind of relationship with a refugee. He seemed irritated with himself for showing emotion, or revealing his desire. He was clearly angry with her for keeping him in the dark about their exact location. He was suffering from post-traumatic stress. He'd been distant while the others celebrated.

She didn't blame him for withdrawing. She couldn't have a torrid affair with an American, anyway. They were from two different worlds. He'd go back to his. If she wasn't careful, he'd break her heart before he left.

The sun rose over the mountains and they ate venison stew for breakfast. Hudson's dark mood hadn't affected his appetite. Ashur sat down next to Layah with his stew. She still had mixed feelings about Ashur handling guns, and she hadn't reacted well to the sight of him covered in blood last night. Now that she'd calmed down, she couldn't begrudge his accomplishment.

He looked taller today, and so much like Hasan her chest ached. She resisted the urge to ruffle his hair.

"You know what I thought when you were born?" she asked.

"What?"

"I thought you were perfect. You had a crumpled-up face like a little old man. You cried so loud, and you held my finger so tight. I knew you would grow up strong and healthy. I thought, when I have a son, I want him to be just like this."

He swallowed a bite of stew, giving her a skeptical look. When she'd come to collect him in Syria, she'd been numb with grief, not overjoyed to see him. They'd staggered along together, from one war-torn country to another. They hadn't spoken about permanent placement for him. She'd been focused on survival and escape, not parenting.

"I imagined having a baby of my own one day. I never imagined that I would become your guardian."

"You don't have to be. I can take care of myself."

"You're not an adult."

"I'm not a child, either."

"Your father would want me to watch over you. So would your mother."

He said nothing.

"I know I can't compare to them. They had thirteen years to learn how to raise you. I will never be what they were."

Ashur made a grunting sound. "You're okay."

She looked away, uncertain. It was difficult to reconcile her girlhood dreams with the crushing reality of the current situation. Instead of Khalil's child, she'd been given a surly teenager. Ashur had her instead of two loving, experienced parents.

"When we get to Yerevan—"

"I don't even speak the language," he interrupted.

"I'll teach you."

"You don't speak it."

"I can get by. We'll learn together."

His brow furrowed at this claim, as if he didn't believe she'd stay there with him. Her parents had fled to Yerevan two years ago. Her cousins planned to settle with their wives in a nearby Assyrian community and look for work. Layah hadn't made any decisions beyond this journey. Since Khalil's death, she couldn't bear to think too far into the future.

After breakfast, they said goodbye to Nadir and his

family, who were heading west to reunite with relatives. Yusef gave Nadir his rifle before they parted ways. Layah offered him one of the tents, which he accepted. Then they continued east as a party of nine.

The route to the Yazidi village followed a steady downhill slope. It was the easiest trek of the journey, and quite picturesque. This side of the Zagros was all green meadows and rolling hills, with a spectacular mountain backdrop. She'd been surrounded by deserts her entire life, and they were majestic, but the rugged beauty of the skyline took her breath away.

It was a struggle to keep moving, nonetheless. She'd been pushed past her limits and she felt it in every step. She never wanted to hike again. Her muscles ached from overuse. She hated her pack and everything inside it. The lovely spring day was too warm, the sun too bright, the birds too cheery, the flowers too fragrant.

They stopped at noon to rest beneath a tree. Its branches were heavy with small green fruits.

"What are those?" Hudson asked.

"Sour plums," she said. "We can eat them."

He picked several handfuls, which they washed and shared. It was an acquired taste. Layah enjoyed the tart flavor, but Hudson grimaced at the first bite. He managed to chew and swallow, with some difficulty.

"We finally found a food he doesn't like," Ashur said. When he repeated it in Assyrian, everyone laughed.

"Is there no sour fruit in America?" she asked.

"We have green apples, dipped in caramel."

"What is caramel?"

"Candy."

"Everything in America is dipped in candy," Ashur said.

"Or fried in oil," Hudson said. "I had a fried candy bar once at the county fair."

"Fried candy?" Layah couldn't imagine it. "Was it good?"

"Delicious."

"Where did you eat this awful thing?" Ashur asked. "Tea-fare?"

"The county fair. You might call it a bazaar, or a market. There's food and amusement park rides."

Ashur's eyes lit up at the mention of amusement parks. He ate another sour plum and stared into the distance, probably fantasizing about roller coasters and guns. Two inventions made infamous in America.

After a short rest, they continued hiking. The sour plums lifted her energy level a little. They reached the outskirts of Baglar well before she expected. She blinked in surprise, as if the village in the valley below might be a mirage. It was quaint and medieval-looking, with stonework houses set into the hillside.

Hanna and Yelda hugged in celebration. For them, this was home. For the others, it was another resting place.

Yelda took the lead as they approached the village. There was a cobblestone bridge guarded by men with rifles. They spoke a different dialect of Kurdish, too quickly for Layah to follow. Yelda was given a warm welcome, however, and the travelers were allowed entry. They continued down a dirt road to a house with a large courtyard. There was a water pump in the center, with a dozen empty plastic buckets nearby.

"If you want to bathe, you can fill a bucket," Yelda said.

Layah went straight to the pump with an empty bucket. The others followed suit. While the men stayed in the courtyard, the women went inside to a private bathing room. There were towels and privacy screens. Layah stripped down behind a screen and scrubbed her body from head to toe. When she was finished, she soaked her hair. It wasn't a warm, relaxing bath, but she felt clean afterwards.

All the women used their leftover water to wash clothing. Layah laundered her undergarments, wrung them out and hung them over a screen. She had two tunics, both dirty. She was trying to decide which one to wear when an old woman came in with a basket of secondhand clothes.

"You can pick whatever you like," Yelda said.

Layah thanked the woman profusely. The travelers gathered around the basket as if it were a pot of gold. Aram's wife found the most colorful dress and twirled around. She was young and brash, like him. Yusef's wife picked something more sensible, but seemed just as pleased. Layah watched them with a smile. Her cousins were both newly married, to brides that suited them. Now they would have a chance at a happy life.

Layah selected a long-sleeved blouse and a long skirt for herself. The items were faded and worn, but comfortable. She didn't want to put on wet lingerie, so she wrapped a scarf around her breasts before she got dressed. Then she combed and braided her hair, humming an Armenian folk song her father had taught her.

"Your American is handsome," Aram's wife said. Her name was Oshana. "Do you wish to keep him?"

"He's not a pet," Layah said.

"He could be a husband. You already sleep together."

Yusef's wife, Nina, made a shushing sound.

"Has he tried to mount you?" Oshana asked.

Layah flushed at her impertinent question. "He's been a gentleman."

Oshana looked disappointed, as if she wanted to hear all about Hudson's bedroom prowess.

"He has a healthy appetite," Nina said. "You could cook for him."

"Good idea," Oshana said, beaming with approval. "If you can't lure him to your bed, tempt him with food."

Layah didn't know whether to be insulted or amused by their advice. She finished her laundry and sat down to rummage through her pack. While she was organizing, she noticed something missing.

Her passport.

Khalil's was still in the side pocket, where she'd placed it. She knew none of the women would take her passport. They had documents of their own.

Hudson must have done it.

She smothered a sound of outrage. He didn't trust her, so he'd searched her belongings and stolen her passport. He'd wanted to have power over her. She should have been more cautious. She couldn't complete the journey without her passport. It was a symbol of freedom, and now it was in his hands.

Taking a deep breath, she removed her medical kit from her pack. No need to panic. She'd get her passport back by whatever means necessary.

She returned to the courtyard to look for him. The men had finished bathing. Her cousins were smoking cigarettes and lounging around. Hudson was sitting nearby, lacing up his boots. His hair was damp. He had on the same pants he'd been wearing earlier, with a red soccer jersey. His eyes traveled down her body and pulled away.

She was acutely aware of her lack of undergarments as she approached him. The loose clothing didn't cling to her curves, but she felt self-conscious, as if he could see though the fabric. His expression suggested that he was trying not to stare. She didn't think she'd need any fancy meals to tempt him.

"I will check your stitches now."

A muscle in his jaw flexed as he tugged his shirt over his head. She sat on the stone bench behind him to examine the wound. It had healed nicely, despite the constant physical activity. He even appeared to have gained a few pounds. He looked healthy and fit, with hard muscles and taut skin. When her fingertips grazed his back, his shoulders tensed.

"These can be removed," she said, reaching for her scissors.

"Are you really a doctor?"

"I went to medical school, but I did not finish."

"Why not?"

"Classes at the university were canceled. Hospitals

all over Syria were understaffed. They were taking medical students to do the jobs of doctors. So that is what I did. I worked in the emergency ward for over a year."

He held still as she snipped the sutures. "What part of Syria?"

"Damascus."

"How was it?"

She paused, searching for the right words. "At the beginning, it was merely difficult. There were some patients like you."

"Like me?"

"Strong and healthy, with minor wounds." She finished removing the sutures. "Toward the end, I had to focus my efforts on the critically injured. There were more than I could help. The month after Khalil died, I worked so much I hardly slept. Then one day I walked away and never returned."

He glanced over his shoulder at her.

She put away her scissors, avoiding his gaze. "You healed well."

He tugged his shirt back into place and rose to his feet. "I was in Syria. I don't blame anyone for getting out."

She acknowledged this statement with a nod. She wasn't ashamed of her inability to continue treating patients amid crushing grief and daily bombings, but she appreciated his lack of judgment. She decided not to confront him about the passport. He could keep it until they parted ways, if it gave him comfort. They had another day's travel between here and Semdinli, where she would leave him. Her chest hitched at the thought. She stared at him with a heavy heart, wishing for things that could never be.

Yelda approached with one of the village elders. "This is Sheikh Faqir. He would have counsel with you and Mr. Hudson."

Layah bowed her head toward the sheikh, who wore traditional garb and a white turban.

"What's up?" Hudson asked.

"The sheikh wants to speak with us."

They followed Yelda and the sheikh to the other side of the courtyard. There was a lattice pergola shrouded in grapevines giving shade to a long wooden table.

"Are we in trouble?" Hudson whispered.

"I don't know," she said, sitting across from the Yazidis.

Sheikh Faqir spoke for several minutes. Layah listened politely, though she had no idea what he was saying.

"He wants to thank Hudson for guiding us to our new home," Yelda said.

Layah repeated this in English for Hudson, who inclined his head.

"There is a problem," Yelda continued. "Three days ago, there was a bomb in Semdinli. It detonated on a bus full of aid workers. Seventeen were killed."

Layah felt the blood drain from her face. "Did anyone claim responsibility?"

"The Da'esh."

"Have they invaded this region?"

"They are here in small numbers. The Kurdish rebels say the Turks have been arming them in secret."

She translated for Hudson, her thoughts racing. There had been conflict between the Kurds and Turks for decades, but the rebels rarely targeted civilians. The Da'esh had no qualms about killing innocents. Even if the invaders weren't involved, a terror attack in Semdinli meant they couldn't travel that direction. There would be an increased military presence, strict curfews and increased tensions.

"The sheikh wanted to warn you before you resumed your journey. He also regrets to inform you that you cannot stay in the village, as an unmarried couple living in sin."

"We're not living in sin," Layah said.

"You have slept together in the same space."

"Not as man and wife."

"He can see the lust in your hearts. That is sin enough."

"What the hell is she saying?" Hudson asked.

"She says we have to leave because we are sinners."

Yelda cleared her throat. "There is a solution. We will cast out your sin by joining you in holy matrimony."

Layah's mouth dropped open. Yelda had predicted a marriage between them at the end of the journey. She also might have overheard the conversation in the bathing room. Layah had been speaking Assyrian, but Hudson's name was the same in every language.

"They want us to get married."

"You've got to be kidding me."

"No."

"Our marriage ceremonies last three days," Yelda

said. "They begin with the groom striking the bride lightly over the head with a stone."

Layah tried not to show her surprise. The Yazidis were allies to the Assyrians, and they had a shared history of persecution, but they had very different beliefs. Layah didn't want to offend them by expressing disapproval or refusing outright. She turned to Hudson and translated without inflection.

His face became a hard mask. "No. No way."

"He'll never do it," Layah said.

Yelda looked disappointed. "You will encounter great danger if you continue the journey without a marriage bond."

The sheikh spoke again.

"Because of Hudson's bravery as a guide," Yelda said, "the sheikh offers you a spiritual cleansing and a boat trip downriver, to Halana. This way you can avoid the conflict areas and we will be purged of your bad luck."

"Thank you," Layah said stiffly. "You are very kind."

They were escorted to an ornate peacock statue in the center of the village. Yelda told them to kneel in front of it. Hudson complied with obvious reluctance. The priest performed a ritual with clay, holy water and a peacock feather. They were cleansed of their sins. When the prayer was over, they were allowed to stand.

"You may gather your belongings now," Yelda said.

Hudson strode back to the courtyard, his irritation clear. Layah hurried after him, nibbling on the edge of her thumbnail. She'd planned to travel to Semdinli, the most populated town in the region, and leave Hudson there. That was no longer an option. After a major terror attack, every foreigner would be a suspect.

Hudson had to stay with them. She couldn't abandon him, for reasons both moral and practical. The sheikh had offered them a boat ride because of *Hudson's* bravery. It was his reward for delivering Yelda and Hanna safely. Without Hudson, there would be no ride, and they desperately needed one.

She stopped him before they reached the courtyard. He scowled, but didn't pull away.

"You are angry," she said.

"I don't like getting jerked around, or praying to peacocks."

"We are guests here. We must respect their customs."

"Should I hit you over the head with a rock? Would that be respectful?"

She ignored his sarcasm. "They are giving us a ride to Halana and saving us three days of travel."

He moved closer and lowered his voice. "What about my freedom?"

"You are free to go to Semdinli and take your chances there. I would not recommend it after a terror attack. You are in the country illegally, with no documents. You could be mistaken for a foreign radical."

He rubbed a hand over his mouth, seeming to recognize the gravity of the situation. Which, admittedly, she'd put him in, but she could not have predicted this outcome. "Why did he want us to get married?"

"Yelda told him we were sleeping together," Layah said.

"Why would she do that?"

"I don't know. The Yazidi have strange ways. She thinks we are destined to marry."

His eyes narrowed with suspicion.

"I did not encourage her," Layah said, placing a palm on her chest.

"Right. You'd never force anyone to do anything against their will."

"I have no interest—"

"No interest? Really?"

"Not in marriage."

"You don't strike me as the casual affair type."

She lifted her chin. "I feel desire, like any woman. I remember the pleasures of the bedroom. That does not mean I wish for a reluctant husband."

He went quiet, contemplating her words. "Will you stay in Halana?"

"No. We head north from there, to Armenia."

"You never said you were going to Armenia."

"There was no need. I had planned to leave you in Semdinli."

"And now?"

"Now I would advise you to stay with us until the danger has passed."

He didn't argue, so she continued walking. They seemed to have reached an understanding. She didn't want to say too much. Admitting her desire for him wasn't a problem; he already knew. Letting him in on their destination was a riskier endeavor. She hadn't told him *how* they would get to Armenia. He wouldn't approve of the route, but she couldn't change it. There was no other way.

She hurried to the courtyard, where she consulted with Yusef and Aram about the new arrangements. They agreed that Hudson couldn't be left at the mercy of hostile Turks or Da'esh invaders. Layah suspected that her cousins had grown to like Hudson. Even Ashur had warmed up to him, and he was made of ice.

The Yazidis didn't send them off hungry. They sat down to a meal of local favorites. The main dish was rolled-up grape leaves stuffed with lamb and rice. It was served with tea, flatbread and a yogurt porridge called *mierr*. True to form, Hudson ate seconds and thirds of everything. Before they left, Hanna gave Layah a sack filled with golden raisins and almonds. Layah thanked her for the kindness.

They collected their packs and walked to the river's edge. There was a rustic fishing boat waiting for them at the end of a wooden dock. Layah noted their dwindling group of travelers. They'd started at thirteen. Now they were seven.

Hanna was saddened by their departure. The girl said goodbye to Hudson in English, and in Arabic to the others. She also surprised Ashur with a kiss on the cheek. He flushed and stepped back, touching his face. They climbed aboard the boat, one by one. As they headed downriver, Yelda slapped Hanna's hand in admonishment. The girl pulled away from her and raced to the shoreline, waving goodbye.

Ashur watched her until the boat rounded the bend. Then he turned forward, focusing on the journey ahead.

Chapter 11

Hud found himself enjoying the scenery along the river.

He wasn't pleased about the circumstances that had brought him here, but it was a beautiful country, and he appreciated the mode of travel. After four days in the mountains, it felt good to be off his feet.

The river meandered through rolling hills and rugged cliffs. Its serene waters lulled him into a more relaxed state. He'd always wanted to visit Turkey. There was a climber's paradise to the west, along the Turquoise Coast. He'd been planning a Mediterranean vacation with Michelle before their split. The funds were in his bank account, untouched. Although this wasn't the trip he'd dreamed of, he couldn't fault the location.

He could fault Layah for dragging him into another perilous situation. She was a magnet for trouble.

He considered what she'd said earlier about having no interest in marriage. It sounded legit, but he didn't know what to believe. She had a new story every day. He was too tired to examine her motives. Examining her figure was a more enjoyable exercise. She was wearing a pale gray hijab with a peasant blouse and a long skirt. Almost no skin was showing, but his pulse still leaped at the sight of her. She looked soft and feminine in Yazidi clothing, her eyes shining with promise. Everything she did aroused him.

He pulled his gaze away from Layah and caught Ashur's warning glare. The resemblance between the boy and his father was startling. Hud didn't know how he'd missed it before, and he felt a twist of guilt for failing Hasan.

They passed under a crumbling stone bridge on the outskirts of Semdinli. Hud stayed alert while they were close to civilization. He scanned the shoreline, his muscles tensed for action. But he saw no law enforcement, no Turkish military, no lurking terrorists. There were a few fishermen along the shore, minding their own affairs.

After a long, lazy stretch, they entered a section of remote wilderness. The river turned turbulent, with a series of churning rapids and narrow channels. The captain didn't seem fazed by the challenges, and the boat was a sturdy wooden dory, well suited for choppy conditions. Layah gripped the underside of her bench seat and held on tight.

They continued to a lower elevation and returned to calmer waters as daylight faded into dusk. An impressive medieval fortress rose up in the distance, its crumbling side illuminated by the setting sun.

"That is Halana," Layah said with pride.

"Who lives there?"

"No one. It is an ancient Assyrian settlement."

The Yazidi captain left them on a muddy bank along the west side of the river. They said goodbye to him and walked uphill to the settlement. There were remnants of old stone houses, cisterns and dirt pathways. Layah stopped to study the details of different relics, chatting happily with her cousins in their native language.

Hud had no idea what she was saying, but her enthusiasm was infectious, and the ruins were stunning. *She* was stunning. It was impossible not to admire her passion and verve. When she got excited about something, her eyes outshone the stars.

When they reached the main building, her face fell. There were broken statues among the rubble, with headless animal figures and piles of debris. Arabic graffiti was painted across ancient stone walls.

She covered her mouth with one hand, horrified. Yusef put his arm around her. She let out a choked sob, her shoulders shaking.

Hud examined the senseless destruction around them. He knew that the Da'esh had destroyed artifacts in Syria and Iraq. They'd bulldozed museums and vandalized historic sites. He hadn't expected to encounter the evidence of their dark deeds in Turkey. Nor had he expected to be so personally offended by it.

The Da'esh had captured and tortured him. They

were his enemies and his targets. He already hated them. What they'd done here ratcheted that feeling up a notch. It was like seeing a swastika scrawled on a synagogue.

The mood was somber as they toured the rest of the site. Most of the damage was limited to one area. Near the top of the fortress, they found the remnants of a fire. Hud crouched down to touch the ashes. They were cold. He had no way of knowing if the vandals had made this fire. Whoever it was, they were long gone now.

Layah glanced around, taking a deep breath. "We should set up camp."

They continued to a small clearing behind a crumbling stone wall. There was a grassy spot for their tents. Hud collected firewood and made a small pit at the base of the wall. They drank tea and studied the crackling flames.

Although the actions of the Da'esh had put a damper on the evening, they rallied. The Assyrians were a resilient sort, determined to make the best of things. Aram had refilled his liquor bottle with Yazidi moonshine, which he passed around the circle. Hud took a swig and gave it to Layah. She gulped the rest, grimacing. Then she handed the empty bottle to Ashur. Everyone laughed at his disappointment.

Yusef teased Ashur about something related to Hanna and they all laughed again. Hud didn't understand the words but he understood the context. Ashur shook his head in denial, scrubbing his cheek as if he had girl cooties. Then Layah told a ghost story. Hud watched her animated expressions and graceful gestures, committing the details to memory. He didn't feel like an outsider anymore, despite the language barrier. He was comfortable among her people. He'd tried to keep his distance, and failed.

Nina sang an Assyrian folk song before they went to bed. Yusef clapped and Oshana danced by firelight, barefoot and lovely. Aram captured his pretty young wife and dragged her into the tent. Nina and Yusef called it a night, as well.

"You should rest," Layah said to Ashur.

"I'll take first watch," Hud said.

Ashur yawned, nodding his agreement. He went to join the others, but stopped short. "I have to sleep in your tent," he mumbled.

She motioned for him to go ahead. The reason for the change became apparent when breathy feminine sounds emerged from the tent. Hud couldn't tell if it was Nina or Oshana. Maybe both, on separate ends.

He arched a brow at Layah. "Your cousins do everything together, don't they?"

She laughed, rising to her feet. "Come. I will take watch with you."

He jumped at the offer, though he knew better. His commitment to proper conduct had cracked under the stress of the circumstances. He was only human. He'd been held captive for two months. If his worst crime after escaping that hellhole was succumbing to the charms of a beautiful woman, so be it.

Not that he planned on sleeping with her. Not tonight, outdoors, with her cousins near. He also didn't have any condoms, and he was supposed to be keeping watch. He brought one of the wool blankets, though. Might as well get cozy while he avoided temptation.

They hunkered down on the other side of the fortress wall, away from the firelight. He set the rifle in a safe place and arranged the blanket. She snuggled against him. He stared across the dark, deserted hillside. The river glittered in the moonlight.

"Why are you going to Armenia?" he asked.

"It is my father's homeland, and we have nowhere else to go. The Da'esh have invaded every Assyrian community in the region."

"Why do they target Assyrians?"

"Some say it is because of American interference. They want to kill all Christians in retaliation."

"They kill Muslims, too."

"Yes. They kill everyone who opposes them. It is sad that we have been forced out instead of them. Parts of Syria, Iraq and Turkey should belong to us. Assyrians have lived here for thousands of years."

"You can't stay in Turkey?"

"It is not safe."

"The Turks won't protect you from the Da'esh?"

"The Turks are not our allies. They are responsible for the genocide that killed two-thirds of the Assyrian population."

"When was this?"

"A hundred years ago, but not forgotten. Also, it is rumored that they have joined forces with the Da'esh to defeat the Kurds."

He nodded his understanding. Like all things in the Middle East, their situation was complicated. Now that he'd seen the evidence of their persecution with his own eyes, he sympathized with her on a deeper level.

"I fled to Syria to escape war," she continued. "I returned to Iraq for the same reason. I do not wish to settle in another unstable place. Armenia has known many years of peace, and our people are welcome there."

"Do you speak Armenian?"

"A little."

"How many other languages?"

"Four or five."

"Which is it? Four or five?"

"I am fluent in English, Arabic, Assyrian and Kurdish. I also know a bit of Farsi and Armenian."

He counted on his fingers. "That's six."

"But I only speak four well."

"I only speak one well. If that."

"You can learn another."

He turned toward her, studying her face. A week ago, he'd had no interest in learning Arabic. Now he wanted to learn her ways. He wanted to know every inch of her. When he cupped her chin with one hand, she didn't pull away. He rubbed his thumb over her parted lips. "What is the word for this?"

"Mouth or kiss?"

"Both."

"*Bosa* is kiss."

"*Bosa,*" he said, touching his lips to hers.

"Mouth is *fum.*"

"*Fum.*" He kissed her again.

"Tongue is *lisan.*"

"*Lisan,*" he said, and gave it to her, plundering

the depths of her mouth. She returned his kiss with a low moan. Her tongue touched his shyly and her fingers laced through his hair. She tasted like Yazidi liquor and female spice, a delicious combination. He settled against her, learning all her sensitive places. His lips traced the silky column of her throat while his hands roamed. Her hijab fell away, and he pulled his shirt over his head. Her fingertips danced across the surface of his chest.

He paused, taking a ragged breath. He was already throbbing with arousal, near the point of no return. "When I have you, it will be somewhere private," he murmured in her ear. "So you can scream my name in pleasure, over and over again, without anyone hearing."

Her fingertips explored lower. "You are very confident."

He captured her hand and molded it over his erection.

"Is this the source of your confidence?"

"It's one of them."

She let out a shaky laugh, sliding her palm along his length. "As a medical professional, I know that size is not linked to female satisfaction."

"But?"

"I think more research must be done."

He kissed her again. He couldn't make love to her here, but he didn't want to stop yet. Her body felt like heaven underneath his. He untied the string over her collarbone, loosening her blouse. Her breasts were bound with a scarf. One tug exposed her bountiful flesh. He lifted his head to stare. He hadn't expected to undress her so easily, or to be so dazzled by the sight. Her breasts were soft and round and perfect.

"How do you say beautiful?" he asked.

"Jamila," she whispered.

He repeated it with reverence, nuzzling her soft flesh.

"Hudson?"

"Call me William," he said.

"William? Is that your name?"

He nodded, wrestling with the fabric of her skirt. He almost swallowed his tongue when he realized she wasn't wearing anything underneath it. "Jesus."

"William."

He lifted his gaze to her face. "Yes?"

"I would also like privacy, when we are together. This is not safe."

He glanced around the dark hillside, considering. They weren't exactly alone, and he needed to stay alert, but he could still give her pleasure. He might never get the opportunity to do this in a real bed. "Let me touch you."

She nibbled her lower lip, uncertain.

He waited for her to say no, but she didn't. A flash of intuition told him that she enjoyed a hint of danger, the same way he did. She'd recognized the trait in him because she shared it. "Lift your skirt."

She seemed scandalized by the order. "What if I scream?"

"I'll cover your mouth with mine."

After a short hesitation, she leaned back against the rock wall and tugged the fabric up her thighs. His arousal swelled to a painful hardness. He pushed her knees apart and left them open. He imagined pressing his tongue to her and tasting her sweetness. Moistening his lips, he returned his attention to her breasts. He suckled her nipples, cupping her soft flesh. Her fingers twined in his hair again and the rest of the world fell away. He left her nipples taut and wet. When his hand moved up her thigh, her breaths quickened with excitement.

She was slippery with arousal, ripe for his touch. He lifted his head from her breasts and watched her face as he stroked her. She wasn't difficult to please. His fingertips circled her swollen bead of flesh. He'd like to know the word for that in Arabic, but he decided not to ask. She gripped his wrist suddenly, shuddering with pleasure. He crushed his mouth over hers to muffle her soft cries.

Although he hadn't planned anything beyond giving her a quick orgasm, he was desperate for release. He fumbled for the buttons on his fly with his free hand. Then he stroked himself with fingers still slick from her body.

She watched him perform the crude task with half-lidded eyes. He was beyond embarrassment, and he knew women liked his size. His gaze moved from her face to her unbound breasts and pouty nipples. He wasn't hard to please, either. He came with a smothered groan, spilling his seed in the dirt.

When his sense of decorum returned, he tucked himself in and buttoned his pants. She fixed her blouse and straightened her skirt. In less than a minute, they were both fully composed, as if he hadn't just brought her to climax and jerked off beside her.

"Should I apologize?" he asked.

"For what?"

"Dishonoring you."

She leaned toward him and brushed her lips over his. "I like your methods of dishonoring, William Hudson."

"In that case, let's do it again."

"Do you have the same appetite for women that you have for food?"

"Not for any woman. Just you."

She smiled at his response, patting his cheek. She didn't believe him. She'd let him touch her because she was a lonely young widow who missed the pleasures of the bedroom. She was still mourning her ex-husband. Hud got the impression that she'd been a well-satisfied wife. He felt another surge of jealousy toward Khalil, along with a grudging respect.

Even if Layah wanted a real relationship with Hud, it was impossible. They had no future together, no hope of permanence. He was a stranger in a strange land, half-broken from months of captivity, still recovering from a painful divorce.

He needed to harden his heart and keep a cool head. If he couldn't enjoy her body without getting attached, he had to back off. He shouldn't be crossing the line with her, anyway. It was personally and professionally risky.

"I will watch with you if you like," she offered.

"No," he said, tugging his shirt back on. "Get some rest."

"Good night, then."

"Good night."

He watched her walk around the wall and crawl into the tent with Ashur. Then he picked up the rifle and trained his gaze on the dark hillside. He'd spent a thousand nights like this, guarding his comrades. Now he was guarding a band of refugees. He had to remind himself that the Assyrians weren't his teammates. They weren't his friends. He was sympathetic to their plight, and he cared for Layah, but he had to go his own way.

He'd brought her people to Turkey in exchange for his freedom. He'd held up his end of the bargain.

It was time for Layah to honor hers.

Chapter 12

Layah drifted in and out of sleep, plagued by strange dreams.

Some were a pleasant rehash of her encounter with Hudson. One involved the peacock ceremony, but they were alone together. She knelt in front of the statue while he painted her naked body with a feather.

Others were nightmares involving the Da'esh. They were chasing her around the ruins, threatening to chop off her head. She ran to the edge of a cliff and jumped, plummeting to the raging river below. Then she was inside the crevasse again, trapped underneath the glacier. Frozen in ice.

She woke with a gasp, her hand over her heart. Ashur slept peacefully beside her. Daylight filtered into the tent.

She emerged from the space and found her cousins sitting with Hudson. She flushed at the sight of him, but he didn't seem fazed in the least. Perhaps he exchanged intimate acts with women as casually as he paid for a cup of coffee.

Yusef and Aram were arguing about who had misplaced the tea, ignoring her. She breathed a sigh of relief as she joined them for breakfast. Her cousins hadn't overheard anything last night. They'd both been too busy with their own wives to worry about what Layah was doing with Hudson.

William.

She banished his Christian name from her thoughts. She couldn't call him that in front of the others. The two of them might never have another opportunity to be alone together. They might never share a bed like husband and wife.

She didn't blame him for rejecting the sheikh's offer. She would have done the same. She wasn't so desperate that she needed to trap a man into marriage. She'd been happy with Khalil. She knew how it felt to be truly loved. She would not sully her husband's memory with a sham wedding to a reluctant partner.

Hudson desired her, obviously. He did not love her. He would return to America, and she would carry on in Armenia.

She felt a pang of sorrow at the thought. She had to start over. She could never go home again, and she could never go back to the way things were. Sharing a piece of herself with Hudson had altered her course forever. It would be him she pined for now, instead of Khalil.

They shared a breakfast of almonds and raisins as the sun climbed over the horizon. Layah changed out of her Yazidi skirt, donning still-damp underwear and pants. Then they packed up and headed away from Halana. Layah glanced over her shoulder at the ruins before they disappeared. She was glad to have visited the site, even though it had sustained damage. She'd always wanted to see the ancient dwellings of her ancestors. Maybe she could return someday for a real vacation.

They walked down into a valley and continued their descent. The river, on their right, flowed into a deep gorge. Danger awaited on both sides, but she didn't want to cross it until they had no other choice. They needed to find a shallow section, because she wasn't a strong swimmer. Oshana and Nina couldn't swim at all.

Around noon, they reached the top of a plateau. The river was thirty or forty meters below, at the base of a sheer cliff. It was even warmer than she'd predicted. The sun beat down on her head and sweat trickled between her breasts. She wished for a shady tree to rest under.

"Stop," Hudson said.

She froze beside him, searching the horizon. There were dark shapes kicking up a cloud of dust in the distance.

"Those are men on horseback," Yusef said.

She translated for Hudson.

"What kind of men? Da'esh invaders?"

"I don't know. They could also be Turkish military or Kurdish rebels."

Hudson studied their surroundings, his brow furrowed. The cliff side was too steep to navigate without ropes. A cluster of boulders nearby would shield them from view, but only for a few moments. On the wide plateau, there were no hiding places. "Do you want to climb down or surrender?"

"Climb," she said, without hesitation. She didn't have to ask Ashur or her cousins. They were already scrambling for the equipment in their packs. They'd left the harnesses behind, but they still had rope and some other random gear. Hudson placed an anchor in the underside of a boulder and threaded the rope through it. Then he doubled the rope into two lines. That was the extent of the safety protection.

"Is the rope long enough?" she asked.

"It's long enough. Hold both ropes and don't let go."

"I understand."

"We'll climb three at a time. You and Ashur come after me. Then Yusef and the girls. Aram will go last."

She translated for everyone. Aram nodded his agreement. He grabbed the rifle and got down on his belly behind the boulder, guarding their escape. The horsemen were getting closer, but they hadn't picked up speed.

"They haven't seen us," Layah said.

"With any luck, they never will," Hudson replied. Then he went over the side of the cliff. She studied his technique, which was similar to the fixed-rope climb. He braced his boots on the rock face and descended in confident motions.

No problem, she told herself. *Just don't let go. And don't look down.*

She took a deep breath and followed him over the edge. It was terrifying, but doable. She focused on holding both ropes in a tight grip and working her way down, hand over hand. About halfway down the cliff, Ashur caught up to her. She tried to climb faster, aware that their time was limited. Her upper body didn't have the strength for the task. Her biceps quivered from exertion and her grip weakened.

Ashur paused, looking over his shoulder at her. "Are you okay?"

She clung to the rope, shaking. She wasn't okay.

"Layah," Hud yelled. "Don't panic. You're almost there."

"I can't do it," she shouted back.

"Wrap your legs around the rope and slide down to me slowly. I'll catch you."

She followed those instructions for the last few meters, until she was in his arms. When her feet hit the ground, her knees buckled. She collapsed in a heap next to Hudson. He kept his gaze on Ashur, who finished the climb without trouble.

They were on a narrow strip of land at the river's edge, exposed to anyone who glanced down the cliff from the plateau above. The only shelter was a deep depression in the sandstone. She dragged Ashur that direction and put her pack down inside. Then she stood by Hudson while the others made their descents. Nina accidentally kicked Yusef in the head, but he held on. So did she. Oshana needed the most help. She didn't even get halfway down before she started to slide. This resulted in rope burns and a minor fall at the bottom.

Layah and the others scrambled into the sandstone cave to wait for Aram and Hudson. Aram joined them first. Oshana clung to him, sobbing. Hudson pulled down the rope so the horsemen couldn't follow them. Then he squeezed in next to Layah.

"Did they see you?" he asked Aram.

"I don't think so."

Although Hudson spoke in English and Aram replied in Arabic, they seemed to understand each other. Ashur put his ear against the sandstone to listen for the sound of approaching hooves.

"They are here," he said quietly. "They stopped."

Aram drew his rifle. Layah prayed the horsemen didn't have their own ropes. If they came down here, there was no escape. There would be an ugly gun battle, and her people would lose.

"Where is your pack?" Oshana whispered to Aram.

He pointed up. Layah's stomach dropped as she realized what had happened. In the rush to get down the cliff before the horseman spotted him, he'd left the pack behind. She prayed the strangers would not disturb it.

Her prayers weren't answered.

Seconds later, the pack landed in the middle of the river with a huge splash. Layah and the others watched in horror as it floated to the surface. The pockets were unzipped, as if the contents had been ransacked. No one moved.

Then the men on the cliff above them opened fire.

Layah clapped a hand over her mouth to smother her scream. Hudson put his arms around her and Ashur, shielding them with his body. Bullets tore through the canvas pack in a chilling display of gun power. The pack jumped and flipped from multiple impacts. Then it sank into the water and didn't resurface.

"They can't get down here," Hudson murmured. "They're just trying to scare us."

"It's working."

The men continued to fire, peppering the surface of the water and the shoreline. Mud and pebbles sprayed up from the ground. Layah closed her eyes, plagued by flashbacks of horror. She'd heard the sound of gunfire too many times. Too many battles, too many bombs. Too many mangled bodies.

She took a deep breath and focused on Hudson. He felt warm and strong and solid. His arms made a heavy band around her and Ashur. Although Hudson was a trained soldier, acting on instinct, she appreciated his protection. There was something comforting, and achingly familial, about their huddle. Ashur couldn't push her away in the cramped space. Hudson might not love her, but he cared about her. He cared about their safety.

After a few minutes, the shooters seemed to lose interest. Ashur put his ear to the sandstone again to listen for the horses as they left. Hudson and Aram emerged from the hiding space with caution. When no one fired at them, the others filed out.

"You think they're looking for another way down?" Hudson asked, studying the cliffs all around them.

"I hope not," Layah said.

"We should have shot them," Ashur said. He always favored the most violent solution.

"We don't know who they are," Layah replied.

"They are the same Da'esh swine who destroyed our relics," Ashur said. "Or they are murdering Turks, who also deserve to die."

"They could be Kurds."

Ashur shrugged. He didn't like the Kurds, either.

"Whoever they were, they had several high-powered rifles," Hudson said. "Shooting at them would have been a serious mistake."

Ashur went quiet, unable to dispute this logic.

They headed downriver, following a narrow edge along the base of the cliff until they found a shallow section. Then they were forced to cross through ice-cold, waist-deep water. There was no time to stop or change clothes after. Hudson insisted they keep moving at a brisk pace.

Layah continued forward in soggy boots and wet, mud-splattered pants. She wondered if the horsemen had been unable to pursue, or decided not to for geographical reasons. The river marked the border between Turkey and Iran. The Da'esh were extremely unwelcome here.

So were Americans, but that couldn't be helped.

Early in the evening, they reached the top of a hill overlooking Rajan, a tiny town in northern Iran.

They'd made it. This marked the end of their journey on foot. They'd escaped Iraq, survived the mountains and avoided being detained in Turkey. Now they would travel across Iran in a vehicle. With any luck, they'd arrive in Armenia tomorrow.

Layah should have been overjoyed. This was the moment she'd planned and hoped for and worked toward for months. But the accomplishment felt empty, because the danger wasn't over. Bringing an American into Iran put everything at risk. If they were stopped and questioned, Hudson would be taken into custody—or killed.

She'd never forgive herself if he got detained here.

She'd meant to warn him at the Turkish border. Then they'd run into trouble and she'd held her tongue. Now they were stuck, and she wasn't sure how to break the news.

"What town is this?" Hudson asked.

"It is Rajan," she said. "My aunt lives near. She will shelter us for the night."

They headed toward a cluster of trees on the outskirts of the village. Then she sent Yusef and Nina to find a pay phone or internet café. They would contact Miri while the others rested. Layah didn't want anyone to see Hudson. European looks weren't that remarkable in this region, but they needed to be extra cautious.

Hudson was the last to remove his pack and sit down. She noticed his wince of pain. Her gaze traveled over his body, settling on a red stain above his knee. His pants were ripped. "You're injured," she said in surprise.

He covered the spot with his hand. "It's nothing. Just a scratch."

She realized that he'd been hit with a bullet fragment or a piece of rock while he'd been shielding her and Ashur.

"Surely you don't expect him to come with us," Aram said in Assyrian.

"What do you suggest?" she returned, bristling.

Aram glanced back the way they'd come.

"He'll be recaptured. He doesn't know where to go."

"He can take care of himself. It's not our concern."

"You agreed to bring him along!"

"To Halana," Aram said. "Not Rajan."

"I won't send him back."

"Will you tell him where we are?"

She crossed her arms over her chest, her stomach roiling. "I'll tell him when it's safe."

"Your affection for this infidel makes you foolish. But then, you have always had a weakness for outsiders."

The dig at Khalil didn't sit well with Layah. Neither did Aram's arrogant attitude. She'd arranged for this entire journey, which Aram had greatly benefited from. She'd spent the last of her money on gear and guide services. "We might not be in this position if you hadn't left your pack at the top of the cliff."

"I had to climb fast, because you women are slow and weak!"

Oshana touched his elbow. "*Shlama*, Aram."

"What's his problem?" Hudson asked, glancing from Aram's angry face to Layah's. "Do you need me to shut him up?"

Layah ignored Hudson. "Was your passport inside the pack?" she asked Aram.

"No. Oshana has it."

"I agree with Aram," Ashur said. "You risk all of us to protect this American who left my father to die in the streets."

"He took a bullet for us," Layah replied. "Look at him."

"It's a flesh wound."

She swallowed her response, aware that Ashur's heartbreaking past colored his opinions. Aram was a young hothead, quick to judge. They both used sharp words without thinking. Instead of arguing with them, she rummaged through her pack for the almonds and raisins. She was in charge of this expedition. She would bring along whoever she liked.

Yusef and Nina returned with good news. They'd been able to call Miri from a pay phone at the pharmacy.

"She'll be here in thirty minutes," Yusef said.

"She won't shelter an American," Aram said. "Her husband won't allow it."

Layah gave him a quelling stare. He was irritating, but he had a point. "We'll see."

Hudson knew they were talking about him, and he didn't seem to care. He stretched out on his back and tucked his hands behind his head.

"Aram wants to leave Hudson here," Layah explained to Yusef.

"Yusef sides with me," Aram said.

"No, I don't," Yusef said.

"What?"

"We are not animals."

Aram took offense to Yusef's strong opposition. "I am an animal for considering our interests ahead of his?"

"We'll let Miri decide," Layah said, ending the conversation. Then she leaned against her pack and closed her eyes. She didn't know what her aunt would do. If Miri refused to shelter Hudson, Layah would have to accept it and say goodbye. She couldn't run away with him. She was going to Armenia with Ashur. She'd made a vow to take him to a safer place.

She owed her brother that much.

Chapter 13

Hud considered making his escape.

The village had a public phone. Yusef and Nina had already used it. One call to his commander would end this farce. He could get up and walk away anytime.

But he didn't, for several reasons. It was difficult to go unnoticed in a village this small. He also wasn't sure what the consequences would be for Layah. As soon as he made contact with the navy, he'd be given specific instructions about where to go and what to do. A plan would be set into motion, with no turning back. Within hours or minutes, he'd rendezvous with personnel from the nearest US air base. There was one in Incirlik, by the Syrian border.

He'd have to tell the truth about how he'd arrived in Turkey. He couldn't claim to have escaped the Da'esh on his own. He couldn't have climbed the mountains without specific gear. If he said he'd agreed to help

Layah, he'd be in violation of military regulations. If he said she'd forced him to act as their guide, she could be prosecuted. No matter what story he told, there would be complications. Her family might get picked up by the Turkish police, or sent back to Iraq.

Whatever happened would be out of his hands, and he didn't want to put her at risk. Waiting until they were in a more populated area would be safer for both of them. He could disappear in the crowd. She could continue to Armenia. Everyone wins.

Decision made, he rested his eyes for a few minutes. They were arguing about him. Maybe Aram had accused him of dishonoring Layah again. Hud was too tired to care. He'd stayed up all night guarding the camp. No one had come to relieve him of the duty, and he'd been reluctant to disturb the love tent. He had nowhere to sleep, anyway.

It rankled a little that Aram was getting in Hud's business, after Hud had given him the privacy to bang his wife and cuddle with her for hours. He'd also saved their asses on the cliff. But whatever. Hud had bigger concerns. His thigh ached like a son of a bitch from the ricochet wound, and he was starving.

He needed to eat and rest. Then he could think about the next step.

A flatbed truck rumbled down the road less than an hour later. The woman who emerged greeted Layah with a warm hug. She cooed over Ashur, who shrugged off her attempt to embrace him. She smiled and pinched his cheek instead. Aram and Yusef introduced their wives. Then Layah grasped Hud's hand and pulled him forward. He didn't understand the words she spoke, but he got the impression she was misrepresenting their relationship. Aram scowled in the background.

Hud wasn't sure how to greet Layah's aunt, so he put his hand on his chest and said hello in Arabic. It must have been okay, because the woman beamed at Layah. There was a flurry of questions and responses. Then it was time to go. Layah took the passenger seat, while the rest of them climbed into the back.

Hud sat next to Ashur. It was a dark night, full of stars. He was happy to be off his feet. After the day they'd had, he was happy just to be alive. As they left the village and traveled down a deserted road, he felt at peace.

"How did Layah introduce me?" he asked Ashur.

"She said you were Khalil."

All his good feelings evaporated. "You're kidding."

"No."

"Isn't he dead?"

"Yes, but Miri doesn't know that. Our family does not speak of him."

"Why not?"

"He was not Assyrian."

Hud fell silent, lost in thought. Something wasn't right, beyond Layah's family secrets. She hadn't mentioned an aunt in Turkey. She'd said her people weren't safe here. They were traveling east, which didn't make sense to him. His mental map of the area was fuzzy, but he was pretty sure they had to go north to reach the Armenian border. East was…somewhere else. Tajikistan? Azerbaijan?

He closed his eyes in an attempt to picture this part

of the world. He'd been all over the Arabian Peninsula. He'd cut his teeth in Afghanistan. In between was a cluster of places he'd never visited. His mind drifted to a tour of duty in the Hindu Kush, a land of snow-capped mountains and jagged peaks.

When the truck came to an abrupt stop, he jolted awake. He hadn't meant to fall asleep. So much for staying sharp.

Ashur gave him a rude shove.

Hud gathered his pack and climbed down from the bed of the truck with the others. They were in a hotel parking lot. Layah urged him into the shadows while her aunt arranged for the rooms. Five minutes later, Layah had a set of keys. She unlocked the door for him and Ashur, ushering them inside.

Hud looked around. It was nothing fancy, just two beds and a bathroom. No phone or television. Ashur collapsed on one of the beds and didn't move. Hud wanted to do the same thing as soon as possible.

"I should care for your wound," Layah said.

"Let me shower first."

She nodded, crossing her arms over her chest. "If you have dirty clothes, I will take them to wash."

Most of his clothes were on his body. He removed a few items from his pack and put them in an empty bag. Then he retreated to the bathroom to strip down completely. His reflection wasn't pretty. He still had a good amount of muscle, but zero padding. He needed a shave. There were minor cuts on his rib cage, left elbow and left thigh.

He placed the dirty clothes outside the door and turned on the faucet. The water was lukewarm and he had to duck his head to wash his hair, but it felt glorious. He enjoyed this shower as much as the last one. Maybe more. He relished the smell of the soap, the lather of shampoo, the feel of his own clean skin.

While he dried off, he noticed a place card on the sink. There were squiggles in Arabic or some other language. In English, it said Hotel Urmia.

Urmia.

He'd heard of Urmia.

Urmia was in Iran.

He wrapped the towel around his waist, his pulse racing. There must be some mistake. They couldn't be in Iran. The name of the hotel didn't mean anything. The soap could be from anywhere. Layah wouldn't bring him to Iran. Would she?

He came out of the bathroom in search of answers. Ashur was still sprawled on the bed, snoring. Layah was sitting on the other bed with her medical kit in her lap. Her eyes traveled down his torso and settled on his rib cage. She rose to her feet, brow furrowed. "You have more than one injury."

He held still while she examined the wound on his side. Her hands were firm and gentle. He gripped the towel at his waist, steeling himself against her touch. His body didn't care if she was a schemer and a liar. It wanted her all the same.

"Come and sit."

He followed those instructions in silence. He didn't ask any questions, because he knew. They were in Iran. There was no other explanation. He knew, but he didn't want to know. He couldn't bring himself to acknowledge her betrayal.

It was so much like Michelle's.

His stomach clenched at the thought. He remembered how it had felt to stand next to his wife in the doctor's office, puzzling over her due date like a goddamned fool. In the two years since, he'd wondered if she'd planned to keep the secret forever. Would she have raised the child as his? Would he have held the baby and loved it and then one day, when the kid was half-grown, noticed her lover's eyes staring back at him?

This moment felt like that one, big and gaping. Swallowing his heart and eating away at his soul.

Layah took care of his side and his elbow before moving on to his thigh. She tried to apply a numbing agent, but he refused. He wanted it to hurt, and it did. She had to dig out a piece of shrapnel with forceps. He endured the pain without flinching. She flushed the wound and covered it with a bandage, then lifted her gaze to his face.

"You know," she said.

"When were you going to tell me?"

"Right now."

"Right now it's too late for me to do anything about it," he said, his jaw clenched. "Why not before we crossed the frigging border? Why didn't you say, 'Hey, Hudson, it's been fun, but we're going to Iran now'?"

"We crossed at the river. I thought we were being pursued."

He stood abruptly, raking his fingers through his hair. Iran was the worst country for him to get stranded in. He'd rather go back to Iraq. There were US air bases in Iraq, and in Turkey. There were allies to contact. In Iran, he was completely isolated.

"I'm sorry," she said.

"Are you?"

"You don't believe me?"

"No. I don't."

Her eyes filled with tears. "I didn't mean to hurt you."

"I think you did."

"For what reason?"

"For Hasan."

She drew in a sharp breath, as if his words pained her.

He didn't buy it. "Why didn't you tell me he was your brother?"

She stood, wiping the tears from her face. "I wasn't sure you remembered him."

"I remember him."

"Would mentioning his name have made a difference?" she asked bitterly. "Would you have rushed to help Hasan's surviving family members?"

"That's not fair."

"I will tell you what is not fair," she retorted. "My brother bled to death in Syria, because he was your interpreter. That is not fair. His wife died in childbirth because the Da'esh threatened to kill anyone who assisted her. That is not fair. Ashur has no parents and I have no husband! That is not fair."

"And you want to make things fair," he said in a low voice. "That's why I'm here. An eye for an eye."

Tears spilled down her cheeks. "No. I care for you."

"Don't you dare say that," he said, closing the distance between them. "You screwed me. You used me to get out of Iraq, you let me get you off, and then you screwed me. But not the way we both wanted."

She slapped him across the face.

The sharp crack echoed through the room and his head tilted to the side. It was a direct hit, but he hardly felt it. He was too focused on his own rage, on the darkness inside him and the blood pounding in his ears. This moment had been coming since he'd left the torture chamber. It had been building to a flash-point.

She retreated a step, her throat working. She was afraid of him.

Good.

He advanced, lightning-quick, as she shrank back against the bathroom door. He braced his hands on either side of her, using his arms like bars to hold her prisoner. She couldn't escape.

"Just admit it," he said, crowding her. "You brought me here as payback. You wanted me to suffer because you blame me for Hasan's death."

She shook her head in denial, lips trembling. He slammed his palm against the door, overwhelmed with fury and frustration. He wanted to shake the truth out of her. He wanted to kiss her until she confessed her sins.

Then he felt the cold bite of metal against the side of his neck. It was Ashur.

"I blame you," the boy said.

A strange sensation came over Hud as Ashur pressed the blade to his throat. He could only describe it as an out-of-body experience. He looked down at himself and saw a man he didn't recognize, using his strength to intimidate a woman. He saw a manifestation of anger and violence and toxic thoughts.

He saw his father.

He took a deep breath and snapped back to reality. The point of the knife cut into his skin, dangerously close to his jugular. Layah stared at him with wide eyes. Hud couldn't make any sudden movements. Ashur had already nicked him. Blood trickled into the hollow of his throat.

"You sharpened your dagger," Hud said.

"Move away from her or I will kill you."

Hud stepped back from Layah, his hands raised. When Ashur lowered his knife, Hud grasped the towel at his waist to keep it from falling.

"Sit," Ashur said to him.

Hud sat down on the edge of the bed. Layah stayed where she was, with her back pressed against the wall. Hud could disarm Ashur easily, but he didn't. They needed to hash this out. "You think I failed Hasan."

"I know you did."

"You're right. I did. We all did."

Ashur blinked at this unexpected admission. A month ago, Hud wouldn't have made it. Now that he'd spent time with Ashur and Layah, he felt compelled to give a deeper explanation. And maybe, Hud wanted to come clean.

"He was a member of our team, but we didn't protect him," Hud said. "We didn't make sure he traveled with an armed guard. We didn't put him in a safe house or insist on bringing his family to live on the base. We let him down."

"You promised him a visa for one year of service," Ashur said.

Hud nodded, though he didn't handle those arrangements. It was the usual reward, and many interpreters didn't live long enough to collect.

Ashur continued, his voice flat. "After a year passed, he was told that he had to wait for visas for my mother and I. So he continued to work for your military. Do you know what happened to him?"

"Yes," Hud said.

"Tell me."

"He was killed."

"How?"

"His throat was cut." Hud omitted the part about the missing tongue. Ashur might not be aware of every detail. "Your mother was heavily pregnant at the time. She went into hiding because of threats made by Hasan's killers. She couldn't get medical attention. We sent a doctor from the base, but it was too late."

Ashur's mouth thinned. "You know these things, but you do not care."

"I do care."

"Liar," Ashur said. He moved closer, touching the blade to the underside of Hud's chin. Layah let out a strangled sob. Hud prayed she wouldn't interfere. "You didn't care enough to protect him! Did you know he was Assyrian?"

"No," Hud said, swallowing hard.

"An Assyrian interpreter is a perfect target for the Da'esh. You should have known this. It is your job to collect information and understand the enemy."

Hud couldn't argue there. He'd assumed Hasan was Muslim. The Assyrians looked like Arabs to him, with their dark eyes and hair. Hud's main concern was how well Hasan spoke the local languages, not his ethnic or religious background.

"I should kill you the way they killed him," Ashur said, his hand quivering.

Layah bit the edge of her fist. Hud held very still, silently imploring her not to move. "I know who did it."

"You lie," Ashur said.

"No. I didn't know enough about Hasan, but he was a good interpreter and a good man. He was a member of my team. I cared about him being murdered in the streets. So I investigated his death, and I went after the men responsible. I went all the way to Telskuf."

Ashur took the blade away from Hud's throat. "Telskuf?"

"I was convinced that the terrorists who killed your father were in a building in Telskuf. I moved in too fast, and I got trapped. I was filled with fury, so much that it made me reckless. That's why I told you emotions and killing don't mix."

"Who?" Ashur demanded. "Who was it?"

Hud shook his head in denial. The name would poison the boy's soul.

Ashur pushed past Hud and grabbed a pillow from the opposite bed. He stabbed it repeatedly, making animal sounds of anguish. Feathers floated into the air. It was a poor substitute for the bloodshed he desired.

Layah slid down the wall and sank to the ground. Her chest rose and fell with ragged breaths. Hud waited for Ashur to vent his emotions. He understood the boy's rage and frustration. He knew how it felt to lose control.

When Ashur was finished killing the pillow, he dropped his right arm. Hud moved in and grasped the boy's wrist. After a short struggle, Ashur let go of the knife. Hud secured it and gave the boy space. Ashur buried his face in the mangled pillow. His thin shoulders shook with silent tears. Layah rushed forward and joined him on the bed. She put her hand on his back, tentative. He turned toward her, seeking the comfort of her embrace.

Hud hid the knife in his pack and retreated to the bathroom. He wiped the blood off his neck and braced his palms on the sink. Summoning calm, he stared at his reflection.

He was in Iran. He was in Iran with a homicidal kid, a band of refugees and a woman who tempted him beyond all reason. This was a total goat screw of a situation. He didn't know what to do about any of it, especially Layah. He couldn't seem to guard his heart against her.

He touched the cheek she'd slapped, contemplative. Despite the wrongs she'd done him, he felt closer to her than to any woman he'd ever known. He admired her daring, even when it worked against him. He sympathized with her struggle for freedom and her concerns for Ashur. He still wanted her.

Yeah. He was clearly an idiot. She'd kidnapped him, wrangled him into an impossible journey and subjected him to nonstop danger. She'd lied to him at every turn. She'd used him as a stand-in for her husband. And Hud wasn't opposed to going another round.

She knocked on the door. "May I come in?"

He let her enter. Of course he did. He might as well lie down and let her walk all over him. She closed the door behind her, moistening her lips. Her hair was uncovered, her eyes wet with tears.

"I'm sorry," he said stiffly. "I shouldn't have gone off on you."

"I should not have slapped you."

He nodded, though he didn't consider the offenses equal.

She crossed her arms over her chest. "Thank you for your help with Ashur. You are good with him."

Hud avoided her gaze. He didn't want to admit that he'd been just like Ashur as a kid, quick-tempered and prone to violence. Maybe Hud was still like that, though he tried not to be. "Is he okay?"

"He is resting," she said. "I wish to explain myself."

"I don't want to hear it."

"William—"

"Don't call me that. Not now."

She flinched at his words. "I hurt you, and I am sorry."

"It's not about hurt feelings. You brought me to Iran."

"There was no other way."

He shook his head in disbelief. He'd rather have taken his chances with the Four Horsemen of the Apocalypse.

"We are here for one day only. Tomorrow we go to

the Armenian crossing. It is an open border, without fees or restrictions. No documents are required. You will be able to enter Armenia in safety."

Hud knew what an open border was, but he didn't trust the Iranians to follow the rules. "Is there a checkpoint?"

"There are customs booths for information."

"What if we're stopped before we cross?"

She didn't have an answer for that.

"Have you been in Iran before?"

"Not since I was a child. It is not safe for Assyrians."

"How does your aunt manage?"

"She married a Muslim and converted."

"Is that what you did?"

Her lips parted in surprise. "No. I did not convert."

He noticed that she didn't deny the first part of his question. "Iranians detain and jail Americans for no reason. And those are just the civilians, who come legally. With my tattoos, I won't be mistaken for a civilian. My presence could even be considered an act of war. If we get caught, I'll be imprisoned, convicted of espionage and executed."

"We won't get caught," she said. "I have a plan."

He let out a frustrated breath. "You always do."

"You can use Khalil's passport."

"I look nothing like him!"

"You are tall. You have dark eyes. If you shave, and cover your hair…"

Hud hated the idea. He hated everything about it. He hated her for risking his freedom, and himself for wanting her anyway. The walls of the bathroom seemed to close in on him like a prison cell. His chest felt tight, his skin crawling. He had to get out. He brushed by her and opened the door, sucking in air.

Ashur was asleep on the bed again. There were feathers all over.

What a goddamned mess.

He stretched out on the opposite bed and closed his eyes. He took deep breaths and pictured tall mountains. Not the snow-capped peaks of the Zagros, but the rugged Sierras, Mount Shasta and the sky-high cliffs of Yosemite. Hud could climb to his heart's content without ever leaving California. He'd always liked California girls, too. He vowed to find a hot blonde to cure him of his feelings for Layah.

"I ordered kebabs," Layah said.

His stomach growled fiercely at the news. He opened one eye.

"You like kebabs?"

"You're evil, you know that?"

She smiled at his expression, spreading a blanket on the floor. She filled plastic cups with water from the bathroom sink. Oshana delivered the kebabs a few minutes later. Ashur woke up to eat, his hair disheveled. They shared a feast of rice, salad, hummus and meat kebabs. Hud's argument with Layah didn't fade away, but it seemed less important after a full meal. Ashur stuffed his face and went back to bed.

Hud climbed into the other bed, exhausted. Layah took her turn in the shower. He listened to the squeaky faucet and didn't even picture her naked. He didn't picture anything. His mind shut off, and he slept.

Chapter 14

Layah tiptoed downstairs at dawn.

She'd borrowed a nightgown from Aunt Miri, but she didn't want to be seen in it. She ducked into the laundry room, which was empty, and removed the clothes from the dryer. Hudson's belongings were mingled with hers. She brought his shirt to her face and inhaled. It smelled like laundry detergent.

Her aunt sailed into the room, startling her. "Good morning," she said in Farsi.

Layah's cheeks heated. "Good morning."

They switched to Assyrian to chat while Layah folded laundry. Miri and her husband owned the hotel, and business was good. Miri was eager to hear any news about family. Like Layah, Miri had married an outsider, so she had very little communication with other Assyrians. Travel between Iraq and Iran was difficult, adding to her isolation. Layah could relate.

She'd been estranged from her parents for years. She still hadn't forgiven them for refusing to recognize her marriage.

"He is a big man," Miri said. "Tall."

Layah was in the process of folding Hudson's pants. "Yes."

"Is he good to you?"

She nodded, avoiding Miri's gaze. He hadn't been very good to her last night, but she didn't blame him. She'd known he wouldn't react well to feeling trapped in a dangerous place. Like Ashur, he suffered from post-traumatic stress.

"He has a charming accent. Where is he from?"

Layah couldn't lie anymore. Not to Hudson, and not to her own family. Miri looked so much like Layah's mother. Layah missed her dearly, despite the rift between them. "He's not Khalil."

"I know."

Layah stopped folding laundry. "You know?"

"Your mother sent me a picture from your wedding."

"She didn't come to my wedding."

"I think she got it from your brother, and she passed it on to me. She gushed about what a beautiful bride you were."

Layah's eyes filled with tears. She had notified her mother about the deaths of Hasan and his wife, but she hadn't said a word about Khalil. It was too painful to speak his name to someone who'd never accepted him. "Hudson is our guide. It's a long story."

"Did something happen to Khalil?"

"He joined the Syrian rebels. He…didn't make it."

Miri wrapped her arms around Layah. "I'm so sorry, *habibi*."

Layah hugged her back, her heart lighter. Then she wiped her cheeks and took a deep breath. "Thank you for helping us."

"I'm glad to. Give your mother a hug from me."

"I will."

"Do you need anything else?"

"Yes," Layah said. "I need a map, a men's razor and a *keffiyeh*."

Miri nodded happily and wished her luck. Miri's husband, Olan, would drive them to the Armenian border.

Layah gathered her stack of laundry and returned to the room. Ashur and Hudson were still fast asleep. Hudson was stretched out on his stomach with the sheets tangled around his hips. She knew he was naked because she had all his clothes in her arms. She could also tell by looking.

She placed his belongings next to him on the bed. He roused at the movement, rolling over abruptly. Her eyes drifted south as he pulled the sheets north. But she'd already seen him, and he was magnificent.

"Good morning," she said in a husky voice.

He said it back in Arabic, the same language she'd spoken. It was the language she'd used with Khalil. She'd forgotten to speak English. For her, Arabic was the language of romance and desire.

Hudson pulled on his pants and disappeared in the bathroom. Ashur rose also, stretching his arms over his head. There were feathers in his hair. She gave him a stack of clothes. When she tried to pluck a feather, he shied away.

"You need to bathe. You smell like a goat."

Ashur scowled at the criticism but didn't argue. As soon as the bathroom was free, he went inside to shower. Breakfast arrived, and Hudson didn't speak to her. He cleaned his plate quickly and drank coffee with relish.

She smiled at his zest. He ate like a man who'd been held captive, but he didn't look it. "Were you heavy, before?"

"Heavy?"

"Fatter."

"I was solid. I lost at least twenty pounds in captivity."

"What is that in kilograms?"

"I don't know. Ten or fifteen."

She considered that amount. It wouldn't make him heavy, just not quite as lean. "Did they feed you?"

"Only enough to keep me alive."

Ashur emerged from the bathroom and sat down to eat. Hudson finished his coffee in silence. She expected him to be angry with her until they were out of the country. Maybe forever. It was ironic that Layah had brought him to a place of grave danger to protect him from the Da'esh. She didn't want to argue with Hudson again, but they had to discuss their travel plans. She wasn't sure how to broach the subject of his disguise. He hadn't seemed comfortable with the idea last night.

"Ashur, go eat with your cousins," she said in Assyrian.

"Why?"

"Because I said so."

"You're not my mother."

"Out!"

He picked up his plate and left the room, giving Hudson a dark look over his shoulder. Layah waited until he'd closed the door behind him. Then she turned to Hudson. He was watching her with wary eyes.

"You know who killed Hasan."

"I have a pretty good idea."

"Will you tell me?"

"No. It's classified."

"I assume it was one of Mohammed Rahim's men."

Hudson didn't confirm or deny it.

"Was the story you told Ashur true?"

"Yes."

"Rahim was not in Telskuf. I would not have gone there if he was."

"He wasn't one of my torturers."

"But you thought he was inside the building where you were captured?"

"I wasn't captured inside the building. I was captured in a tunnel underneath the building after it exploded."

"Was it a trap?"

"I think so."

"Who were your captors?"

"The faces changed. There were some high-level guys the first week. Near the end, they were just guards."

She nodded, understanding. Rahim certainly could have planted a bomb in Telskuf. He was responsible for a number of atrocities in Syria and beyond. He'd ordered the execution of the rebels outside Palmyra, where Khalil had been killed. She didn't know if Rahim was involved in Hasan's death, but he'd been in Hasakah at the time, and he had a band of butchers at his disposal. She'd always suspected one in particular, Abdul Al-Bayat.

"Are you plotting revenge, like Ashur?" Hudson asked.

"No. I am concerned that your escape from Telskuf was communicated to Rahim."

"I wouldn't be surprised."

"It is possible that those men with rifles were sent to look for us."

"How would they know where to look?"

She swallowed hard, thinking of Ibrahim. She'd told him not to go back to Telskuf, but he was old and stubborn. "Ibrahim knew my travel plans. He is Assyrian, and has access to a vehicle. He might have been questioned."

"Would Rahim's men follow us here?"

"They can't get into Iran or Armenia, but they can get close." She reached into a colorful bag Miri had brought up with breakfast. It had a map, two razors and a checkered headscarf. She unfolded the map and spread it across the floor.

Hud's expression turned flat. "You've had this all along?"

"No. Miri gave it to me this morning." She pointed to their location. "Today we are going to Nordooz, where we will walk across the border. As you can see, it is only a few kilometers from Azerbaijan. The Da'esh may be able to travel freely there from Turkey. I do not believe they will come so far for us. I only wish to offer you information."

"How generous."

She moved her finger across the border, ignoring his sarcasm. "My parents will meet us on the Armenian side. They live in Yerevan, which has a US Embassy."

"You're going to introduce me to your parents?"

"If you like."

"What do you expect me to say to the authorities?"

She hadn't considered this problem. She'd been so focused on the journey, she couldn't see past the end. She rose to her feet and paced the room. If he told the truth, she might be considered a war criminal.

He stood with her. "You know why I stayed with you in Rajan?"

"No."

"I wanted to give you a chance to get away before I called my commander. I didn't want to interfere with your quest for freedom."

She crossed her arms over her chest, guilt-struck. Another apology would make no difference, and it might set him off, so she didn't bother. "You don't have to lie for me. I will face the consequences of my actions."

"You could be deported."

"If God wills it," she said in Arabic. "I made this journey for Ashur, not for myself."

A muscle in Hud's jaw flexed, as if he wanted her

to argue, or to beg and plead with him. "What if we're stopped in Iran?"

"I will say you are my husband."

"I don't look like him."

"You can cover your hair, and shave."

"I'm supposed to pass for Arab by shaving my beard?"

"Many Arab men shave. Especially young, professional men like Khalil."

"What profession?"

"He was in law school."

"A lawyer and a doctor."

Now a desperate refugee and a dead soldier. She pushed aside her emotions, which threatened to crash over her like an ocean wave, and brought him the headscarf. "This is a *keffiyeh*."

"I know what it is."

She supposed he'd worn one before. Military men from all over the world found them useful in the desert. She handed him the razor also. "If we are stopped on the way, stay silent. I will say you are dumb."

"Dumb?"

"Unable to speak or hear."

"Mute," he said, shaking his head. "Deaf-mute."

"Deaf-mute," she repeated.

He turned the razor over in his hands. "You can do all the talking, but I don't trust Iranian officials. If something goes wrong, I won't cooperate. I won't let them take me in. Do you understand?"

"You will kill them."

"If I have to."

She knew without asking that he'd rather die than

be held captive again. Whatever the Da'esh had done to him, it was worse than death. "I have Khalil's passport."

"I saw it."

"Do you have mine?"

He rummaged through his pack and tossed it at her.

She picked it up in silence. Then she folded the map and handed it to him. "You can keep this until we are in Armenia. For good faith."

He accepted the map and pocketed it, avoiding her gaze. He would leave her in Armenia. He'd probably never speak to her again.

She couldn't force his forgiveness. She couldn't make him confess his feelings for her. Maybe he didn't have any. It wouldn't be easy to say goodbye to him, regardless. Somehow, over the course of this journey, the pieces of her broken heart had knit together, and she'd found a place for him. She'd thought she'd never love another, after Khalil. She'd been wrong.

Fighting tears, she secured her passport with Khalil's. She would hold both in case they were asked for documents. Hudson's eyes darkened at the sight of her binding the two booklets with a rubber band. He'd been angry with her for withholding the map and travel information. Now he seemed angry about the passports.

He walked into the bathroom and slammed the door. She made a rude gesture, like she was flinging dirt at him. Then she yanked the nightgown over her head and got dressed. The Yazidi skirt looked nice with her dark blue tunic.

Ashur returned from breakfast as she was tidying up the room.

"Get ready to leave," she told him.

"Did he tell you the name?"

"I didn't ask."

"You don't care who killed my father?"

"Knowing won't bring him back."

"Al-Bayat was in Telskuf."

Her stomach clenched with unease. Abdul Al-Bayat was Rahim's top executioner. They called him The Butcher. Layah's sources hadn't revealed any specific information about Hudson's captors. She only knew that Hudson been left in the care of local guards who were waiting for the kill orders.

"Who told you that?"

"Ibrahim."

"That doesn't mean anything," she said. "Hudson didn't say the men who killed Hasan were in Telskuf. He said he *thought* they were."

"Was Al-Bayat in Hasakah when my father was murdered?"

"I have no idea," she lied. "Why fixate on this when we are so close to freedom? We need to look forward, not back."

Ashur stretched out on the bed and stared up at the ceiling. She hoped he would let it go. Al-Bayat was a likely suspect for Hasan's murder, but they couldn't retaliate. The Da'esh were in power. Challenging them would bring more death and pain.

Hudson emerged from the bathroom fully dressed

and clean-shaven. He had the *keffiyeh* wrapped loosely around his head. There were light-haired Arabs and Kurds in this region, so his coloring alone wouldn't cause a stir. The problem was his face. Shaving had refined his rugged appearance more than she'd anticipated. With his strong jaw and chiseled features, he took her breath away. A man this tall and attractive wouldn't go unnoticed.

"Well?" he prompted.

She blinked a few times. "Well?"

"How do I look?"

"You look like an actor from a Turkish soap opera."

Ashur smirked at the comparison.

"What does that mean?"

"You are too handsome. We want to look ordinary."

"Ordinary? You couldn't look ordinary to save your life. Especially in that outfit."

She glanced down at her tunic and long, flowing skirt. She tugged on the fabric. "What is wrong with this?"

"Nothing. I'm just saying that you'll attract attention at the border. It doesn't matter what you wear. Men look at beautiful women, without fail. If they notice me, it will be because I'm standing next to you."

She grabbed her hijab and covered her hair, irritated. She already felt guilty about bringing him to Iran. Now he was trying to pre-blame her for turning heads at the border. Her skirt wasn't colorful or clingy. Maybe the garment caught his eye because she'd let him hike it up to her waist the other night. She flushed at the memory.

They left the hotel room and joined the others in the parking lot. Miri smiled at Hudson's attempt to assimilate. She introduced her husband, Olan, who would drive them to Nordooz. Then she said goodbye, and they piled into the stake bed of the pickup. Olan had stacked two large bundles of old hotel towels in the back. He would sell the towels in Tabriz. He covered everything with a tarp, tied down at the edges.

The passengers were well hidden, but uncomfortable. It was dark and cramped in the bed of the truck. Although Layah was exhausted from the long journey and happy to be off her feet, she didn't enjoy the ride.

Hudson settled near a tear in the tarp, which offered a small amount of light and air. Aram and Yusef took the opportunity to cuddle with their wives. Ashur slumped against the towels and slept.

Layah tried to give Hudson space. She felt alone, even though she was sandwiched next to him. She hadn't expected him to express his tender feelings toward her or beg for her hand in marriage, but she wanted a different end to their story. A hint of passion and emotion, instead of his cold dismissal.

After a few hours on the road, everyone was asleep except her and Hudson. His body was taut as a bowstring beside hers. This experience must have been agonizing for him. She imagined that it reminded him of his time in captivity, and she understood why he'd do anything to avoid recapture.

He took off his *keffiyeh*. Beneath the scarf, his hair was soaked in sweat. Although the air was warm in the confined space, it wasn't sweltering. She felt a stirring of sympathy, despite the tension between them. The least she could do was offer him comfort.

"Lean back against me," she murmured, massaging his shoulders.

After a pause, he reclined against her lap. She stroked his damp hair to soothe him. She remembered the day she'd discovered that he had a sensitive scalp. He'd strained toward her touch as if she had magic hands. He did the same thing now. He didn't relax enough to sleep, like the others, but some of the tightness in his muscles eased. Perhaps his anger toward her faded, as well.

He was a resilient man. She was a reasonable woman. Although they couldn't repair their relationship or make any future plans, they could part ways in peace.

"Why did you tell your aunt I was Khalil?" he asked quietly.

Her hands went still in his hair. "Aram thought she would turn us away if we had an American among us."

"Is that what you argued about?"

"Yes, but there was no need to lie. Miri knew you were not Khalil. She'd seen him in a wedding photo."

"She didn't come to your wedding?"

She started stroking again. "No. Most of my family did not attend."

"Because of the war?"

"Because of the war, and because it is forbidden for Assyrians to marry outsiders. My parents refused to give their blessing. They never met Khalil."

"Ouch."

"Yes. Ouch."

"Do they know he's dead?"

She flinched at the blunt words. "They do not."

"Have you spoken to them at all since you married?"

"I notified them of Hasan's death. I could not bear to mention Khalil at the same time. I thought they would be relieved, instead of saddened."

"That's harsh."

She cleared her throat. "It is part of our culture."

"Harshness?"

"Ferocity, perhaps. We are the descendants of ancient warriors. My people ruled this land for thousands of years. Now our numbers have been greatly reduced by genocide. The only way to protect our bloodlines and keep our culture alive is to intermarry."

"And yet you didn't."

"No."

"Why not?"

"I was young. I fell in love."

He turned to face her, his eyes glittering in the dim light. "Do you regret it?"

"I regret nothing," she whispered.

A new awareness passed between them. They'd been attuned to each other from the first touch. Maybe the first glance. That feeling had developed into a strong connection and a deeper understanding. He'd loved and lost under completely different circumstances. He'd suffered at the hands of the Da'esh. They were bound by more than desire. It felt like fate.

His mouth descended on hers and the world fell

away. She forgot that they were in a cramped space, on a dangerous journey, in a hostile country. She forgot that they weren't alone. She forgot everything except him. His touch, his taste, his tension. She threaded her fingers through his hair and twined her tongue around his. He kissed her as if her lips held the secrets of the universe. He kissed her like she was his last meal.

Then he stopped and lifted his head. They couldn't share more than kisses here. Even that was risky, because they were both too bold, too hungry, too adventurous. They were both living at full-throttle, reluctant to pump the brakes.

She wanted to express all her feelings, to bare her soul in a messy spill of emotions. But she held herself back, just as he did. There was no hope for them. They couldn't be together. They probably couldn't even stay in contact. It didn't matter how strong the attraction between them was, or how true the bond. It didn't matter how well suited they were. The obstacles between them were insurmountable.

He shifted to one side, and she snuggled against his chest. They couldn't share a bed, but they could share this. A few stolen moments together and a private conversation. "Will you forget me after you return to America?"

"I'll try."

"How long will it take?"

"Not long. Ten or twenty years."

She smiled at his sad joke. "I would like for you to find a woman to make love to. In a month or a year, whenever you are lonely and need to touch someone. For only one night, pretend she is me."

He inhaled a sharp breath. "Will you do the same, with a man?"

"Should I?"

He shook his head. "I can't decide what's worse, picturing you with a stranger for one night or picturing you married with children."

"I'd prefer the second."

"I know."

She brushed her lips over his neck, sighing.

"I can't pretend anyone else is you, Layah."

"You can't?"

He lifted her chin to meet her gaze. "No, I can't. Because there's no one like you. Even if I found someone who looks like you, she wouldn't be the same. She wouldn't talk like you or think like you. She wouldn't make me feel the way you do."

Her eyes filled with tears and her throat closed up.

"I wish I could fulfill your fantasy. You can tell me all the hot details, if you want."

"I can't," she said, biting his earlobe. "You will get excited."

"Too late. What are you wearing under this?"

She pushed his hands away from her skirt. The combination of teasing and tenderness made her chest tighten with emotion. If only they could always be like this, without the ugliness of the world threatening to tear them apart.

If only she could tell him what he meant to her.

Instead she hugged him close and engaged in her favorite fantasy. It involved just the two of them, twined together on a blanket under the stars, sharing a night of passion in a peaceful place.

Chapter 15

Hud roused with the other passengers as they traveled through a busy city.

This must be Tabriz. It smelled of smog and spice. The sounds of traffic were deafening. People weren't afraid to lay into their car horns here. Layah shared a snack of flatbread and dates from her backpack. Soon they were on a quiet, winding road again.

Hud focused on the piece of gray-blue sky visible through the ripped tarp above his head. He felt trapped in more ways than one, assaulted by memories of days in captivity. Getting a glimpse of the outside world helped to keep the monsters at bay. Making out with Layah helped more.

He couldn't stay mad at her. He understood why she'd brought him here, and why she'd kept secrets from him. He'd let his anger take over last night, and he'd gone to a dark place. But he didn't want to stay there. He didn't want to be that kind of man. They'd both made mistakes, and they'd suffered enough. He'd rather look forward, toward the light.

Whenever she got close to him, he lost himself in her. It was impossible to ignore his feelings or hold his desire in check. He was tired of beating himself up for giving in to their attraction. He was hungry for a woman's touch, and her touch affected him like no other. It soothed and inflamed him.

The truck came to a stop about an hour later. Hud put his turban back on. He also slipped Ashur's knife into his boot, just in case. They had no other weapons. Aram had left his rifle in Urmia.

Olan removed the tarp and they piled out.

"We walk from here," Layah said.

It would be easier to cross the border in a vehicle, but Hud didn't blame Olan for leaving them on the side of the road. He'd already taken a huge risk by transporting them. Hud nodded his thanks as Olan drove away.

Layah had a short conversation with the others in their native language. Aram gave Hud a disapproving look. Whatever Layah's plan was, he didn't like it. Ashur didn't like it, either. When she tried to hug him, he said sharp words and avoided her embrace. There were tears in her eyes as they started walking.

"What was that about?" Hud asked.

She adjusted her pack. "Nothing."

Hud felt a surge of irritation. Instead of demanding answers, he summoned patience. Sometimes she was too independent for her own good.

"I told them not to wait for us," she said, after a

pause. "If we're questioned, I want Aram to keep going. He will take care of Ashur and get everyone across the border."

"Aram doesn't want you to stay with me," Hud said.

She didn't answer.

"I agree with him."

"Don't be ridiculous. You speak only English. You need me beside you."

"Are you ready to go to prison with me?"

"We will not go to prison. We will run."

"You'll get in the way, and slow me down."

"Was I slow on the mountain?"

"You're not trained for survival situations."

"And you have no language skills."

He let it go. They were on a quiet road about a mile from a cluster of buildings and a bridge that marked the border crossing. Speaking English wasn't a great idea. The area could be under video surveillance. He didn't know what kind of technology the Iranians used at their borders, but it was better to be safe than sorry.

Glancing around, he didn't get the sense of a well-guarded fortress. Open borders weren't that common, and they tended to be in remote locations with minimal security. Although Hud would feel uneasy anywhere in Iran, this place seemed pretty mellow. A truck driver passed by with a cheery wave. Maybe everything would be okay.

He was overdue for a break. He'd had a string of bad luck, starting with his bitter divorce. Then Hasan's death in Al-Hasakah, followed by the bomb in Telskuf,

Hud's stint in captivity and this entire messed-up journey. Layah had experienced more than her share of hardship, as well. They were in for some good days.

The mood was positive among the group. Aram ruffled Ashur's hair and put his arm around Yusef. Oshana linked hands with Nina, smiling with excitement. Layah looked nervous, but hopeful. They were almost home. Almost free.

Hud studied their surroundings as they moved forward. There were checkpoint stations on both sides of the bridge. Iranian officials were on the left, Armenians on the right. Vehicles were driving through without stopping. Hud didn't see any other pedestrians, which wasn't a surprise. Hikers wouldn't be crossing here often. On the other hand, it was a mountainous area, well suited for climbing. Backpackers probably passed through on occasion. They prided themselves on visiting the most far-out locations.

Hud spotted an Armenian customs official sitting in a booth on the opposite end of the bridge. Two border guards in battle fatigues were monitoring activity on the Iranian side. They were armed with batons and nothing else. Hud evaluated both men as low-level threats, but he braced himself for action anyway. The Iranian guards noticed the group and began their approach immediately.

Although border and customs officials were supposed to focus on who was entering the country, rather than who was leaving it, Hud wasn't surprised by the attention. He expected an exchange of some sort. The guards might ask them for passports, information or an itinerary. They might ask for money.

Layah took the lead, saying hello in a language he assumed was Farsi. She repeated the greeting in Arabic and offered a bright smile. They stared at her the way all men did, tongue-tied and agog.

So far, so good.

She pointed to the bridge. They nodded agreeably. She bowed her head in thanks and they continued forward. One by one, they walked by the Iranians. Hud went last. He put his hand on his chest in a show of respect. The first guard said something about him to the second, and Layah's smile faltered.

Hud knew better than to pause or act guilty. He walked on as if he had no worries. The second man drew his baton and held it like a crossbar to halt Hud's progress. Hud considered breaking his arm, stealing the baton and taking out his partner. All of this could be accomplished in two or three seconds.

Layah gave him a warning look. She wanted to handle the guards her way, with words and fluttering eyelashes. She motioned for the others to go ahead while she brandished her passports and some bribe money. Hud shrugged out of his backpack, moving his gaze from the baton to the bridge. The Armenian official didn't even come out of the booth. Aram held Ashur's elbow in a firm grip as they crossed. When the boy glanced over his shoulder at them, Hud's throat tightened. Ashur tried to break free, but Aram wouldn't let go.

Hud returned his attention to Layah. She was doing her best to charm the Iranians, who had become impervious. The man with the baton had a flat stare. Hud's gut clenched as he realized they were stalling.

This wasn't a routine shakedown. It wasn't general questioning. They'd been stopped for a specific reason.

An armed guard emerged from the checkpoint station, shouting orders. Now Hud had three men to fight, and this new one was a real contender. Six feet tall and solidly built. Layah rushed toward him, displaying her passports. He didn't even look at them. When she grabbed his arm, he shoved her away in annoyance. She stumbled backward and fell down in a dramatic sprawl. Then she used the opportunity to swing her legs at the armed guard. She connected with his ankle and caused him to stagger.

Hud couldn't believe she would dare to grab his arm, let alone kick him. What a woman. She was completely fearless. And he was totally in love with her.

He didn't have any time to process this epiphany. She'd given him a split-second opening, and he was taking it. His hand locked around the baton and twisted. The guard's arm bent into an awkward angle and the bone snapped. He let go with a muffled cry. Hud didn't even need to hit him again. He thwacked the man's partner across the temple, knocking him out. Hud advanced toward the third target while the second crumpled to the dirt.

The armed guard wasn't stupid or slow. He drew his weapon and squeezed the trigger as Hud launched his attack. The baton connected with the man's elbow, and not a second too soon. His shot went wide, and the gun flew out of his hand. Unfortunately, Hud's baton flew with it. The reverberations caused his grip to slacken.

Hud flexed his fingers as he squared up with the big guard. He heard the sounds of another struggle behind him, but he didn't take his eyes off his opponent. The man charged him and took the fight to the ground. Hud was okay with that. They exchanged a few punches, rolling across the dirt. Then Hud went for the knife in his boot. He drew the blade and buried it in the man's thigh.

The guard cried out in pain. He'd had enough. He didn't remove the knife. Keeping his gaze locked on Hud, he cupped his hand around the wound, which was bleeding profusely.

Layah stood behind them like a lady warrior. She held the baton over her head. The gun was beneath her boot. One guard was cradling his broken arm nearby. The other was on the ground, half-conscious.

"Give me the gun," Hud said.

"More are coming," she said, moving her foot aside. "Look."

Hud picked up the weapon and trained it on the man with the knife wound. Two squad cars were tearing down the road. Someone had called them in. Hud could try to cross the bridge, but the police cars would overtake him. A tree-lined ravine on this side of the border offered immediate cover. It was his only hope.

"Go," he said, gesturing to the bridge. "They'll follow me and you can make it across."

"I'm coming with you."

He pointed the gun at her. "Go."

She narrowed her eyes and started running—toward the ravine. She knew he wasn't going to shoot her. He wasn't even going to shoot these guards.

Cursing, Hud tucked the weapon into his waistband and ran after her. The guards would give away his location and description, but so be it. Hud didn't have the heart to execute three unarmed men. He also didn't want the heat associated with being an American cop-killer in Iran. He could evade a small group of officers over rugged terrain. If they launched an extensive manhunt, he'd never get out of this country alive.

He caught up to Layah quickly. She wasn't slow, but he was faster. He pulled her toward the trees, with seconds to spare. As soon as they reached the ravine, they jumped together. Bullets peppered the trees above them.

Hud let go of her hand as they tumbled into the creek bed. She scrambled to her feet and almost fell down in the mud. He drew the weapon he'd just stolen. He couldn't hit a target with a handgun at this range, but he returned fire anyway. He wanted his pursuers to think twice about following them.

"This way," he said to Layah, crashing through the shallow water. They stayed in the ravine for several anxiety-filled moments. When he spotted a copse of trees that appeared thick enough to disguise their exit, they climbed the bank. Although he was desperate to get out of Iran, moving away from the border was a safer bet. They ran through a forest of bushy pines. He stuck to low ground as much as possible. Soon they reached a point where the only way forward was up.

He looked over his shoulder again and saw no one. "We have to keep going."

She nodded her agreement. They climbed over boulders and continued uphill as fast as she could manage. He carried her pack, because he'd left his own behind. They jogged and scrambled and clawed their way to safety. He pushed her as hard as he dared, and then he pushed harder. When they reached a cluster of craggy rocks that might offer a good hiding space, he stopped.

He was winded. Sweating. His muscles burning. He braced his hands on his knees, sucking air. Layah collapsed behind a boulder nearby. She drank water from her container between ragged breaths. He checked the position of the sun in the sky. Several hours had passed since the altercation at the border.

After a moment of rest, he investigated the rock formation. He found a convenient nook to duck into. She joined him in the dark space, hugging her arms around her body. It smelled damp and faintly wild inside, as if an animal had lived here at some point.

"Do you think we lost them?" she asked.

He shrugged, raking a hand through his hair. If the Iranians had a team with dogs, they were in serious trouble. If not, they'd gained a short respite. Either way, their odds of escaping this little detour weren't great.

"I don't understand," she said. "We did nothing. Those guards did not care to look at the passports. They did not want money."

"They were tipped off."

"What does this mean?"

"They knew we were coming."

"How?"

"I don't know. Rahim has connections all over.

The Iranians might not be friends with the Da'esh, but they'll take information from them."

She leaned back against the rock wall. "We'll have to cross somewhere else."

"You think?"

Her brow furrowed. "You are angry."

"Yes. I'm angry."

"I should be angry. You pointed a gun at me."

He closed the distance between them, bracing his palm on the boulder behind her. He wasn't proud of his actions, but desperate times called for desperate measures. What she'd done at the border had been beyond reckless. Her refusal to follow his orders and her insistence on risking her life infuriated him. She'd gone too far. "I told you not to come with me," he said in a low voice. "I told you to run across the bridge while you had the chance."

Her eyes filled with tears. "I saved you."

"You endangered yourself."

"What should I have done?"

"You should have left me!"

"They wanted to detain you."

"Now we'll both die. Is that better?"

She lifted her hand to his tense face. Like always, her touch affected him. It changed him. "I could not leave you, William Hudson."

"Don't call me that."

"I could not leave you, because I—"

He crushed his mouth over hers to cut her off. He couldn't let her say the words, because then he might say them back. He'd been pushed past the limit already. He was at the end of his rope, over the edge, in too deep. They were combustible together, and the only way to fight this fire was to let it burn.

She accepted his kiss with a breathy moan. Their mouths met in an explosion of heat and energy. She parted her lips wide and tangled her fingers in his hair. He thrust his tongue inside her silky mouth. She tasted wild and sweet and forbidden.

He couldn't get enough of her.

His hands roamed the curves of her body and settled on her perfect bottom. He groaned, lifting her against his erection. He was rock-hard and ready to go. Her breasts were soft, her hips were lush and her mouth was magic.

He needed more. He needed all of her.

Breaking the kiss, he fumbled with her clothing, seeking bare skin. She pushed his hands away and pulled her shirt over her head helpfully. Her hijab went with it. He didn't know what he'd expected to see under her clothes, but a sexy bra wasn't it. Her breasts were almost too full for the lace cups, which strained to hold their bounty.

She tugged at the hem of his shirt with impatience. He was so stunned by her beauty that he didn't want to look away, even for a second. He yanked his shirt over his head and took her mouth again, filling his hands with her breasts. Her nipples jutted against his palms and his erection swelled harder.

He couldn't stop—and she didn't ask him to. He pushed her bra straps off her shoulders and her breasts tumbled free. Her taut nipples brushed his bare chest. She explored the bunched muscles in his back and tried to unfasten his belt. He made a strangled sound of enthusiasm. They were totally on the same page. His hands roamed under her skirt. She was wearing panties today. He yanked them down to her knees and slid his hand between her legs. She was damp with desire, her thighs quivering.

"Yes," she said, and that was all he needed to hear.

He knelt at her feet to remove her panties completely. He could smell her arousal as he drew her skirt up to her waist. He wanted to taste her, but he just looked. His gaze rose from her bare thighs to her flushed face.

Beautiful.

"Hold this," he said, indicating her skirt.

She held the gathered fabric and watched him unbutton his fly. When he freed his erection, she moistened her lips in anticipation. He lifted her against the wall and positioned himself at her opening. Then he was pushing inside her, inch by inch. Her body stretched to accommodate his. She was slick. He was hard. It worked.

It worked so good, he was close to finishing before he'd started.

He groaned, thrusting deeper. She grasped him like a hot fist. Her inner muscles fluttered around his shaft. He slid out and drove back in, harder. She closed her eyes and made little sounds of pleasure, driving him wild.

God. Her body was heaven.

He gripped her hips and gave her all he had, his jaw clenched tight. Her breasts jiggled from the impact and his shaft glistened with her moisture. She clung to his shoulders, letting him take what he wanted. He was moving too fast, leaving her behind, but it felt too good to stop. He lost himself in her. Spools of pleasure unraveled inside him and he shuddered against her. With a hoarse cry, he climaxed.

When he came back down to earth, he withdrew from her body. Warning bells clanged in the back of his mind. He hadn't used a condom. He also hadn't given her an orgasm.

Damn. Those were the two basics. Failing either was grounds for immediate dismissal from a lady's bedroom. This was the woman he was in love with, too. He should be impressing her with his best moves, not banging her against a rock like a caveman.

He buttoned his pants and sank to a sitting position. He'd have to impress her later, after he'd caught his second wind. She didn't seem disappointed. She fixed her clothes and snuggled against him.

"I didn't use anything," he said.

"It's okay."

"Are you protected?"

"No."

He frowned at her answer. "Then it's not okay, Layah."

She sighed, touching her lips to his neck. "It is the wrong time of month."

Her confidence didn't reassure him, but he set aside that problem for now. "I'm sorry I didn't bring you pleasure."

"You brought me pleasure."

"You didn't come. I was out of control."

"I liked that. It was very exciting."

He shook his head in wonder. He'd never met a woman as adventurous as her. She took his breath away, over and over again. "If we live through the night, I'll make it up to you. Slowly, for hours, in a real bed."

She kissed his lips. "We will live."

He rose to his feet and donned his shirt. Her optimism was rubbing off on him. They'd made it this far. They'd already overcome insurmountable odds. Maybe they'd evade the Iranian authorities and ride off into the sunset together. Stranger things had happened. "Are you ready? We should try to find a road before dark."

She nodded her agreement and they started hiking again. It was late afternoon. He felt anxious, but invigorated. Yeah, he was in Iran, and he'd attacked three border guards. They were in a boatload of trouble. What else was new? This wasn't the worst situation he'd been in. He'd just gotten laid, and that always improved his outlook. He was with a beautiful, sexy, passionate woman who couldn't keep her hands off him.

They reached the other side of the mountain and looked around. He didn't see any police. There was a road at the base of the hill that headed away from the border. He consulted the map from his pocket. It was in Arabic, so he couldn't read it.

"I think this road goes to Hadishahr," she said.

"Is that a big city?"

"No, but it might have a hotel."

"It's too far to walk."

"We can get a ride. People in Iran are very friendly."

"Yeah, those guards were super nice."

She smiled at his sarcasm, unoffended. They made their way downhill and reached the road at sunset.

Hud kept his eyes peeled for police cars. There wasn't a single vehicle for miles. When a truck appeared in the distance, he stuck out his thumb.

Layah grabbed his hand, eyes wide. "That is not how you get a ride in Iran!"

"How do you do it?"

She made a gesture to slow down, with her palm flat.

"What does the thumb mean?"

"It is a crude sexual suggestion."

He held his palm flat, chuckling at his mistake. The driver pulled over immediately. Hud let Layah do the talking. Whatever she said gained them a ride. There was only one seat, so Hud climbed in first. Layah sat on his lap.

The driver didn't seem suspicious about foreigners. Layah spoke to him in Farsi, or some other language, and she said a few words to Hud in Arabic every so often. He nodded as if he understood and tried to ignore the feel of her delicious curves against him. Memories of their last encounter made it difficult to concentrate on anything else. Her bottom wiggled and shifted with every bump in the road.

Soon it was full dark, and he was at half-mast, but Hud had no complaints. They were a safe distance from the border crossing, headed toward a town they could hide in. They hadn't been harmed in the scuffle. It was a miracle they were alive.

He didn't know what the future held. He had no idea how he'd get out of Iran, or if he'd ever be free again. All he knew was that he had to make the most of every moment with Layah before their time ran out.

Chapter 16

Layah relaxed against Hudson, her back cradled to his chest.

She couldn't believe they were on the run together in Iran. He'd warned her of this possibility, but she hadn't imagined it would actually happen. She'd expected to cross into Armenia without incident.

She considered what he'd said earlier. Maybe someone in Rahim's circle, like Abdul Al-Bayat, had told the guards to look for an American in a group of backpackers. Hudson was easy to pick out of a crowd. The guards might have been paid to detain him at the border or even transport him to neighboring Azerbaijan. Al-Bayat was known for his ruthlessness and tenacity. The Da'esh executioner despised Assyrians and Americans. He would travel to the ends of the earth to recapture an enemy.

Her thoughts moved from Al-Bayat to Ashur,

who'd been distraught at the border. She hoped he would forgive her for staying with Hudson. At least she knew Ashur was safe in Armenia with her parents and her cousins. The Da'esh would find no allies there, and they weren't interested in her family. They wanted Hudson, their prize catch.

She couldn't allow anyone to recapture him. She would do anything for him.

She was in love with him.

He hadn't let her say the words, and they hadn't made a commitment to each other. She didn't know how long they could be together, but she couldn't worry about tomorrow. If tonight was all they had, she would enjoy it.

They reached Hadishahr in the early evening. The driver dropped them at a small hotel across from an internet café. She thanked him for the kindness and climbed off Hudson's lap. He winced in discomfort as he exited the vehicle.

"Is your injury bothering you?" she asked.

He shook his head, his mouth quirking. She made a mental note to examine his wound after they checked in. Then she handed him a few bills from her pocket. Miri had given her some cash before they left the hotel. "You should pay for the room. It is customary."

"What do I say?"

She told him the right phrase in Arabic, which he repeated perfectly. He could learn the language if he applied himself. When they reached the front desk, Hudson asked for a room. The clerk said they could have one ready in thirty minutes. Layah nodded. Hudson overpaid, but Layah didn't interfere. She tugged on his arm and mentioned the internet café in Turkish. He pretended to understand.

"What happened?" he asked when they were outside again.

"They have to prepare the room. We will eat."

He didn't argue with that.

"I have to send a message to my parents in Yerevan. Do you wish to contact someone? Your family?"

"I can't risk it," he said, after a pause. "Any communications between here and the US could be monitored."

"Who would you notify, if you could?"

"My mom, and my commander."

"Are you close with your mother?"

"Yes."

Layah wanted to ask more questions, but they'd arrived at the café. "We are pretending to be Turkish."

"I'll just smile and nod."

"Perfect."

They entered the café, where Layah took a seat across from Hudson. She ordered tea and *khoresh*, a type of stew with rice. Her mother, who'd been born in Iran, used to make the dish for their family. Layah excused herself to use one of the computers. She wrote an email to her parents to let them know she was okay. She said she would come to Yerevan soon, and she asked them to give Ashur a hug from her.

When she returned, the stew had arrived. Hudson ate most of it, though Layah enjoyed the flavor. She couldn't speak Turkish well enough to fake an entire conversation, so she stayed quiet. She sipped her tea and watched him. She was nervous about their night together, and eager to be alone with him.

"Do you like the food?" she asked in Arabic.

"*Iaa*," he said, eating more.

She knew a few Turkish phrases. "I love you."

He smiled and nodded.

She looked away, her throat tight. She was setting herself up for heartbreak. It was one thing to confess her desire for him. It was quite another to confess her feelings like a character in a Turkish soap opera. He had no idea what she was saying.

They finished the meal and walked across the street together. The night sky twinkled with far-off stars. He grasped her hand and held it. They got a key for the room. The accommodations appeared comfortable. He locked the door behind her, his eyes on her mouth.

She held up a palm to stop him from advancing. He looked ready to lift her against the nearest wall and take her. Which was fine, but they had a nice bed and a private bath. She was dirty and sweaty and sticky from the day's various activities. "If you wish to make love to me properly, I will bathe."

He backed away from her, nodding. She ducked into the bathroom and stripped naked. She took her time in the shower, washing every inch of her body and shampooing her hair. When she was finished, she felt like a new woman.

He showered next. She sat at the edge of the bed and waited. He was quick. He emerged with a towel around his waist. Her eyes took a leisurely path from his well-muscled torso to his bare feet. Her stomach fluttered with awareness as he approached the bed. She drew the towel up to expose his injured thigh.

"Does it ache?"

"A little."

She pressed against his hard flesh. "There is no swelling."

"You're looking in the wrong place."

She moved her gaze to his erection, which was definitely swollen. She removed the towel for a closer inspection. Her throat went dry at the sight of him. "Oh my."

"What's your diagnosis?"

She wrapped her hand around his thick shaft. He was like a stone under hot, tender skin.

"I think you have a fever."

He strained toward her, his jaw tight.

She stroked him up and down. "You need immediate attention. This organ is dangerously enlarged."

He choked out a laugh. "Can you treat me?"

"Yes. I have the cure right here." She took off her own towel, exposing her naked body. "I recommend immersion therapy."

He stared at her as if he'd never seen a nude woman before. He'd seen everything, but not all at once. A pulse throbbed at the base of his throat. He pushed her back on the bed and climbed on top of her, his gaze smoldering. "I'm not ready for immersion."

"No?"

"I'll have to work up to it."

She twined her arms around his neck, smiling.

He smiled back at her. "I like the way you play doctor."

She touched her lips to his. "You're a good patient."

"Remember how you said I should find another woman to make love to?"

"Yes."

"What did you want me to do to her?"

Heat prickled over the surface of her skin. "Kiss her breasts."

He dipped his head with relish, nuzzling her ample flesh. His mouth closed around one taut nipple, then the other. He used his tongue and lips and teeth until she was lost in pleasure, her hands buried in his damp hair. A greedy pulse throbbed between her legs.

"Where else should I kiss?"

She moaned, pushing his head lower.

"Her stomach?"

"Lower."

"Her inner thighs?"

Layah spread hers wide. He kissed the inside of her knee and moved his way up. By the time he reached the apex of her arousal, she was quivering with anticipation. He skipped over her center and moved toward the other knee.

"You are teasing this poor woman," she panted.

"She likes it."

With a groan, Layah took matters into her own hands and stroked her needy flesh. She was slippery and swollen.

"That's cheating," he said. "Now I have to start over."

She gasped as he flipped her onto her stomach and gave the same treatment to the backs of her thighs. He kissed every inch of her spine, from the cleft of her bottom to the nape of her neck. When he moved south again, she was writhing with impatience. She rolled over and pushed him on his back. Then she lowered her mouth to his erection, and she didn't tease. She parted her lips and took him deep.

He let her pleasure him, burying a hand in her hair. She couldn't manage his entire length, but she tried. His face was exquisitely tense as he watched her mouth move up and down. He pulled her away after a few moments, shuddering.

She touched her tingling lips. "I have bad news about your condition."

"What's that?"

"If you refuse treatment, you could erupt."

He smirked at the warning, climbing on top of her again. He held her thighs apart and buried his tongue between them. She didn't expect him to be shy or tentative, and he wasn't. He sucked and licked her in bold strokes. She was so primed for orgasm that she couldn't hold off. She bucked against his mouth, exploding in pleasure.

He laughed at her lightning-fast climax.

"That was unfair," she said, light-headed.

"I agree. You're too easy."

She slapped his shoulder in a weak protest. He stayed where he was and reapplied himself to the task, tasting her leisurely. She didn't object to a second round. She'd never been loved like this before, as if her body was a delicious dessert. It was clear that he relished the act. He was a man of strong appetites in more ways than one. He flicked his tongue over her clitoris until she screamed his name. She came again, clutching his hair.

He wore a satisfied expression. "Should I go for three?"

"I can't," she panted.

"I bet you can."

"I want you inside me."

"I won't last that way."

"I don't care. Just fill me."

He gave her what she asked for. Stretching out on top of her, he held her gaze and pushed inside. She was slippery from two orgasms, and accommodated him easily. Her eyes fluttered closed as he filled her to the hilt.

"Look at me," he said, withdrawing a little.

She opened her eyes.

He thrust inside again.

On the mountain, they'd been rushed and desperate. In this room they were safe, and he had time to do it right. Not that she was complaining about their earlier encounter. She'd loved every second of it. His heat, his size, his roughness. Their first coupling had been explosive. It had doused the fire that threatened to consume them both.

What he was doing to her now was different. It was gentler, more focused and more deliberate. It was a culmination of everything that had been building between them, and a response to her unspoken confession. It was a communication of the words he could not say. He buried his hands in her hair and took her to heaven. He kissed her, loved her, completed her, breathed life into her. Tears spilled from her eyes. He kissed those, too. When she cried out in pleasure, he drank the exaltation from her lips. She watched him fill her, and it was beautiful. They were connected, body and soul.

He withdrew at the moment of climax, his face taut. She wanted to feel him, so she wrapped her fingers around his thick shaft. He was hot and slick from her moisture, pulsing in her hand. He spilled across her belly with a hoarse groan. She marveled at the sight. Perhaps because she was riding a sexual high, the by-product of their union seemed precious. His seed glistened on her skin, painting her in warmth.

He rolled onto his back, completely spent. "I'm dead. You killed me."

She laughed, her tummy quivering. He passed her a tissue from the box next to the bed, so she wiped his seed away. "You don't have to withdraw."

He made a grunting sound.

She cuddled against his side. "I want your child."

His eyes flew open. "You said it was the wrong time of month."

"It is. But I wish to pretend otherwise. The next time, you can stay inside me."

"Give me a minute. I'm still dead."

She walked her fingertips down his chest. His manhood twitched at her touch.

"Half-dead," he corrected.

She laughed, and he moved on top of her again. He kissed her and tickled her until she was gasping for breath. Instead of starting another round, they took a break. The room had a television, which seemed like a divine luxury. He turned it on and flipped through the channels until he found a news station. Her Farsi was rusty, but she didn't hear anything about an American fugitive or an attack at the border.

"Bring me that map," he said, patting her bottom.

She retrieved the map from her backpack and spread it on top of the bed. There were no easy ways out of Iran.

"Is there another border crossing into Armenia?" he asked.

"Not from Iran."

"What's this place again?"

"Azerbaijan."

"Why are there two countries named Azerbaijan?"

"It is one country, two land masses."

"Can we go there?"

"There is a crossing in Jolfa, but it will be heavily guarded."

"What about here?"

She considered the route he was suggesting, in a remote area that stretched from Iran to Azerbaijan and ended in Armenia. "We would have to enter illegally, and travel over rough terrain."

"Now you're worried about breaking rules?"

"Iran is a militant nation. They have a large, well-organized police force, and they are diligent about border security."

"Do we have a choice?"

"There is another problem with going through Azerbaijan."

"What's that?"

"Abdul Al-Bayat."

She knew Hud recognized the name, because he went quiet.

"Ashur told me he was in Telskuf before we came. Ibrahim mentioned it."

"So?"

"Was he one of your captors?"

Hud rubbed a hand over his mouth, not answering.

"Perhaps you are familiar with his yearly ritual to celebrate spring." It involved the beheading of a high-profile enemy, live-streamed for maximum exposure and to rally their bloodthirsty followers.

"You think he planned a public execution?"

"You are a Navy SEAL. He would revel in your death. Also, Rahim might have sent him after you. The Da'esh cannot allow an escaped captive to live. It damages their image."

He digested that without arguing. "Al-Bayat and his men can get into Azerbaijan."

"Yes."

He studied the map again. She saw what he saw: a vast expanse of unfriendly territory with no clear path to freedom.

"We can stay here in Iran," she said.

"*You* can stay here," he countered.

"I go where you go."

He put the map away and came back to bed. Discussing his beheading wasn't the most romantic way to spend their time together. The future was uncertain, but her love for him was not. He cradled her close and held her until she drifted to sleep.

Chapter 17

Hud eased away from Layah in the wee hours of the morning.

He rose to his feet and got dressed in the dark. Then he stood by her side of the bed and watched her sleep. Her hair spilled across the pillow in tousled black waves. He memorized every detail of her lovely face. The sweep of her eyelashes. Her exquisite body, all soft curves and smooth skin. He was desperately in love with her.

Too bad he'd never see her again.

He forced himself to take a step back. Then another. Swallowing hard, he picked up his boots and carried them to the door. He hated to leave without saying goodbye, or even writing a note, but he couldn't risk waking her up. She'd insist on coming with him. He had to go now, before dawn.

He padded down the hall, then paused to put on his

boots. The lobby was dark and quiet as he ventured
outside. He continued down the road, not looking
back. He tried not to think about how Layah would
feel when she realized he was gone. She'd given him
the best night of his life, and he'd ditched her. But he
had no other choice. He couldn't stay with her. If he
was going to die, he was going to die alone.

According to the map, he was about twenty miles
from the border with Azerbaijan. It was another ten
to Armenia. He'd have to cut across a mountainous
area and face challenging terrain. He also needed to
stay out of sight as much as possible.

He ignored his clenched gut and kept moving. He
was hungry, but food wouldn't fill him. The empti-
ness inside him was all about Layah.

It was killing him to walk away from her. He didn't
know how he'd live without her. When he'd started
this journey, he'd been eager to abandon her and her
family. He'd searched for opportunities to escape.
Now he was finally free of her, and it felt like hell.

He knew she'd be safer on her own than with him.
She was an extremely capable woman. She'd get to
Armenia without any trouble. She could speak five
languages. She had her looks, her connections, her
wits. Her daring. He thought about the way she'd
jumped to his defense at the border. She was a fighter.

He didn't have to worry about her suffering in Armenia. She had a medical degree, or close to it. She
had her family. She wouldn't be destitute. He wished
he didn't have to leave her, but he didn't see a path for
them. He had to go home, and she couldn't come with
him. For all he knew, she'd get sent back to Iraq. He

didn't know what he'd say about her actions, or his own. He'd crossed the line with her so many times.

He pushed away those thoughts. Right now, he had to focus on survival.

By dawn, he'd traveled past the outskirts of town and cut across a series of green fields. He climbed a path that zigzagged along a rocky hill. As he came over the top, he startled a sheep farmer with his herd. The man seemed to think Hud was lost. When Hud shook his head and continued walking, the farmer followed him.

Hud increased his pace in an attempt to lose the farmer. Two squad cars appeared on the road at the base of the hill he'd just climbed. Hud's stomach dropped as he recognized them. These were the police cars from the border. They weren't doing a casual sweep of the area. They were moving at top speed toward Hadishahr.

Hud dived to the ground in the middle of the herd, his pulse racing. Sheep bayed and trotted around his head. He was sure the farmer would alert the authorities, but he didn't. The man stood by with a gnarled staff, his face brown and weathered.

After the cars passed, it dawned on Hud that they were going to the hotel. It was the only one in this area, and a likely place to look. Maybe the guards had called around and discovered two guests matched their descriptions.

His heart plummeted. They were going to find Layah.

Hud leaped to his feet and tore across the hillside, leaving the farmer in the dust. The hotel was several miles away. He couldn't catch a moving vehicle, but he ran as hard as he could. He had to get there before they left with Layah.

If these Iranian cops were clean, which Hud doubted, they'd take her in for questioning. If they were dirty, they'd deliver her to whoever was paying them. The second possibility chilled his blood.

Hud was intimately familiar with Al-Bayat's treatment of prisoners. The Da'esh executioner had been in Telskuf during the first week of Hud's capture. He'd supervised the torture proceedings and participated with relish. Al-Bayat had no qualms about hurting women, though he might not televise it like one of his celebratory beheadings. He wouldn't hesitate to use Layah as bait to lure Hud back into captivity.

Hud couldn't let that happen. He couldn't let those bastards touch her. He sprinted down the middle of the road, his arms and legs pumping. The streets were still quiet at this early hour. The hotel loomed in the distance. Before he reached it, both squad cars pulled out of the parking lot and continued down the road.

He was too late.

He kept running until he reached the front of the hotel. Then he stopped, bracing his hands on his thighs. The police hadn't seen him. They weren't coming back. They'd taken Layah, and there was nothing he could do about it.

He entered the hotel lobby, ignoring the curious clerk, and barged into their room. There was no sign of her, of course. The bed was unmade, the sheets tangled. He sat down on the edge of the mattress, stunned.

He'd failed her.

He'd abandoned her, and she'd been captured. They'd found her sleeping *naked*, because he hadn't warned her. He'd left her alone and unprotected, after using her luscious body. He'd taken what he wanted and then some. He could still smell her on the pillows. He sank his fist into his thigh, his teeth gritted in anguish.

A moment later, he heard the telltale creak of an intruder in the hallway. He leaped to his feet and crossed the room in swift silence. Standing next to the door, he drew the gun he'd taken from the guard yesterday.

His heart pumped with adrenaline as he waited to attack.

Layah dreamed of Khalil.

It was the same dream she'd had before. She was following him through the busy streets of Damascus. He kept moving farther away, getting lost in the crowd. She finally gave up and sat down to cry. Then he was right there in front of her. She stood to embrace him. He hugged her and stroked her hair.

"Why did you leave me?" she asked in Arabic.

"I didn't want to."

"You promised you'd come back."

"I tried, *habibi*. I tried."

She pressed her face to his chest and wept. "You never said goodbye."

"Don't be sad anymore."

"Hold me for a little longer."

"I must go," he said, shaking her shoulders gently. "Wake up now. Wake up."

Layah opened her eyes and sat upright. Khalil wasn't there, of course—but neither was Hudson. It was near sunrise, judging by the light in the window. The open bathroom door revealed empty space. She wasn't just alone in the bed, she was alone in the room.

She clutched the sheets to her chest, frowning. Something was wrong. The dream had been so vivid, as if Khalil had actually visited her. She could still feel him in her arms. The most disturbing part wasn't that he'd come to her, or that he'd said goodbye. It was his urgent suggestion to wake up. She slipped out of bed and dressed quickly. While she was lacing up her boots, she heard a commotion in the lobby.

Several intruders had entered the hotel. They were coming up the stairs.

She checked the door to make sure it was locked. Then she circled the room in a panic. There was nowhere to hide. She rushed toward the window and looked out. It was too far to jump, but there was a ledge to stand on. She glanced over her shoulder, pulse racing. A fist pounded on the door.

"Come out now! This is the police!"

She swung her leg over the window jamb. The distance to the ground appeared daunting, and the ledge narrow. The doorknob started turning. She smothered a sound of distress and climbed all the way out.

Trembling with anxiety, she stood on the ledge with her stomach pressed against the building. She tried not to look down. It was only about twenty feet, but she'd be risking a serious injury if she jumped. Men burst into the room, their voices raised. They stomped around, smashing things.

Layah assumed they'd look out the window any second. She inched along the ledge, terrified.

Where was Hudson? Had they taken him?

She reached a drainpipe that prevented her from continuing along the ledge. She could climb down the pipe, but it looked weakly supported and unsafe. While she hesitated, a man stuck his head out the window. It was the tall border guard from Nordooz. The one she'd kicked, and Hudson had stabbed.

She stared at him. He stared at her.

"Here," he shouted in Farsi, loud enough to wake the dead.

She had no choice but to climb. She gripped the pipe and prayed for strength. The men didn't shoot at her, which was good. The pipe didn't hold her weight, which was bad. She got halfway down the building when it broke loose. She went careening sideways and landed in a pile of garbage bags.

It wasn't a soft cushion, but she bounced off the pile and scrambled to her feet. She started running as fast as she could. She didn't know where she was going. Alleyways, buildings, homes, gardens. Everything passed in a blur.

Hudson had left her. He'd left her.

She kept running and found herself tangled in a laundry line. Damp linen covered her face, obscuring her vision. She fell down hard and stayed down. Crawling behind a brick wall, she huddled in the corner of a small backyard.

She waited there, breathless, to be discovered.

She waited sixty seconds, and counted sixty more.

Then she was found—by a child. A boy of no more than three or four years. She touched her finger to her lips in hopes that he'd be quiet.

"Who are you?" he demanded.

"I am Layah."

"What you doing?"

"Hiding."

He picked up the damp linen and waved it around like a flag. "A strange lady is hiding in the garden. Come and see!"

Layah clapped a hand over her eyes. When he continued to shout about his discovery, perhaps to get the attention of his family members, she scrambled to her feet and fled the yard. As soon as she stepped into the street, she saw them.

Two officers in uniform.

She turned to run the opposite direction and met with a broad chest. It was the border guard Hud had grappled with yesterday. His arms locked around her like a vise. She screamed and kicked, but there was no one to help. No one but a noisy little boy, gaping at her distress.

The guard picked her up and carried her down the street. She was handcuffed with a plastic tie and tossed into the back seat of a squad car. The doors locked automatically. A metal grate separated the front from the back. There was no escape.

One of the officers got behind the wheel and drove forward. They were followed by the second squad car. The border guard stayed on the street, watching their departure.

"Where are we going?" Layah asked.

"Quiet," the man replied.

"Please," she said, tears spilling down her cheeks. "I am a doctor. I have money. My family has money."

The officer ignored her.

"Please, let me go!"

He told her to be quiet and said something that sounded like a threat. She didn't speak Farsi well enough to catch every word. She repeated her plea, sobbing. When that didn't work, she rolled onto her side and started kicking the door. She kicked the window, the seat, the door handle. The officer drove on, unconcerned.

She stopped kicking, because it was exhausting. She'd hurt herself, not the vehicle. Tears of fear and frustration leaked from her eyes.

"Where is the American?" the officer asked.

"What?"

"The man you were with. Where is he?"

She straightened, realizing they hadn't captured him. "I don't know."

"He was in the hotel?"

She didn't answer.

"Speak, you dirty rag! If you do not, I will make you."

"He went to the police station to report your corruption," she said in Arabic. "Now everyone knows you are a traitor for the Da'esh."

The officer must have understood her, because he stopped asking questions and turned on the radio.

Layah felt no satisfaction in his silence. She was too distraught about Hudson. They hadn't caught him. He'd left of his own volition. He'd sneaked out like a thief in the night—after saying goodbye to her in bed, instead of with words.

Just like Khalil.

The similarities were gut-wrenching. Her dream had been a warning and a memory combined. She was ready to let go of Khalil. She was in love with Hudson. What they'd shared together had been incredible. His passion for life was infused in his touch. He'd taken her to dizzying heights of pleasure. Then he'd walked out on her before the sheets were cool!

Now she was heartbroken and abandoned, in enemy hands.

She couldn't bring herself to regret their encounter, even under these circumstances. She didn't regret falling in love with him. Maybe she shouldn't have kidnapped him or forced him to be her guide. Maybe she shouldn't have brought him to Iran. Maybe she shouldn't have given herself to him, body and soul.

She blinked the tears from her eyes, taking a deep breath. She would not cry over the choices she'd made. She'd relished every moment in Hudson's arms. One night wasn't enough, but she would cherish it always.

She set aside her hurt feelings and focused on the present. She was in serious trouble. These men wanted to track down Hudson. They'd use her to recapture him. They'd harm her to make him suffer, and vice versa.

She had to escape before they got the chance.

Chapter 18

Hud jumped into action as soon as he caught sight of the gun barrel.

He swung down hard in a chopping motion, hitting the intruder's forearms. The gun discharged with a loud blast and skittered across the floor. Hud struck again, pounding his left fist into the intruder's rib cage. The man bent forward, stunned from the blow. Hud finished the job by slamming the butt of his pistol into the back of his head.

He slumped to the ground, unconscious.

Hud pointed the gun at him and checked the hallway for more assailants. They were alone. The man on the floor was the tall border guard Hud had tangled with yesterday. He was wearing his green uniform. Hud set aside his gun and stripped the man quickly. They were about the same size. Hud removed his own clothes, tossed them at the guard and donned the uniform. The boots didn't work, but everything else fit well enough. Hud tugged on his green cap while the guard groaned and rolled over.

Hud trained the gun on him again. "Where's Layah?"

He held up his palms in supplication.

"Where is she? Where is the woman?"

"No English," he said.

Hud kicked him in the thigh he'd stabbed yesterday. The man screamed in pain and clutched his leg. "Answer my questions or I'll shoot you," he said with careful enunciation. "Where is Layah? Where is Al-Bayat? Where did they take her?"

"Jolfa," he said. "Jolfa, Azerbaijan."

Hud recognized the name of the border town. It was the location of the land crossing from Iran into Azerbaijan.

"Get up," Hud said. "Get dressed."

The guard muttered something in his native language and tugged on the clothes. He moved slowly, his jaw clenched. Hud grabbed a pillowcase from the bed while he was waiting. He also found a zip tie in the uniform pocket, which he used to secure the man's hands behind his back. Hud dragged him to his feet and shoved him out the door. He covered his weapon with the pillowcase before they continued down the hall.

They passed the hotel clerk on their way out. Hud nodded politely. There was a Jeep with a government insignia parked on the street about a block away. Hud found a set of keys in his pocket. He moved toward the Jeep, his gun pressed against the guard's ribs.

"Get in," he said.

The guard climbed in the passenger side. Hud took a seat behind the wheel. He didn't know how he'd save Layah, but he'd worry about that later. He traveled down the main drag and past the outskirts of town. Then he headed north, to the border.

He drove as fast as he dared, checking his rearview mirror for flashing lights. The hotel clerk might have called the police. Hud could get pulled over any time. Even if he made it across the border, there was little hope of a good outcome. But what else could he do?

Hud considered his options as he continued driving. He didn't know who to turn to. Alerting the Iranian authorities wouldn't help. They'd arrest him on the spot. He could stop the vehicle and try to call his commander, but he needed immediate assistance. The SEALs couldn't mobilize quickly enough to save Layah. The nearest air base was hundreds of miles away. They'd have to deploy a Blackhawk, and they couldn't even fly over Iran. It was a risky undertaking with astronomical costs, for a refugee of little consequence. His commander would never get clearance.

Yeah. Hud was on his own.

When he reached Jolfa, he followed the signs to the border. It was a small town with a land crossing in the form of a bridge. The layout was similar to what he'd seen in Nordooz. Security was tight on the Iranian side.

Hud had no idea if the guards here had been compromised by the Da'esh. He assumed there was a plan in motion that involved the Iranian police. They'd made a deal with the devil. Hud put the pillowcase over the guard's head before they reached the checkpoint. He didn't want anyone to recognize his captive.

"Stay silent or I'll shoot you," Hud said. He gave the guard a hard tap against the temple. "You got that?"

"Iaa."

Hud honked his horn in greeting as they approached the bridge. It seemed like the thing to do, and it worked. He was in a border guard uniform, driving a government vehicle. The guards didn't blink an eye at Hud or his hooded passenger. They waved him through without any hesitation. He accelerated across the bridge and kept going.

Then he was in Azerbaijan. That was it. He'd escaped Iran.

Hot damn.

He glanced in the rearview mirror, his blood pumping with adrenaline. No one was coming after him. There was plenty of trouble ahead, but none behind him. So far, so good. He reached out to tug the pillowcase away from the guard's face.

"Now where?"

The guard gritted his teeth and jerked his chin to the right. It was in his best interest to cooperate. Hud was more than willing to shoot him in the leg or toss him out of the vehicle if he didn't. The guard was at his mercy. Hud would try to exchange the man for Layah. He was a bargaining chip, nothing more.

If Al-Bayat was running the show, there would be no exchanges. Al-Bayat didn't make deals; Hud knew that for a fact. The terrorist leader wouldn't negotiate with him or release Layah for any reason. Hud wasn't sure how to defeat him. He had no plan of action. He wasn't used to flying solo, without a SEAL team to back him up.

The rendezvous spot was only a few miles from the bridge. The guard indicated a road on the right, which Hud followed to a large dirt lot. There were white boxes stacked in neat rows in the middle of a clearing nearby. Two squad cars were parked in the shade at the end of the lot.

Al-Bayat wasn't here.

Hud couldn't believe his luck. This was the ideal scenario. If Hud rescued Layah before the Da'esh executioner arrived, the two of them could escape this nightmare and make a run for the Armenian border.

He parked about thirty feet away from the squad cars. The officers didn't come out to greet him. Hud couldn't see anything but two vague shapes through the rear window of the second squad car.

The scene made him uneasy. It was too quiet, but he didn't have time to do any more reconnaissance. Al-Bayat and his henchmen might arrive any moment. He couldn't ask his captive to evaluate the situation, either. The man spoke little or no English. Hud made sure the guard's face was covered with the pillowcase before he exited the vehicle. Moving swiftly, he circled around to the passenger side. He opened the door for the guard, his gun raised. They walked toward the squad cars together.

Hud thought about car bombs and other traps. His last assignment as a SEAL had ended in a huge explosion. He'd been reckless in Telskuf, and he'd paid the price. He was lucky he hadn't been killed. Now his instincts told him to proceed with caution. He could be walking into another trap.

Hud studied their surroundings as they continued

forward. The white boxes in the clearing were for bees. He could hear the faint buzz of insect activity. It was the only sound. Two men were sitting in the front seat of the squad car on the left. Both were facing forward, not looking back. They were way too still for Hud's tastes. His gut clenched with trepidation.

He decided to make a sharp detour. He cut to the right instead of walking in a direct line toward the squad cars. He entered the clearing and circled around for a better view. As soon as he got a glimpse through the front windshield, his heart dropped.

There was a reason the officers weren't moving.

They were dead.

Layah wasn't in either vehicle. She must have been taken to another location and delivered to Al-Bayat. Hud felt a sharp twist in the center of his chest. If he couldn't save her, nothing else mattered.

Layah had become his entire world. She was his woman. She was his assignment. She was his reason for living.

He would not fail her again.

Hud knew there was trouble coming. He had no more use for the guard, no reason to keep a gun trained on him. The uniform Hud was wearing had helped him cross the border. Now it felt like a target on his back. Al-Bayat would want to keep Hud alive, if only to torture him some more or behead him in a grisly celebration. The guard was disposable, like the police officers. Al-Bayat was clearly cutting ties with his Iranian comrades.

Two men in black emerged from the trees on the

opposite side of the dirt lot. Two Da'esh militants with rifles.

"Get down," Hud said to the guard.

The man didn't understand, or just didn't comply. Hud left him standing there and ran toward the clearing, his head ducked low. When he reached the first row of white boxes, he jumped over them and kept going. Bullets tore across the clearing, peppering the ground at Hud's feet. He hurdled another row of boxes. A third man appeared at the edge of the clearing, cutting off his escape route. Hud dropped to his belly to avoid more gunfire. The box in front of him exploded in a dark swarm.

Angry bees and chaos erupted.

Layah watched the bridge to Iran disappear behind them.

Her hopes of being rescued plummeted. Hudson couldn't follow them across the border. They were in Azerbaijan now, on their way to Al-Bayat or whoever was in charge of her fate. Her throat closed up with emotion.

They stopped in a dusty parking lot in a secluded place. She stared out the window and prayed for Hudson, for Ashur and for herself. A voice over the radio broke her concentration. The police officer picked up the receiver to answer.

"Go ahead," he said.

"They just crossed."

"Who did?"

"Your guard and his captive."

The policeman seemed surprised by this news. He

thanked the other officer for the notification. "One guard captured your man without any trouble," he boasted to Layah. "This American is not so smart or strong, is he?"

Hudson had defeated three guards at Nordooz yesterday, but Layah didn't say that. "Who are we meeting?"

"You'll see."

"How can you work for Da'esh monsters? They kill women and children."

"Propaganda," he said in a dismissive tone. "How can you sleep with an American? They steal everything they touch."

"I have not betrayed my people or my country."

"Silence," he hissed. "You have no honor, trash woman."

She watched the officer from the second squad car approach the passenger side. He climbed in to consult with his friend. Although the conversation was in Farsi, Layah understood most of it. The second officer was concerned about the border guard, who wasn't answering his phone. The first officer insisted that the guard was on his way with Hudson. While they argued about it, a black SUV barreled into the parking lot. Its passenger side window lowered to reveal a masked gunman.

Layah ducked her head, swallowing a scream. The executioner took aim before the officers could draw their weapons. Their deaths were swift and brutal. Blood sprayed into the air like red mist. There was an ominous gurgling sound, then nothing.

Layah cowered in the back seat, but there was no escape. A man dragged her out of the car and tossed her into the SUV. The vehicle drove a short distance before stopping again. She got shoved from the SUV and landed in a heap on the dirt floor of a barn. Straw was scattered all over the ground.

Al-Bayat stood there like a lord in his realm. Layah had never met the man before, but she recognized him. She'd seen his execution videos. He was young, no more than thirty, with a stocky build and a full beard. His eyes glinted with menace, and a hint of madness. She didn't know if he truly believed in the twisted teachings of the Da'esh, or if he simply enjoyed killing. He wore a military-style uniform in black.

"Layah Anwar of Nineveh," he said, bowing. "I knew your brother."

She spat out a piece of straw. If she could spit in his face, she would.

Al-Bayat held two passport books in his hands, hers and Khalil's. She must have left them behind in the melee at Nordooz. "Perhaps I knew your husband, as well. Was he in Palmyra?"

Tears filled her eyes, against her will. She didn't answer.

"I removed the heads of so many rebels, it is difficult to keep track. But one stands out in my mind. If I remember correctly, he begged for mercy and swore his fealty. He kissed my hand so sweetly. So sweetly."

She tugged at the plastic tie binding her wrists, her throat tight.

"What happens when an Assyrian woman marries a Sunni dog? She becomes a mongrel, fit only for an American."

"He's ten times the man you are."

"Which one? Your husband or your lover?"

"Both."

He walked in a circle around her. When he stopped, he trapped her hair under his boot. She hadn't put on her hijab before she'd fled the hotel. "Look at you. Uncovered and dirty."

The SUV backed out of the garage, leaving them alone together.

Al-Bayat knelt to stroke the hair he'd soiled. "For an Assyrian mongrel, you have a pleasing face."

Layah tried to generate enough saliva to spit again, but her mouth was dry.

"I will strip you and bathe you in the blood of your American. Then I will purify you with my essence."

"I will purify you with my vomit."

He yanked her hair cruelly. Then a phone sounded in his pocket. He straightened and walked toward the barn doors to answer the call. She couldn't hear the conversation. He seemed agitated, as if his plans had been thwarted.

She curled up on her side and prayed for Hudson.

The SUV reappeared outside the barn. The driver slammed on the brakes, kicking up a cloud of dust. A man was dragged from the vehicle. His face was covered, but she recognized his clothing as Hudson's. Her heart seized in her chest.

No. Please, no.

Khalil had been executed while wearing a hood. The Da'esh had videotaped the mass shootings in Palmyra. She hadn't been brave enough to watch the footage, but she knew he'd been among the victims. His body had been positively identified.

Now she was confronted with the same nightmare, all over again.

The Da'esh militants dropped him to the straw-covered ground. The pillowcase over his head was from their hotel room. His hands were bound behind his back, like hers, and his shirt was covered in blood. He didn't move.

He was dead.

She scrambled onto her knees, smothering a sob. This couldn't be happening. Her mind went blank with grief. She couldn't think, couldn't speak, couldn't breathe.

"I told you I wanted him alive," Al-Bayat said. "I told you to shoot the *Iranians*."

Three men bowed their heads in shame.

"Were my instructions difficult to understand?"

"No, sir."

"His hands are tied! How can you shoot a man whose hands are tied?"

"It was an accident. There were bees—"

"Who is responsible for this travesty?" Al-Bayat interrupted.

The three men looked at each other. One had reddish lumps all over his face. His eyes were swollen, his hands bumpy. He stepped forward to be judged. "I am."

Al-Bayat drew a gun from his waistband. "Kneel."

The man knelt.

"Pray."

He bent forward, his lips moving in silent prayer. Al-Bayat shot him in the back of the head with cold precision. He slumped onto his side, eyes open. Layah's stomach lurched with nausea. She stared at the horrific scene, unable to look away. She couldn't process what she was seeing, or accept it. There were two corpses on the ground, and one was...

No.

That man wasn't Hudson. It wasn't him. The clothes didn't quite fit his body. His muscle mass and skin tone were different. The dead man was larger than Hudson, with a heavier build. It wasn't just a trick of her desperate imagination. Her heart knew the truth, too. She searched for the tattoo on the inside of his forearm. It wasn't there.

Hudson wasn't dead. He was alive, and fighting!

Al-Bayat seemed aware that something was amiss. He followed her gaze to the body. Striding forward, he yanked the pillowcase off the man's head.

It was the border guard.

"This isn't him," Al-Bayat said.

His men looked perplexed. "It isn't?"

"No," he roared. "Where's the guard?"

"He ran away."

Al-Bayat paced the dirt floor, swearing at the top of his lungs. He didn't execute any more men, but he shot several holes in the roof of the barn.

Layah was amazed by the turn of events. Hudson must have switched clothes with the guard. He'd made it out of Iran. He'd survived a clash with Al-Bayat's men. Now he was free, and he would save her.

"Should we go look for him?" one man asked.

"No," Al-Bayat said. He gave Layah a measured glance, as if weighing her importance. "He'll come to us."

Chapter 19

Hud was saved by a swarm of bees.

Bees.

After he dropped to the ground, the third assailant fired a few shots that went widely off target. One of the bullets struck the guard in the side of the neck. He fell to his knees, making choking noises. Hud drew his gun to return fire, but the bees did all the work. They descended on the Da'esh terrorist like a tornado, stinging his hands and face. Hud jumped up and ran away while the man was distracted. The other two rushed forward to check the guard, who was bleeding out in the dirt.

Hud escaped with a few bee stings and no tail. The militants didn't even follow him. Two of them were focused on the accidental shooting of the man they thought was Hud. The other was in the throes of a violent insect attack.

Hud found a group of cypress trees to hide in. It was the only cover in the area, so he climbed up high and watched the scene unfold. The bee sting victim ran away from the clearing while the other two men stayed with the guard. They did nothing to help him, of course. Hud figured he was already dead. There was a black SUV on the opposite side of the parking lot. They loaded the guard into it and headed down a dirt road to a barn.

Al-Bayat would be there. In a barn like an animal.

Hud waited a minute to make sure they stayed inside the structure. He heard the faint pop of gunfire from the building. His gut clenched at the sound. Layah was in there with them. He could imagine what Al-Bayat would do to her, or wanted to do to her. Hud had to get there and stop him.

Once again, he didn't really have a plan. He couldn't count on another swarm of bees, or any more freak accidents. He'd have to enter a confined space, where he'd be outnumbered and outgunned. He was risking his life. Worse, he was risking recapture. He could be tortured for weeks before his public beheading.

It wasn't the way he wanted to go out, but he'd do anything for Layah. He'd take on the whole world for her. He'd die for her.

That was love.

He'd loved before, on a different scale. He loved his mother, and his teammates. He'd even loved Michelle, though he wouldn't compare her to Layah. What he felt for Layah was on another level. It was mountainous, majestic, epic. It was like climbing to the summit and touching the sky. It was everything.

Of course he would die for her. He couldn't live without her.

He dropped down from the cypress tree and returned to the parking lot. The government vehicle he'd driven here still had the keys in the ignition. Hud moved it closer to the squad cars and got out. He transferred the smaller of the two policemen from the squad car to the Jeep. He put the body behind the wheel, with one dead foot on the gas pedal and the other on the brake. Then he shifted into a low gear and fired up the engine. The Jeep lurched forward. Hud walked along beside the open door.

The road leading to the barn started on a gentle downhill slope. Hud paused there, shifting the Jeep into Park. He wondered if Al-Bayat knew his men had shot the wrong person. Al-Bayat would want to see Hud's dead face. Maybe the pop of gunfire indicated that Al-Bayat had discovered the mistake.

Hud assumed they'd be ready for him. The barn would be well guarded, with at least three men in addition to Al-Bayat. He couldn't just stroll up to it and rescue Layah. He had to create a diversion first. If he tried to drive the Jeep into the barn himself, he'd get taken out by gunfire before he arrived. This body was the perfect driver, immune to more bullets. A corpse wouldn't take his foot off the gas. Hud decided to add a surprise twist just in case the Jeep failed to catch their attention.

He walked around to the passenger side and searched the glove compartment for an old rag and a lighter. He stuck the end of the rag in the gas tank. Then he shifted into Drive. As the Jeep rolled forward, Hud lit the rag.

Now it was sure to cause a scene.

He started running at full speed, putting distance between himself and the moving vehicle. He sprinted through the trees and made a wide circle toward the back of the barn, where he could stage an attack from the rear.

His diversion worked a little too well. The Jeep rolled straight to the front of the barn, drawing gunfire from multiple assailants. Then it kept right on going. It crashed through the entrance and exploded on impact. Everything went up in flames.

Holy hell.

Hud ducked his head low as he crept along the side of the barn. There was a rear exit, so he stood next to it with his gun drawn. The first man out was unlucky. Hud took him down with a single shot.

The next man didn't make the same mistake. He stopped at the sight of his fallen comrade and retreated into the recesses of the burning building. Hud pursued, because the element of surprise was gone. The man lifted his weapon a split second too late. Hud eliminated him with two to the chest.

His eyes adjusted to the dark space, which was rapidly filling with smoke. He crept forward, staying low. There were two more men on the ground. Both were dead. Hud followed a blur of movement into the corner of the barn. Al-Bayat stood with Layah. He had a gun pressed to her temple. His face was sweaty, his eyes crazed.

"We meet again," Al-Bayat said in heavily accented English.

Hud gestured with his weapon. "Let her go."

"Why would I do that? I want to watch her bleed."

"Let her go, and you can have me."

"No," Layah protested, struggling to break free.

"You sacrifice yourself for a woman?"

He nodded. "I'll put my weapon down. You release her. As soon as she's out the door, I'm all yours."

"You are a fool."

"Do you want to return to Rahim a success or die here a failure?"

Al-Bayat considered this question. He was sweating profusely. The interior of the barn was blazing hot and airless. Hud was impervious to the discomfort; he'd suffered far worse in the torture chamber.

"Don't do it," Layah said.

"Think of my beheading," Hud suggested, ignoring her. "It will be your best show. So many views. So many converts."

"You aren't that important, American."

"Sure I am," Hud said. "That's why Rahim sent you after me. You're far away from the battle zones, aren't you? Rahim must not need you on the front lines. Maybe he found a replacement killer."

"Shut up," Al-Bayat said, his hand fisted in Layah's hair. "You know nothing."

"It can't be that hard to cut off heads. Any village butcher can do it."

Al-Bayat didn't like this conversation. He was a madman, but a calculating one. He was ambitious and self-aggrandizing. His favor with Rahim could be in jeopardy. "You are eager to return to my prison?"

"It wasn't so bad."

"I have a recording of your screams as I burned your flesh."

"That didn't even leave a scar."

Al-Bayat's mouth thinned with displeasure. Hud knew he wouldn't release Layah. Al-Bayat knew Hud wouldn't back down. It was a standoff. Hud didn't care if the roof was on fire. He didn't care if his *clothes* were on fire. He wasn't leaving without Layah.

One of the ceiling beams plummeted to the ground next to them. The moment of distraction was all he needed. Layah shoved away from Al-Bayat and Hud pulled the trigger. Al-Bayat fired at the same time.

Hud's aim was true. Al-Bayat's wasn't. The Da'esh executioner dropped his weapon and careened forward, clutching his chest.

Hud didn't wait to make sure he was dead. The roof was caving in on them, raining flames and debris. He covered his nose with the crook of his arm and grabbed Layah. They ran through the smoke together.

Then they were outside, tripping over the bodies of their enemies. Hud pulled her forward and kept moving, as if the fire might chase them. He didn't know how many locals Al-Bayat had paid to assist his scheme.

When they were at a safe distance, he paused to free her wrists. She sobbed in relief, throwing her arms around him. He held her for several seconds, his chest tight with emotion. Then they broke apart and started running again.

They ran because they were in Azerbaijan, at the scene of a horrific crime. The authorities would respond to the fire and discover the bodies. Even if the police here were friendly toward Americans, not allies of the Da'esh, Hud didn't want to get detained. Layah ran with him, matching his pace.

They ran across fallow fields and over rocky hills. They ran until Layah couldn't run anymore. She collapsed at the base of a gnarled oak tree, gasping for breath. Hud rested with her, his hands on his knees. When her shoulders shook with silent tears, he sat down and put his arms around her.

"Shh," he said, stroking her hair. "We're okay."

"I thought you were dead," she choked.

"I know."

"You don't know, William. You don't know how it felt to see the body!"

He kissed the top of her head. "Tell me."

She pushed away from him, her lips trembling. "There was a man wearing your clothes, with his face covered. Soaked in blood."

He rubbed a hand over his mouth, silent.

"They put a hood on Khalil in Palmyra."

"I'm sorry."

"Al-Bayat said he begged for mercy."

"Al-Bayat is a liar. And now he's gone."

"You killed him," she said in a flat voice. "You killed all of them."

"Yes."

Her eyes shone with tears again. He didn't expect her to celebrate his actions. She wasn't a battle-scarred soldier, like him. He'd fantasized about taking down Al-Bayat for years, and he wouldn't lose any sleep over the bloodshed. Sometimes victory was empty, or void of triumph. This wasn't one of those times. He felt a grim satisfaction in dispatching The Butcher. He'd done what he had to do to survive, and to save Layah.

He cupped her chin, checking her for injuries. "Did he hurt you?"

"No."

"Did any of them hurt you?"

She shook her head.

"How do we get to Armenia from here?"

She wiped her cheeks and took a ragged breath. "I'm not sure. The borders between Armenia and Azerbaijan have been closed for a long time. The two countries are not at peace with each other."

"Of course they aren't."

"It is easier to cross from Iran."

"I'm not going back to Iran. Ever."

Sadness flitted across her features. "I understand that. We can take the bus, or get a ride closer to the border. Then we will find a place to cross."

"Let's go."

There was a road on the opposite side of the hill, with sparse traffic and a bus stop. Hud waited there with Layah, his mind quiet. A man with a cart passed by, selling leather sandals. Layah declined the sandals but inquired about the flannel shirt tied to the cart. She paid for it with coins from her pocket.

Hud shrugged out of the border guard's shirt,

which was conspicuously decorated with blood, and put on the faded flannel. When the bus arrived, they boarded without incident. They rode to the last stop, a small village called Ordubad. Then they got off the bus and walked. A truck driver offered a ride to the end of the road. By noon, they were only a few miles from the Armenian border.

"Do you want to keep going?" he asked Layah.

"Yes. We're too close to stop."

It wasn't as difficult to reach Armenia as he'd imagined. The border was in a remote location, quiet and unpatrolled. There might be tension between the two countries, but there was peace within them, and stable borders.

They followed a set of old train tracks for three or four miles at the most. Then they reached the outskirts of an idyllic little town in a green valley. Layah stopped and grasped his hand, inhaling a sharp breath.

"This is Agarak," she said in a hushed tone.

"Yeah?"

Her eyes, which had been dark from the day's trauma, brightened like stars. "It is Armenia."

"We made it."

She moved her sparkling gaze from the town to his face. "We made it."

He was mesmerized by her beauty, astounded by her strength and resilience. He brought her knuckles to his mouth for a kiss. She had a red mark on her wrist from the plastic tie, so he kissed there, too. His throat closed up and his heart thumped hard inside his chest. He had to tell her how he felt, right here and now. "I love you."

To his surprise, she pulled away from him. "No."

"No?"

"This is where we say goodbye."

He flinched as if she'd struck him.

"We are finally in Armenia, my father's homeland. I have been dreaming about this moment for so long. I've been striving for it, saving for it. But it is my destination, not yours. This is where you leave me."

He shook his head in denial. "It doesn't have to be."

She crossed her arms over her chest. "Oh?"

Frustration welled up within him. They'd just survived impossible odds. He'd rescued her from certain death. They'd finally reached a safe place, and he'd shared his deepest feelings. He didn't want to be brought down by harsh reality. They were alive! He wanted to kiss her and embrace her and celebrate the moment.

"You left me this morning," she said. "Do you remember?"

"I remember."

She gave him a pointed look.

"You think that was easy for me? You think I *wanted* to?"

"It is not a matter of want, William. You will leave again."

He grasped her shoulders. "Come with me."

"Stop."

He didn't stop. He wouldn't stop until she agreed to be his. "I can't live without you, Layah. I'm in love with you. I don't care how impossible you think it is

for us to be together. I'm going to make it happen.
I'll do whatever it takes. In case you haven't noticed,
I'm pretty good at challenges. I can overcome any ob-
stacle in my way, and I don't quit, ever."

She held up her palm. "I refuse."

"You refuse what?"

"To let you break my heart with this fantasy."

"Tell me you don't love me, and I'll give it up."

Her brow furrowed at his request. She didn't deny
that she shared his feelings, but she turned her back
on him, looking across the hillside. "The night Khalil
left, we argued. I begged him not to join the rebels.
He wasn't a soldier. I said he was throwing his life
away. He told me he would think about it, and we...
made peace."

She meant that he'd made love to her. Hud's gut
clenched at the comparison.

"When I woke up, he was gone. I never saw him
again."

"I'm not him, Layah."

"You are worse. Twice as stubborn and ten times
as fearless."

"I'm trained for combat."

"The problem is not your profession. It is your
failure to see the truth. Our parting is inevitable."

He wanted to argue with her, to convince her that
they could overcome any obstacles. But he didn't
know what the future held. He *would* have to leave
as soon as he talked to his commander. He couldn't
stay in Armenia indefinitely.

"I'll come back to you," he said, wrapping his
arms around her again.

She accepted his embrace, if not his words. Her fingers threaded through the short hair at his nape. "Let us proceed with eyes wide open. This is temporary. It is a passionate affair we will remember always. I enjoy your hands on my body and your mouth on my skin. Let us have that, without the promises."

"I want both. I want everything."

"You can't have everything."

He could, and he would. He'd have her by whatever means necessary. Because this wasn't a fantasy for him. It wasn't a short fling. He'd made bad choices with women before, and he'd learned from his mistakes. As a SEAL, he'd learned to take calculated risks, instead of stupid ones.

Marrying Michelle had been a stupid risk. They'd had nothing in common outside of the bedroom. He'd needed space, and she'd needed the opposite. They hadn't communicated or connected on a deeper level.

With Layah, he knew he'd met his match. He felt it in his bones. She was the one. They were right for each other. She was fiercely independent, and more than willing to speak her mind. He could tell her anything. They'd forged an unbreakable bond on this journey. He wasn't going to let go now.

Sure, they'd hit some rough spots along the way. She'd deceived him a few times. The difference was that she hadn't done it thoughtlessly, or for selfish reasons. She'd sworn to protect her family, just as he'd sworn to protect his team.

If they could get out of Iran, they could do anything. They could overcome any obstacle. He wasn't going to stop fighting until he convinced her.

They had all night.

He removed her hand from his hair, because he was already getting aroused. She smiled, aware of the effect she had on him. He smiled back, intent on making her his.

They continued down the hill to Agarak. There was an inn at the end of a cobblestone street, across from a café. He wasn't in the mood for a feast, for once. Maybe his body had finally recovered from the days of near starvation.

He was hungry for her and only her.

She ordered a light meal of chicken soup with flatbread and mineral water. There were pistachio cookies for dessert. They walked to the inn at sunset. She used the last of her money to pay for a room. It was a budget-friendly place, clean and basic, with a bed that wasn't big enough for what he intended.

"I'll have to sleep on top of you," he said.

"Will we sleep?"

He pulled her into his arms. "Not if I can help it," he said, kissing her soft mouth. She smiled against his lips, acquiescent. He lifted her up and carried her into the tiny bathroom, where he set her down on the vanity sink. "Let's shower."

"Both of us?"

"That's the best way to do it."

"I don't think we fit."

"I'll show you."

He stripped off her tunic, which smelled like smoke. His flannel shirt smelled worse, like sheep and sweat. They struggled out of boots and pants and undergarments. Then she was standing naked before him.

"God in heaven," he said, ogling her nude form. She took his breath away. She was all soft skin and dark hair and lush beauty. Her nipped-in waist made a dramatic contrast to her full breasts and flared hips. "You're perfect."

She laughed at this claim, as if he was exaggerating. He dropped to his knees before her, spanning her waist with his hands.

"I love this spot," he said, touching his lips to the curve beneath her belly button. Her abdomen wasn't flat and hard like his. It was cushiony and feminine. She had the kind of shape that a fashion magazine might airbrush into a sleeker profile. Which was a crying shame, because the sight of her rounded hips cradling his thrusts was incredibly erotic. He kissed both hip bones, watching her little belly quiver.

He could smell her womanly scent, rich and warm. His mouth watered for a taste of her, but she shyly covered her mound with one hand. He could wait until she was begging for it. He rose to his feet, his erection rising high. She studied him with half-lidded eyes. He turned on the shower to let the water heat up. Then they stepped inside the stall.

It was a tight fit. Deliciously tight. Her slippery wet body plastered against his. Water rained down his back as he filled his hands with her buttocks. He shuddered with pleasure. His staff nudged her slick belly.

"Damn," he said, gritting his teeth.

"What's wrong?"

"You feel too good."

"This is very stimulating."

He slid his erection back and forth, unable to resist. "I'm already close."

"Your organ is enlarged again."

His hips jerked forward. He moved his hands to her breasts, stroking her wet nipples. "Touch it."

She found the soap and started at his shoulders. Then she worked her way down, lathering his chest and stomach. By the time she encircled his shaft, he was trembling with need. She squeezed him with soapy fingers.

He endured her attention for about thirty seconds, moaning helplessly. Then he peeled her hand away, his jaw clenched. She smiled and reached for the shampoo. He watched her breasts jiggle enticingly as she washed her hair. Bubbles dripped down her smooth skin, over her sexy stomach and into the cleft between her thighs.

Jesus.

She tilted her head back to rinse her hair, eyes closed. He took his shaft in hand and strangled it into submission. When she was finished, he turned her around and made a fist in her hair. She gasped, bracing her palm on the shower tiles. He kissed the nape of her neck and slid his fingers down her belly. His erection nestled against her ass as he parted her plump folds. She was very wet.

He could take her like this, from behind. He could take her standing up, against the tiles. He could have her on her knees. He could make her come with his fingertips and finish himself off with a quick jerk.

All of that sounded hot, but too expedient. He

wasn't just trying to get her off. He was trying to win her heart.

He removed his hand from between her legs and released her hair. She glanced over her shoulder at him, her lips parted. She looked disappointed, as if she'd enjoyed that hint of roughness. His erection throbbed like a sore thumb. He shut the water off and helped her out of the shower stall. Then he lifted her against the sink, her legs spread.

Again, he wanted to take her. The tip of his shaft was right there at her opening. Her thighs shimmered with droplets of water and her sex glistened. He kissed her sweet mouth, plunging his tongue deep. She kissed him back with equal fervor. She wanted this as much as he did. She needed him deep inside her.

He broke contact with her mouth and brought his thumb to her lips. He encouraged her to suck it, and she did. His erection throbbed at the sight of her hot mouth stretched around him. He removed his thumb and swept it across her cheek. He pinched her taut nipples, making her moan. Then he went down on his knees.

She was ripe for his tongue. So ripe and wet and swollen. He speared his tongue into her hot flesh. She buried her hands in his hair and cried out for more. He gave it to her. He replaced his tongue with two fingers, plumbing her silky depths. Then he swirled his tongue over her clitoris. He sucked it and kissed it and loved it. He relished her taste, her scent, her uninhibited responses. He'd never enjoyed pleasuring a woman more. Her moisture flooded his fingers as he thrust them in and out.

She made breathy sounds of excitement, close to

ecstasy. He flicked his tongue slower to draw the moment out. She bucked against his mouth and gave a hoarse scream. He smiled at the sharp tug of her hands in his hair. When her grip loosened, he slid his fingers from her sex.

"What did you do to me?" she murmured drowsily.

He rose to rinse off his mouth at the sink. "I'm just getting started."

She chuckled at this claim, as if she didn't believe it.

He carried her to the bed and tossed her on the mattress. "Are you ready?"

"For what?"

He climbed on top of her. "This," he said, gripping her hair. He entered her in one thrust. She gasped at the feel of him. Her slick channel squeezed him like a fist. He withdrew a few inches and drove home again, harder.

"Ooh," she said. "Yes."

"Tell me what you want."

"You. Inside me."

He groaned, thrusting deeper. Her moisture glistened on his shaft as he pounded into her. Her delicate parts stretched wide around his flesh. Everything was swollen and tight and slippery. It felt so goddamned good, he couldn't stand it.

He wanted her to come with him, so he slid his hand between them. She mewled her encouragement, her mouth contorted in pleasure. She was so hot, so wet, so perfect. She cried out his name, hips bucking under his. He buried himself to the hilt as her inner muscles fluttered around him.

God.

It was just good sex, and great chemistry, and healthy bodies performing well together, but it felt special. It felt like magic. It felt like no one had ever reached this peak before.

He pulled out at the last second, shuddering with the power of his own climax. Hot seed erupted from him in heavy spurts. It jetted across her belly and arched higher, reaching her quivering breasts.

When he was finished, he collapsed on top of her. The bed wasn't big enough for him to roll away. He could have fallen asleep like that, but she shifted with discomfort. He remembered that part of being a generous lover was cleaning up the mess, so he lumbered to his feet. He soaked a washcloth and took care of her. He wiped her breasts, her belly, between her legs. She trembled at his touch, still sensitive. His shaft thickened with interest.

"Don't even think about it," she said.

He set aside the washcloth, smiling. "You can't handle another round?"

"Please. Let me rest."

He climbed into bed and put his arm around her, content to wait. He'd rushed things by telling her he loved her earlier. She was rattled from the day's events. She'd believed him dead. Putting on the emotional brakes was a natural reaction to trauma. If she needed him to slow down, he'd slow down. If she needed time, he'd give her time. He'd do anything for her—because what he felt wasn't temporary.

It was forever.

Chapter 20

Layah didn't dream of Khalil.

She dreamed of William, locked in battle. Jumping through fire, guns blazing. Shielding her with his body, protecting her from harm.

She woke at dawn in the safety of his arms. He cradled her for a few moments, his breath fanning her ear. Then he eased away from her and sat at the edge of the bed. She tugged the sheets up to cover her naked body, studying him. He had broad shoulders, rippled with muscle. She felt deliciously sore from last night's activities, but eager to touch him again. She crawled across the mattress and wrapped her arms around him. The sheet fell away, leaving nothing between them.

He glanced over his shoulder at her. "This is how I'd like to wake up every morning."

She cuddled closer, pressing her bare breasts

against his back. She could hear his heartbeat, strong and sure. He lifted a hand to her hair and cradled her head. He held her in place behind him, as if he never wanted her to move.

"I've decided to take you captive," he said.

She inhaled a sharp breath. "Captive?"

"It's only fair."

"Will I stay in this room?"

"Yes. I'll tie you to the bed."

"Naked?"

"Naked, or covered with a sheet. I'll rip it off you whenever I want."

Her nipples tightened into fine points and heat settled between her legs. She could hear the edge in his voice, the near seriousness of his words. She understood his desire to take control of the situation. To take control of her. He was an idealistic American. He wanted a happy ending to their story, and he couldn't accept anything less.

She touched her lips to his shoulder. "I will be your captive, if you like."

"Can I tie you up?"

She stretched out on her back and brought her wrists together in offering. His eyes darkened at the supplicant move. Instead of playing her game, he rose from the bed and put on his pants. He paced the room, raking a hand through his hair. He didn't want her submission. He wanted her heart.

She covered herself with the sheet again. "We can take a bus to Yerevan. My parents will wire me money for tickets."

"I have to call my commander first."

"And your mother? You will call her?"

"Yes."

"Tell me about her."

"She's a nurse. She lives in Kansas City."

"Is that where you're from?"

He nodded.

"Where do you live now?"

"San Diego. California."

"Where is your father?"

"He died when I was eleven."

"I'm sorry."

He shrugged, sitting down next to her.

"What was he like?"

"He was a womanizer and a drunk. It was hard on my mom."

"Not on you?"

"It was, but I think she got the worst of it. She had to raise me on her own."

"Were you a good boy?"

"Hell no. I was a nightmare."

She smiled at his description. "How so?"

"I was angry and impulsive. I liked to fight. I climbed everything. I fell and broke bones and drove her crazy."

"She must be proud of you now."

Hud gave Layah a measured look. "Aren't your parents proud of you?"

"I don't know." She stared up at the ceiling, clutching the sheet to her chest. Her parents wouldn't approve of this affair, but maybe it didn't matter. She'd already fallen far from grace. "I've disappointed them."

"Because of Khalil?"

"They also didn't want me to leave home, or to study English in Baghdad. I was never a good Assyrian girl."

"You went to medical school. Isn't that good enough?"

"Marrying an Assyrian doctor would have been better."

He shook his head in disbelief. "My mother would love you."

She was touched by the compliment, and she didn't think he gave it lightly. "Did she like your first wife?"

"She did not."

Layah laughed at his wry expression. He curled up beside her, his arm draped across her waist. She studied his hands, which were as hard and strong as the rest of him. His veins stood out in harsh relief.

"I'll come back for you," he said against her neck.

"Don't."

"Why not?"

She turned to face him, her throat tight.

"Is it Ashur? Are you doing this for him?"

"I want to see him settled, but he's not my only concern. I can't bear to hope for something that will never be."

A muscle in his jaw flexed. "What if I can get you a visa?"

"How will you do that?"

Hud didn't answer.

She traced the insignia on his chest with her fingertip. "Do not lie for me. This job is who you are. It is too important to risk."

"You're important, too."

She rose from the bed, denying him. "I meant what I said last night."

He followed her across the room and grasped her shoulders. "Tell me you don't love me, and I'll walk away. I'll let you go."

Her eyes filled with tears. "I don't love you."

He flinched as if she'd struck him. She didn't think he believed her. She thought he'd kiss her until she admitted the truth. Either that or throw her down on the bed and make love to her roughly, like he had several times the night before.

Instead he released her and backed away.

She wished she could explain her feelings to him. It had been easier to confess her love for him in a language he couldn't understand, or at a moment when she thought they were both going to die. Now they were safe, and she was terrified to surrender her heart. Because she'd been down this road before. She'd waited a year for Khalil to return from the war zone. He'd called every week to say he loved her.

She couldn't endure another relationship like that. The distance, the worrying. The fear that she'd never see him again, followed by the cold reality.

It was better to make a clean break.

They got dressed in yesterday's clothes. She'd bought a hairbrush and some toiletries at a convenience store. Getting a bus ticket was as easy as walking to the transit station and calling her parents. They were happy to hear from her. Even Ashur got on the phone.

"How are you?" she asked him.

"I'm fine."

"Do you like Armenia?"

"It's okay," he said grudgingly. "Is Hudson with you?"

"He is."

"He's coming to Yerevan?"

"I'm not sure."

Ashur fell silent. She couldn't guess what he was thinking.

"I'll be there soon. Be good to your grandparents, okay?"

"Okay," he said, and hung up.

She returned the pay phone to its cradle. William arched a brow at her teary eyes. Though he couldn't understand her words, he could read the emotions on her face.

He picked up the phone to make his own calls. She retreated a few steps to give him privacy. He spoke to someone in a gruff tone, laughing a few times. This was his commander. She stared at his strong profile, her heart breaking.

He hung up and took a deep breath.

"How did it go?" she asked.

"Good. I had to answer a bunch of security questions to convince him it was really me. He couldn't believe I was still alive after that explosion in Telskuf. He told me what happened to my teammates."

"Are they okay?"

"Yes," he said, smiling. "I was the only casualty."

She smiled back at him.

"He's sending someone to meet me in Yerevan tomorrow. I'll take the bus with you."

Some of her tension eased away. They didn't have to say goodbye yet.

"I'm going to call my mom now."

"Should I…" She gestured to a bench nearby.

"You can stay."

She stood close to him, nervous on his behalf. His mother thought he was dead. She couldn't imagine how difficult it would be for him to make this call. She hadn't even been able to tell her parents that Khalil was dead.

Hud dialed the number and waited. "It's going to voice mail," he said to Layah. Then he spoke into the receiver. "Hi, Mom. It's William. I'm…alive. I've been in an Iraqi prison, but I got out, and I'm coming home." He had to pause to clear his throat. "I know this is a shock. You can contact Commander Doheny's office if you have questions. I'll call back later." His gaze met Layah's, and her eyes filled with tears.

I love you, she mouthed, as a reminder for him to say those words.

"I love you," he said, and hung up.

They stared at each other for a long moment, sharing the experience. She didn't know if he realized she was speaking the truth. She'd denied it before, but she couldn't deny it now. She was desperately in love with him. The pain she'd hoped to avoid was unavoidable. Hearts didn't make clean breaks.

He got a money transfer from his commander. They ate breakfast at the station. When the bus came, they boarded it together. She rested her head on his shoulder as they passed through a series of small towns. They hadn't slept much in the inn last night. They slept on the bus instead. They reached Yerevan at sunset.

"Stay with me tonight," he said, kissing her hand.

She agreed without hesitation. Yerevan was a modern city, full of small luxuries. He had a pocketful of cash to spend on incidentals. They went shopping first. While he browsed for men's clothes, she found a simple dress and some pretty lingerie.

After he paid for their items, they had a casual dinner at the food court in the mall. Most of the women weren't wearing hijabs. She marveled at the sight of so many hairstyles. It was a completely different world here.

"What are the women like in America?" she asked.

"Depends on where you go."

"In California they are all blondes in bikinis, no?"

He smiled, drinking his tea. "There are brunettes in bikinis, too."

"I changed my mind about you making love to another woman."

"Oh?"

"Now that I know how you do it, I don't want to share."

He laughed at her possessiveness. "This problem is easily solved by you coming to California. You'll look great in a bikini, and I'll never be with anyone else."

She regretted steering the conversation into dangerous territory. They were having a nice time together. It was like a casual date. She didn't want to spend their last night arguing. She had better things to do with him. "I can't imagine wearing a bikini. I feel self-conscious about my uncovered hair."

"I love your hair like that."

She touched her flyaway locks. "You do?"

"It's beautiful."

"Thank you."

"You aren't shy about your body with me."

"That's different. It's private."

"You've never worn a swimsuit?"

"I have, but it was a long time ago."

"Sounds like you're overdue for a vacation. *I'm* overdue for a vacation."

"Where would you go?"

"I wanted to go to Turkey."

"You're kidding."

"No. The climbing there is supposed to be world-class, and I like traveling to far-off places. Right now, I'd rather hang out at home, though. I live near a beach called Sunset Cliffs. It's gorgeous."

She knew what he was doing. He was trying to convince her to come with him, but there was no way she'd get a visa unless he lied about her involvement in his kidnapping. She wouldn't ask him to do that. Even if she did, what kind of woman went halfway across the world for a man she'd known only a few weeks? Falling in love with him was foolish enough. They were both emotional from yesterday's near death experience. They'd been through hell together. These feelings would fade after he left. She hoped.

They found a nice hotel in a quiet area a few blocks from the mall. While he ducked into the shower, she called her parents to let them know where she was. She expected her mother to ask a dozen questions, but she didn't.

Layah hung up the phone, shrugging. Then she took her turn in the shower. She bathed and brushed her hair, smoothing out the tangles. The lingerie she'd purchased was black lace. When she came out of the bathroom in the new bra and panties, William's jaw went slack.

He stood, wearing only a towel around his waist. She gave him a little fashion show, turning in a circle. He whistled appreciatively.

"Too shy to wear a bikini, but not this?"

She followed his gaze to the mirror on the vanity behind her, which displayed her mostly bare bottom. He skimmed his hands along her sides, where lace met flesh. "We are not in public."

"Good thing," he said roughly. He cupped her buttocks and squeezed. "I'd get arrested for lewd behavior."

It was clear that he liked her curves, and she felt the same admiration for his body. The sight of him in a towel gave her hot flashes. He seemed to get stronger every day. He was in excellent health, for a man who'd been held captive. She explored the contours of his broad shoulders and well-developed chest. Her fingertips trailed down his flat abdomen. He'd kissed her belly last night. It was only fair that she return the favor.

She couldn't have a real relationship with him, but she could give him another night to remember before he left.

He inhaled a sharp breath as she dropped to her knees. She pressed her lips to the trail of hair below his navel. Then she traced its path lower, to where his erection jutted at the front of the towel. She pulled the damp terry cloth away. He was magnificent, long and hard and thick.

She wrapped her fingers around him in a loose ring, barely skimming his flesh. He threaded his hand through her hair. She let him guide her forward. She touched her tongue to him delicately, making him groan. He shuddered with excitement as she brushed soft kisses along his shaft. His fingers tangled in her hair, pleading. She parted her lips and took him deep.

He seemed mesmerized by her swirling tongue and stroking hand. She didn't think her skills were mind-blowing, but she enjoyed what she was doing. She enjoyed his size, his heat, his firm flesh. His gaze moved to the mirror periodically. She looked there and saw herself kneeling before him, her bottom tilted and her mouth full. She could see him sliding in and out, jutting against her cheek.

No wonder he was mesmerized. It was incredibly erotic.

She moaned, taking him deeper. He made a fist in her hair, his jaw clenched. Need pulsed between her legs. She squeezed her thighs together, squirming. He withdrew from her mouth, which was fine. She had other uses for him.

He reclined on the bed, at her urging. She removed her panties quickly. She felt warm and slick and ready. She straddled his waist and sank down on his length, inch by inch. He gritted his teeth at the heady sensation. She kissed his tense jaw. Then she started moving, and he was lost. He gripped her hips, thrusting higher into her.

Yes.

She tugged down her bra straps and he cupped her breasts. His hands were all over her, his mouth on her taut nipples. He sucked them, one by one. She clutched his hair, riding him harder.

Yes, yes.

He looked down at where their bodies were joined, watching her take him to heaven. His hand followed his eyes. He strummed her sensitive nub in swift circles. Then he pinched gently. She cried out in ecstasy.

He kept stroking and she flew apart, sobbing his name. Her hips bucked in a wild rhythm. A second later, he went still beneath her. She cradled his head to her chest as he found his release.

They came back down to earth together, panting. She released her grip on his damp hair. He lifted her off him. She curled up on her side.

"I didn't pull out."

"I told you. I want your child."

"You won't let me make you any promises, but I can fill your belly with a baby?"

She rested against the pillows, drowsy and satiated. "It is the wrong time of month."

"Are you sure?"

"Yes."

He didn't seem convinced. She rose from the bed with a sigh and walked into the bathroom to wash away his seed with cool water. When she returned he wrapped his arm around her, kissing the top of her head. She understood how he felt about an unplanned pregnancy. It wasn't fair to ask him to father a child he couldn't raise, but she wouldn't mind being a single mother. She was almost thirty, and she doubted she'd fall in love again. She'd already had two great loves in her life. She wouldn't find a better man than William Hudson.

She couldn't bear to think about their uncertain future, so she didn't. She closed her eyes and snuggled against him, relishing the present.

Right now, they were together, and it was perfect.

Chapter 21

Hud didn't leave without saying goodbye this time.

Commander Doheny was sending a US Marshal to escort Hud back to the States, and their flight wasn't scheduled until noon. He enjoyed a leisurely breakfast in bed with Layah. They got up and put on their new clothes. She looked pretty and fresh in a flower-print dress. He wasn't too shabby himself.

They walked to the mall, hand in hand, to meet her parents. Hud spotted Ashur first. Layah hugged him and cried. Ashur endured the embrace, narrowing his gaze at Hud.

He expected her parents to be stern and disapproving, but they weren't. Her father shook his hand politely. Her mother was too busy crying and hugging Layah to notice him. Finally, she wiped her cheeks and Layah introduced him.

Hud had no idea what her parents thought Layah

had been doing with him last night. It was clear Ashur knew. Hud pulled the boy aside for a private conversation while Layah chatted with her parents.

"Protect her for me, will you?" Hud asked.

"You are going back to America?"

"Yes."

Ashur stared at him for a long moment, seeming both relieved and disappointed. "She's too good for you."

Hud didn't argue. "You were right about Al-Bayat."

"He killed my father?"

"He did, and I took care of him."

"He is dead?"

"Yes."

The boy's brow furrowed. "That was my job."

"You'll have to find something else to do."

Ashur nodded, as if he already had a second victim in mind. Hud didn't ask. He didn't want to know.

Layah approached him again before she left. They'd had plenty of contact in the hotel, all night long, but he wished for one last embrace. He didn't get it. She rose on tiptoe to give him a demure peck on the cheek.

"Take care of yourself," she whispered.

"I love you," he said, not caring who overheard.

Her eyes filled with tears. She kissed her fingertips and waved goodbye. Then she linked arms with Ashur and walked away with her parents. Hud stared after them until they disappeared, his chest tight with emotion.

She claimed she didn't love him. She didn't believe he would come back for her. She thought there was no hope for them.

He'd prove her wrong.

He took a cab to the airport, his heart heavy. He met the US Marshal who was escorting him back to the States. They boarded a twenty-hour flight to Los Angeles via Paris. When they arrived, a vehicle was waiting for him at the tarmac. Hud was taken to Commander Doheny's office at the Coronado Naval Base.

The mood on base was subdued. No Team Twelve members came to greet him. Hud felt self-conscious about his street clothes as he entered the office buildings. Doheny's secretary put him in a private interrogation room, which was strange.

Doheny entered a moment later. Hud rose to shake his hand.

"Welcome back," Doheny said.

"It's great to be here."

They sat down to go over the details of Hud's adventures in Iraq and beyond. Hud spoke without inflection, giving just the facts, and he tried to be as honest as possible. It was difficult to recount some of the darkest days of his captivity. His memory was fuzzy, as if he'd blocked out the pain. He skipped ahead to the journey with Layah. He didn't mention the fact that he hadn't been given a choice about being her guide, and he kept the intimate details private. Doheny didn't need to know everything.

When he was finished, Doheny leaned back in his chair. "I spoke to an Azerbaijani official yesterday. Al-Bayat's remains were identified."

Hud was encouraged by this news.

"It's an incredible story."

"Yes."

"Are you aware that you were in violation of military law when you left Iraq with a group of refugees?"

"Yes, sir."

"Is there a reason you ignored regulations?"

"They needed help, and they rescued me from a torture cell. I felt obligated."

"You felt obligated."

"I wasn't thinking clearly, sir. I'd suffered multiple head traumas, daily beatings, dehydration and poor nutrition. I was desperate to avoid getting recaptured. When the refugees offered a way out, I took it."

"And when you followed them into Iran? Were you thinking clearly then?"

Hud rubbed a hand over his mouth. This was the most problematic part of his story. He couldn't explain a decision like that. "We'd encountered some unexpected complications in Turkey, like I said. Al-Bayat's men were following us. I didn't realize we were in Iran until it was too late."

Doheny brought out his laptop and opened a file. He turned the screen toward Hud, showing him a picture of Layah. It was a staff photo from Damascus Hospital. She was smiling, her eyes bright.

"Is she the reason you weren't thinking clearly?"

Hud swallowed hard, unsure what to say.

Doheny brought up another picture, taken from a distance. It was of him kissing Layah outside their hotel room in Yerevan. Hud's blood went cold at the sight. He hadn't realized they were being watched.

"You had me followed?" he asked.

"You've been on your own behind enemy lines for months. I had to check up on you."

"You think I went AWAL? That I was *radicalized*?"

"I believe you were taken captive. I'm questioning your claim that you went with this woman willingly."

He gestured to the photo. "Do I look unwilling?"

"According to your statement, which matches our intel, Ms. Anwar blew up the side of a building to get you. It doesn't make sense for her to go to all that trouble and then give you the choice to decline to help her."

Hud drummed his fingertips on the table. "Let's focus on the big picture. She busted me out of that hellhole and saved me from a public beheading. In return, I helped her family get to Armenia. There's no harm done, and Al-Bayat is dead. Everyone wins."

"Al-Bayat is the problem," Doheny said. "He was on the top ten list. Every detail of your story will be examined at the highest clearance levels. I can't give you a free pass for withholding information, or for having inappropriate contact with a refugee."

"I'm not asking for a free pass," Hud said. "Punish me however you see fit. Put me on leave without pay."

"Why are you so intent on protecting this woman?"

"Because I'm in love with her," Hud said, his jaw clenched.

Doheny's brows rose. "You're in love with her."

"That's right. I plan to apply for an expedited visa for her and her nephew. I think we owe them that, after what happened to her brother, and I won't do anything to jeopardize their chances of getting accepted."

Doheny took off his glasses and pinched the bridge of his nose. "Your story won't change?"

"No."

"There is no statute that allows you to stay silent to protect a foreign national."

"What if she's my wife?"

Doheny wiped the lenses of his glasses and put them back on. "You're the victim of head trauma, weeks of torture and near starvation. By your own admission, you're not thinking clearly."

"That was bullshit. I'm fine."

"Bullshitting a superior officer is grounds for dismissal."

Hud scrubbed a hand down his face, caught in his own trap.

"You have a perfect record, Hudson. Your bravery in combat has been noted time and again. Your ability to survive in extreme circumstances and to defeat our enemies is part of what makes you an exemplary SEAL. I'm willing to overlook your involvement with Ms. Anwar, because your feelings toward her seem genuine, and I want to keep you on Team Twelve. I need more men like you, to be honest."

"Thank you, sir."

"You're not off the hook yet. You need to take some time off to recover. Get a full physical with a psych eval. If you're cleared, you can go back to Armenia and visit this girl. Make sure you're making the right decision."

Hud rose to his feet. "I'll get a physical right away."

"I'm grounding you for three weeks. No travel."

Hud nodded and thanked him again. He could handle a few weeks of rest, and he knew he'd ace his physical. He'd never felt better. Doheny wasn't going to punish him for a minor violation, because Hud had taken out a very high profile target. This was a huge score for the SEALs. Sometimes results mattered more than methods.

The biggest challenge now was convincing Layah to marry him.

Chapter 22

Layah did her best to settle into a quiet life in Armenia.

Her parents lived in Verin Dvin, a small community on the outskirts of Yerevan. It boasted about three thousand residents, the majority of whom were Assyrian. The schools taught lessons in Assyrian, Armenian and English. Ashur fit right in, to Layah's relief.

He'd been a good student in Syria. He had an ear for languages, like his father. After his parents died, Ashur had lost interest in school. He'd often refused to go to class when it was in session. The lack of resources and general instability in Iraq had chipped away at his desire to learn. Layah had given up on making him attend regularly.

In Verin Dvin, there was a real schoolhouse, a nice brick building surrounded by green football fields.

The playground was full of noisy children. There were books and desks and even a gymnasium. When she brought Ashur to the office for registration, the headmaster was thrilled by his fluency in English. He'd asked if Ashur wanted to get started right away. He'd shrugged an agreement, and that was that. He'd fallen in with a group of rowdy boys who lived in her parents' neighborhood. They created mischief, but it was tolerable mischief.

Aram found work on a farm, and Oshana was serving drinks at a local pub. He didn't approve of her job, so there was tension between them. They argued passionately and made up on a daily basis. Layah predicted a child in their immediate future.

Sadly, there was no child in hers. She'd hoped there would be, despite the timing, but her monthly cycle came as expected.

Yusef and Nina had stayed in Yerevan. Layah would have to return to the city at some point to inquire about her career options. There were online records of her transcripts from Damascus University. She didn't know if the units were transferrable, or if she had any hope of securing a position at a local hospital. Not being fluent in Armenian was a major obstacle. It would be easier to complete her residency in the United States. Medical professionals with her language skills were in high demand there, and she could apply for student loans for any additional schooling. Here, she was at a disadvantage.

On Sunday, nearly a month after they'd arrived, her parents hosted a picnic lunch in the park. Yusef and Nina came in from Yerevan. Layah and Ashur had been staying in her parents' cottage, along with Aram and Oshana. There weren't enough rooms for everyone, but they made it work.

Layah sat on the blanket she'd brought and watched Aram play football with Ashur. For all Aram's faults, he was a natural father figure. Ashur needed someone like him to wrestle around with. She felt a pang of sorrow for Hasan, who would never see his son grow up. Ashur was adjusting to their new home better than she'd expected. Now that Al-Bayat was dead, the boy's need for vengeance had faded.

They didn't speak of Hudson. Layah was afraid to say his name, for fear that her own longing would swallow her whole.

She'd prayed that her feelings for him would ebb away. She'd hoped for a swift recovery from heartbreak. She'd achieved her goal of escaping Iraq and finding a better place. She'd worked so hard to get here. But she couldn't enjoy her accomplishment. She'd been as listless as a lovesick schoolgirl, daydreaming about a romantic reunion.

She hadn't heard from him since they parted ways. She'd wanted a clean break, but it still hurt. He'd claimed to love her. He'd sworn to come back to her. He'd said he'd do anything for her.

She rested on the blanket and closed her eyes, wishing she'd been wrong about him. Wishing she didn't care.

A shadow fell over her, blocking out the sun. She squinted up at a man with broad shoulders standing next to her blanket. He was holding a bouquet of flowers. She straightened abruptly, her lips parted in shock.

"William."

He knelt beside her, handing her the flowers. Fresh tulips. Her heart lodged in her throat as she accepted the bouquet. She wanted to throw her arms around him and never let go, but she restrained herself. What if he'd come to say goodbye? His face was tense, and he wasn't smiling. "Layah."

"What are you doing here?"

"I came to visit."

"You didn't call."

"You told me not to."

She stared at the colorful bouquet, blinking tears from her eyes. She'd told him not to make promises he couldn't keep. She hadn't wanted him to string her along with phone calls and romantic messages that prolonged the inevitable.

"I'm going to say hi to Ashur," he said, rising to his feet.

She watched him join the others. He walked in long strides, like always. Her chest tightened with emotion. Aram shook his hand as if they were best friends. Ashur passed him the ball. Everyone seemed pleased to see him. Layah couldn't believe he'd shown up. She'd convinced herself that it was over.

Now he was here, and she didn't know what to do. She'd have to make a decision about continuing their relationship. She couldn't escape the future. She couldn't escape her feelings.

Ashur kicked the ball into the trees, where it got

stuck on a high branch. Her mother appeared beside her.

"Did you know he was coming?" Layah asked.

"He called to ask for our address."

"Why didn't you tell me?"

"He wanted to surprise you."

Layah was surprised, all right. "You approve of his visit? You gave him your blessing?"

"Should I have turned him away?"

Layah shook her head in confusion.

Her mother reached out to pat Layah's shoulder. "You are my only daughter and I love you. I almost lost you. Life is too short and too precious. I do not wish to repeat the mistake I made with Khalil."

Layah wiped the tears from her eyes. This was the first time her mother had mentioned Khalil.

"I was wrong, and I'm sorry."

Layah hugged her tight.

"If this man loves you, he has my blessing."

"What if he wants to take me to America?"

"Does he make you happy?"

"Yes."

"Then go with him."

Layah didn't mention the obvious—that she had Ashur to consider. She'd already spoken to both her parents at length about his guardianship. They wanted the boy to stay in Verin Dvin. Layah hadn't decided her own fate, but his was secure. He seemed to like it here with Aram and his grandparents.

William returned before Layah was ready. He said hello to her mother in Arabic, and he called Layah a treasure. Her mother beamed with approval. Layah gave her the tulips. Then she took him by the elbow and walked away for a private talk.

"You've been practicing Arabic."

"I wanted to impress your mother."

"You did."

They fell silent, watching Aram and Ashur try to rescue the football out of the tree. "Does Ashur like it here?"

"Yes."

"Do you?"

Her throat closed up with emotion. "It is peaceful."

"That's not what I asked."

"What do you want from me?"

He stuck his hands in his pockets, contemplative. Now that she'd calmed down a little, she could appreciate his appearance. He looked fantastic clean-shaven. He'd gained weight, and it favored him. His clothes fit well. He was devastatingly handsome.

While she studied him, he studied her. "You're more beautiful than I remember."

"I'm wearing makeup."

"Are you expecting?"

The question robbed the breath from her lungs. "Is that what you came to discuss?"

"No. I have other topics."

"I'm not expecting."

"Okay," he said, smiling.

"Are you relieved?"

He shrugged. "I could go either way."

She kept walking toward a cobblestone path in the distance. He followed, grasping her hand. The warm contact tingled through her palm and danced across her skin. She could smell his aftershave, or some other enticing male scent. He was wonderfully tall. She felt the overwhelming urge to stand on tip-toe and kiss him.

"I can't stop staring at you," he said.

"How long are you here for?"

"I have three more weeks off. We can stay here, or go somewhere else."

"Then what?"

"Then your visa will be approved."

"My visa?"

He nodded, squeezing her hand. "I made some inquiries for you and Ashur, based on the promises made by Team Twelve to Hasan. INS was already in the process of approving visas for two of Hasan's family members. We owe you."

Layah couldn't believe what she was hearing. She'd hoped there would be no criminal charges pending against her. Securing a visa was beyond her wildest dreams. It was incredibly difficult for an Iraqi national to begin the citizenship process in the US.

"There's a catch," he said. "I told immigration officials we were engaged."

She clapped a hand over her mouth.

He fumbled in his pocket for a velvet box. Taking a deep breath, he got down on one knee and presented it to her.

"What are you doing?" she asked, glancing around them. They were alone.

"I'm asking you to marry me."

She took the box and opened it. There was a diamond ring inside, sparkling like a star.

"I love you, Layah. I can't live without you. I told you I'd do anything for you, and I will. I want you to come to California and be my wife."

Her eyes filled with tears again. She shut the box. "I don't know what to say."

"Say yes."

"I have to talk to Ashur."

William arched a brow. "You're going to let him decide?"

"No. I'm going to think about it, and ask him how he feels. This is important."

"Take all the time you need."

She rushed away before he could draw her into his arms and make her melt. She'd been ready to throw herself at him the moment he'd appeared. She needed a minute to collect her thoughts. It was important to be calm and deliberate in her decision-making process. She returned to the picnic area and found Ashur. He walked along the path with her.

"William asked me to marry him."

"Who's William?"

"Hudson. William Hudson."

"Oh."

"How do you feel about that?"

He just shrugged. "I don't know. He's okay, for an American."

"He wants us to live with him."

Ashur's brow furrowed. "Us?"

"He can get you a visa. You can come to America."

"No. I like it here."

She took a deep breath, fighting tears again. "I don't want to leave you."

"I never thought you would stay."

"Why not?"

"Because of him."

"I'm your guardian."

"You're not my mother. I'll be fine without you."

Her face crumpled with sorrow. Ashur didn't pull any punches.

"Don't cry," he said, putting his arm around her. "You're my favorite aunt."

"I'm your only aunt."

"I want you to be happy."

She hugged him close, weeping on his thin shoulder. By the time she was finished, she'd made her decision. Ashur was doing well here, and he might not adjust to another move easily. He could always come visit. Maybe in a few years, when he was ready for college, he'd reconsider.

She wiped the tears from her cheeks and returned to William's side. She opened the box to remove the ring and place it on her finger. The diamond sparkled cheerily. She held her hand in the sun to catch the light.

"Well?"

"My answer is yes. I will marry you."

He let out an excited whoop and lifted her off her feet. They whirled around in a circle. "I love you," he said, setting her down.

She stroked the short hair at the nape of his neck. "I love you, too."

"You do?"

"Of course."

"Since when?"

She thought back, trying to pinpoint the moment. "When you put your arms around me and Ashur to protect us from bullets. I knew then that I would no longer pine for Khalil. You had replaced him in my heart."

"I don't expect you to forget him."

She nodded her understanding.

"Is Ashur coming with us?"

"No. He wants to live here."

"I'm sorry."

"You are?"

"He's grown on me."

"You are a good man, William Hudson."

"You're a good woman, Layah Anwar."

"We are lucky to have found each other."

"I'm the lucky one."

She wanted to argue, but he crushed his mouth over hers in a passionate kiss. She kissed him back with relish, her toes curling. They were both lucky. Lucky to have escaped, lucky to have survived, and lucky to start a new life together—forever.

* * * * *

Don't miss the first TEAM TWELVE *story
from Susan Cliff*
STRANDED WITH THE NAVY SEAL

*Working on a cruise ship was supposed
to be the perfect distraction for chef
Cady Crenshaw. Instead, it made her the
perfect target. Abducted and thrown
overboard into foreign waters, she has only
one shot at survival...and it comes at the
hands of an irresistible ally.*

*Navy SEAL Logan Starke's protective instincts
were locked and loaded the moment he met
Cady at the ship's bar. When a violent struggle to
take down her captors leaves Logan and
Cady stranded on a deserted island,
he leaps into rescue mode. But the hot sand
and the even hotter attraction between them
can't be denied...and temptation could
be the deadliest threat yet.*

Get 2 Free Books,
Plus 2 Free Gifts—
just for trying the Reader Service!

SPECIAL EXCERPT FROM

⊕ HARLEQUIN®
™

ROMANTIC suspense

*US marshal Trina Lopez never expected the fugitive she
captured to be navy SEAL turned undercover agent
Rob Bristol, the unwitting father of her son. But the Russian
mob is closing in around them and they'll have to survive
that before they can even begin to try to become a family.*

*Read on for a sneak preview of
THE FUGITIVE'S SECRET CHILD,
the next installment in Geri Krotow's breathtaking
SILVER VALLEY P.D. miniseries.*

"You didn't like seeing me with a child?" It could have been
anyone's; how did he know it was hers? He clearly didn't know
the real truth of it. That the baby was his. Theirs.

"The kid wasn't the problem. It was the man you handed it
over to."

"The man I…" She thought about her time assigned to
Commander, Naval Surface Forces Atlantic, a staff in Norfolk,
Virginia. It had been a horrendous juggling act to deal with her
grief while adjusting to life as a new single mom. There had
been only two men who'd been close enough to help her at
the time. Craig, another naval officer who worked on the same
staff, and her brother Nolan, who'd just completed law school
and was working as a lawyer in Virginia Beach.

"Not so smug now, are you?" His sharp words belied the
stricken expression stamped on his face.

"There's nothing to be smug about, you arrogant jerk." She
turned into the parking lot of a suite hotel and drove around to
the back, out of sight of any main roads. As soon as she put the
gearshift into Park, she faced him.

"I was with one of two men during that time. One was my brother, Nolan."

She waited for him to turn, not giving a flying fish how much it hurt him. Because she'd hurt for so long, had finally moved on past her loss, and here he was, telling her he'd seen her and their child but had done nothing to broach the divide?

He turned, and she saw the glimmer of fear in his eyes. Fear? It couldn't be.

"The other man—did you marry him?" His voice was a croak.

"He was, and is, one of my dearest, best friends. As a matter of fact, I was at his wedding this past spring. To his husband. He's gay. I never married, and even if I'd wanted to, that was what, only eighteen, twenty months since you'd died? Scratch that, I mean went missing, right? Because you were alive all along." She shook her head, followed by a single harsh laugh. "You know, a big part of me never believed it, that you were dead. As if I could feel you still alive on the planet. But my brother, my family, they all told me I had to move on. To get past what had happened."

"Did you?"

"Did I what?"

"Move on."

She didn't answer him. Couldn't. Because the man next to her, Rob, wasn't Justin anymore. He was a stranger to her. And she had no idea what a man who hadn't told her he'd survived would do once he discovered he had a son.

Don't miss
THE FUGITIVE'S SECRET CHILD by Geri Krotow,
available May 2018 wherever
Harlequin® Romantic Suspense books and ebooks are sold.

www.Harlequin.com

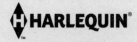